A Rampage of Grace

A Rampage Of Grace

Where Love and Forgiveness Meet

by
Anne-Marie Alexander

Copyright © 2015 Anne-Marie Alexander

The right of Anne-Marie Alexander to be identified as author of this work has been asserted by her in accordance with the Copyright, Designs, and Patents Act 1988

No part of this publication may be reproduced or transmitted in any form or by any means, electronic or mechanical, including photocopy, recording, or any information storage and retrieval system, without permission in writing from the author.

All of the characters in this book are fictional.
Any similarity to persons alive or deceased is purely co-incidental.
All of the companies in this book are fictional.
Any similarity to companies current or historic is purely co-incidental.

First published by AuthorHouse 2015

This book is dedicated to my beautiful children:

Eve

Thomas

Phoebe

With grateful thanks to:

Joy Maddison, the editor, for her supportive style and encouragement.

God, without whose grace I would never have survived.

INTRODUCTION

So here I am, standing in front of the church doors waiting to marry Ben, my best friend and now husband-to-be. It has been such a journey to get here, an emotional roller coaster of comical calamities, chocolate and catastrophic relationships.

Disaster was my constant companion for the first twenty something years of my life but through every disaster came learning and eventually wholeness. If you have not read *A Rampage of Chocolate*, then let me recap:

So why Ben? Well, he is the one who loved me unconditionally through all those disasters and tirelessly picked up the pieces of my broken heart. He is also the one that I failed to notice for all those years. He was hidden from me by his foppish fringe. Taken for granted. Part of the scenery. A treasure hidden for me in my back garden, whilst I fruitlessly mined elsewhere.

Still, I am not going to beat myself up for overlooking him because I am convinced that the eventual timing of our union was right. I would never have been ready for him before. I was too self-focused and insecure and had needed to complete my journey to womanhood; to establish my self-worth in something greater and to understand the promise that was nestled within me all along. As I stabilised emotionally, my reliance on chocolate dwindled and my episodes of clumsiness, whilst still dramatic, became less frequent. From this new-found platform of stability, I was finally free to discard lust-filled, selfish relationships and to prepare myself to enter one based on love. Only then was I ready for Ben.

I remember so well the evening when, after years of knowing each other as friends, Ben took his courage into his hands and made his position known to me. He bared his heart and soul and I responded… with a dumbstruck silence! It was shock on my part. The fireworks were exploding loudly inside my heart; I just forgot to let them out!

I am not sure who was more shocked, me or my flatmates - Liz, Bronie and Tina. They, alongside Ben, had accompanied me through many nightmare encounters and had always rallied around afterwards helping to pick up my broken pieces. As per most house shares, we were an eclectic mix of personalities, but somehow it worked. Tina, an air-head with a surreal sense of normality, invariably kept the mood light; whilst unemotional (in a grumpy sort of way) Bronie ensured that all our feet remained firmly planted on the ground. Liz, on the other hand, was more streetwise and balanced. Consequently, she was the first to spot the signs of Ben's hidden agenda towards me and alert me to his cause.

Two other key friends had partnered with me throughout my life. My friendship with Darcy dominated my former years, leaving a trail of fond memories behind; memories laden with laughter, mud, innocence and fun. Regretfully, our childhood friendship was not robust enough to survive the buffeting of our teenage years. The first forays into love were all that were required to cause us to drift apart. Thankfully, my friendship with Reeta fared somewhat better over time, but even then our distant phone relationship was a far cry from the intimacy that we once shared throughout our university years and on our European adventure together. Unexpected parachute arrivals and smelly, Turkish train carriages seemed a lifetime away from the sterile, corporate worlds that we now inhabited.

Aside from Ben, the mainstay of my life has remained my flamboyant, flirtatious, kind-hearted mother, Davina. A single-mother from my birth, her frequent injections into my life have resulted in a joyous, rainbow-filled mix of delusion and sense peppered with a sprinkling of fun. This heady cocktail, whilst often frustrating to me over the years, has proved irresistible to a never-ending stream of optimistic suitors, none of whom have ever been capable of taming her for any length of time. Like an unbroken unicorn, Davina has consistently refused to conform to the template of 'normal' society boundaries. Instead she has confined herself to freedom at every opportunity. Unpredictability is her stability. Shock and laughter are the fragrant trails that she leaves behind.

So this is where you find me – about to enter uncharted waters, to embark upon a marriage with no parental template to follow and no insight into the palaces and pitfalls of a lifelong union. As always, I am filled with naïve optimism at the adventure ahead and have a determination to enjoy the journey, not just the destination. No doubt there will be laughter on the way, no doubt tears, but it's the undertow of truth that will propel me into those hidden, sweet lagoons of rest that we all so often crave.

Chapter 1
Unorthodox Approach

It was hardly the best start to my wedding day; not exactly what I had dreamt of as a little girl. However, despite everything, here I stood at the door of the church about to step into the most important day of my life; to step into a life-changing, life-lasting commitment. My heart raced at the enormity of what I was embracing and my legs turned to jelly. I felt the reassurance of my Uncle George's plump, protective arm. I gripped it tight and looked up at him. The kindness in his eyes and the warmth of his smile melted away my fear and I returned the gesture as best I could.
"This is your last chance to dash for freedom you know," he whispered, winking. "You can still make a run for it."
"Oh, very funny!" I replied, somewhat irritated.
"Are you ready?" asked the vicar sombrely (clearly he used the same demeanour for both weddings and funerals). I composed myself and nodded. With that he opened the great oak doors and the swell of organ music heralded my arrival.
"Best foot forward!" Uncle George quipped.
"Not funny!" I snarled under my breath.

I watched as heads turned to catch the first glimpse of the

bride. Today that bride was me. I smiled. They gasped. I edged my metal walking frame forward down the aisle! The Bridal March, played with gusto by the overenthusiastic, spindly, old organist, filled the church, drowning out the clunking of the metal frame and the thudding of my plaster cast on the flagstone floor. So often I had watched brides glide gracefully down the aisle, like swans on a crystal lake, but my clumsiness had dictated otherwise for my grand occasion. Instead I was forced to approach my husband-to-be with all the elegance of a tip-toeing elephant.

My generous train and restrictive dress bodice had rendered the use of wheelchairs and crutches an impossibility: Crutches had been my preferred choice, but their effect on my bosom and buttons were both dramatic and breath-taking! For the sake of the vicar and my own modesty, I was forced to try something less risqué and somewhat more practical. Davina had pushed a wheelchair into the centre of the lounge.
"Try this!" she had offered optimistically. I hobbled over to the drab, khaki chair and reluctantly lowered myself into it. As I did so I disappeared under a quagmire of silk and netting, so that only the very top of my bosom remained visible - two pink melons perched on an oversized meringue!
"Oh dear!" Davina exclaimed horrified. "That will never do! I'm afraid there's only one thing for it… You'll have to use the metal monstrosity!"
"No!" I whimpered, as we both turned and stared at the drab metal frame. I could not believe that this ugly beast was about to take centre stage on one of the most important days of my life!

The next 24 hours were spent converting this dull, metal frame into a must-have, glamorous, bridal accessory - desperately disguised with satin ribbon and ornate pink and white trailing flowers. By the time we had finished, it resembled my very own portable hanging garden, which, whilst beautiful to look at, was still an unwelcome addition to my bridal ensemble. Unfortunately in the process we got a little carried away with our creativity and decorated my plain white cast too. By the time we had taken a step back to view our handiwork, it was too late; the glue had dried. My cast, bedecked with pink ribbon, now resembled a deformed candy cane and my heart sank a little lower.

As I clunked down the aisle I was at least grateful for my long, white flowing dress that so easily accommodated the unexpected bulk of my leg and hid it from view. However, the train of my dress kept getting caught in the walking frame. Tina and Liz, my chief bridesmaids, worked hard behind me to gather the flowing, white material and keep it out of harm's way, but at one point I heard a small ripping sound followed by Liz's muffled whimper. I glanced around and she hurriedly shoved her bouquet in front of my train so that I could not see the damage. She smiled guiltily. I shrugged my shoulders and carried on.

I consoled myself with the knowledge that my dress was not the important part of this day, nor my leg. What counted were the vows that I was about to undertake. I had pored over them for weeks now, pondering the implications of each one... *Til death us do part*. That was the vow that scared me the most. Not because I was scared of death, but because I was scared of life. If I lived to 80 then I was committing the next 50 years of my life to this man! That

A Rampage of Grace

seemed to be an eternity. There were no get outs, no caveats (*for better for worse* took care of that one). This was a covenant and it felt scary. The enormity cascaded over me as I negotiated the hobble down the aisle. Uncle George's (albeit impossible) option of a final dash for freedom started to feel appealing.

I suppressed my fears and fixed my eyes resolutely ahead of me. For the first time, I caught sight of Ben, standing in his morning suit waiting expectantly for me at the altar. The stability of his stature and his peaceful demeanour reassured me of my decision to entrust him with my life. Alerted by the huge clunking sound, he turned towards me and I saw his familiar foppish fringe, bluebell eyes and warm smile. My heart engaged with his, my love for him bubbled up and I knew that I would keep my vows with every breath in my body.

Chapter 2

The Hen Night

Of course, my wedding day was never meant to have been that way. Up until two weeks before, I had been fighting fit and at the gym every morning, toning and honing my perfect, wedding day body. Determined to look my best for my big occasion, I held nothing back, attacking my training program with gusto. The perfect body was within my grasp. I only made one mistake… letting Tina organise my hen weekend!

My instincts had cried out *Nooooooo!* when she had approached me, but I ignored them, feeling powerless to refuse her enthusiastic offer:
"Let me organise your hen weekend, pet. It'll be fun! I have something in mind that you're ganna enjoy!" she had trilled with a wink and a broad Geordie accent. "

Tina had never been fully grounded on this planet, constantly evading the reality of this world. Married life with Greg had not improved this situation. It seemed his hippy ways had combined with her dizziness to produce a completely alien species, totally separated from earth but lovable nonetheless. Tina's dress sense now mirrored that of my mother – psychedelic colours, floaty fabrics and platformed heels. Even knowing all that, I agreed and entrusted my hen weekend to her. Maybe it was the lyrical tones of her Newcastle accent, her innocent smile or a misplaced sense of loyalty to our friendship. Whatever my reasoning at the time, I decided that it was only one weekend and it could not possibly do much too damage!

The hen weekend had started well. Tina, complete with neon clipboard, was the first to arrive at the house that I shared with Liz and Bronie. She rang the doorbell several times to the tune of *Here comes the bride*.
"That'll be Tina then!" muttered Bronie in her usual sarcastic tone. I sauntered over to the door to let her in and was bowled over by a huge hug and a sprinkling of rose petals. She discarded her coat in the middle of the hall and floated into the lounge.
"Ah Hinny," she sighed, "this is ganna be so canny! I've got some real treats lined up for ya." With that she waltzed over to the window and winked at Liz, who was sitting grumpily in the corner.

Liz and Dean had been seeing each other for about five years now and there was not so much as a hint of marriage on the horizon. The nearer we got to my day, the more focused Liz became on her situation. Tina understood and inserted some Geordie wisdom.
"Now divn't go getting all huffy on us. You're a canny lass and your time'll come, pet. Let's focus on Laurie today. We're ganna make this a weekend to remember!" Liz opened her mouth to form a retort but was interrupted by the doorbell. I hastened a speedy retreat from the looming storm and went to open the door.

My heart leapt as I saw Reeta standing there. Her wavy, black hair cascaded down her front, contrasting beautifully with her crisp white shirt and purple, pencil skirt. I had never seen her look so chic. In fact, I just had not seen her! She had matured so much in the last couple of years. For a second I considered the inadequacies of my own casual attire - I was still a jeans girl at heart and had not really progressed from our student days. Maybe progress was overrated I decided and leapt towards her.

"Reeta!" I screamed, hugging her tight. "You look amazing! How long's it been?"
"Too long!" she replied and she was right.
"Come on in. What's new with you? Are you... I mean do you..." Overcome with excitement, I tripped over my words... and Tina's coat... landing spread-eagled in the middle of the lounge, much to everyone's amusement.
"Good to see that you haven't changed!" Reeta laughed. "I was only thinking about you on the train this morning."
"Really?"
"Yes. The toilet was blocked. Reminded me of..."
"STOP!" I yelled. "I DON'T want to be reminded of that incident. I was never able to wear those shoes again."
Reeta giggled. I gave her another hug. It was so lovely to be around her once more. "So how's work? Vice Principal no less! I'm so proud of you." Reeta blushed.
"It's not as glamourous as it sounds. I'm still quite hands on, especially when we're short-staffed. I've been helping out in the nursery all week. In fact there's one of the children that reminds me of you."
"Really?"
"Her name's Phoebe. She's very funny, always laughing, but just a little on the clumsy side. Yesterday she got her leg stuck in the safety gate and had to be cut out by the headmaster. She's so used to disasters that she didn't fret at

all; she just sat there with her juice and fruit snack until it was all over."
"No chocolate then?"
"No. No chocolate."
"And there the similarity ends," I retorted.

The doorbell rang a final time. It was Davina.
"Hi, Mum," I said, sneaking my arms under her scarlet poncho to give her a hug.
"Hello darling," she purred. "I've brought you a surprise."
"Really? What?" I asked with trepidation. Davina's surprises over the years have proved to be rather extreme and wide-ranging in content, although mostly they have resulted in an injection of rainbow fashions into my otherwise moderate wardrobe. Davina grinned and took a step to the side so that I could see her car. A tousle of ginger hair appeared behind the bonnet, closely followed by a freckled, beaming face."
"Darcy!"
Darcy stood up. I ran forward to meet her and squeezed her so hard that she struggled to breathe. Tears started to flood my eyes.
"So am I welcome then?" she asked sheepishly. "I realise that it's been a long time. It's just that I bumped into your mum and she said that you were getting married. Well... I just wanted to come..." I interrupted her with another hug.
"You will ALWAYS be welcome!" With that we both cried tears of joy, our reconciliation complete. Sometimes friendships get lost in the sea of forgetfulness and busyness. It is so precious when they resurface and we get a second chance to treasure them again.

"Divn't just stand there. Let the lass in!" ordered Tina in an uncharacteristic outburst of northern authority. "Let's get this hen weekend underway!" She beamed at us both and then produced a veil and 'L' plates for me to put on. Just then a minibus pulled up. "Howay man! All aboard!" she enthused.

We all piled out of the house and squeezed ourselves into the available seats. Davina positioned herself in the front next to the male driver, rearranged her poncho and then shot him her best, red-lipstick smile. He simpered a smile in return, averted his eyes to the road ahead and reached nervously for the gear stick. With all the concentration of a mouse sitting next to a crouching tiger, he applied himself to the journey ahead.

A general kerfuffle in the back of the minibus ensued as the rest of us redistributed luggage, coats, legs and bottoms, until we were all comfortable. Finally, when we were all settled, Tina passed around a big bag of chocolate bars. I pulled out a *Clock Off* bar and smiled.
"I guess this one's for me?"
"Why aye! What else would I give you, Hinny?" Tina grinned impishly.
"Where to exactly?" asked the minibus driver.
"The airfield, please." Tina looked at me and winked. I raised an eyebrow.
"Airfield?"
"Why aye. We've clubbed together and paid for you to do a parachute jump!" she announced proudly with a grin. My heart sank and my countenance dropped to the floor. Thankfully, she failed to notice my reaction and chirpily carried on. "We decided against the tandem jump – it wouldn't be right to strap yourself to another man just before your wedding day! You and Liz'll be doing the static-line jump instead." I looked at Liz.
"Really?"

"Yes. Dean bought it for me for my birthday. I guess he thought that the thrill would keep my mind off marriage for another year!"
"You kept that a bit quiet," I muttered resentfully.
"Well I didn't want to give your secret away. It'll be fun. I've always wanted to do one. I bet you have too?" I looked around at the sea of faces in the van, all looking expectantly for me to show appreciation for the terror ahead. I racked my brains and came up with the most appreciative, yet truthful response that I could think of: "Wow! An opportunity of a lifetime, eh? Thanks guys!"

The journey to the airfield seemed long and bumpy, allowing plenty of time for my concerns to build. By the time we finally arrived, I discovered that this 'airfield' was exactly that – a lot of air and a very large field! The simple addition of a concrete hut did nothing to assure me of their credibility; *amateur* was written all over this set-up. My remaining confidence left as fear and dread entered the minivan and sat down beside me.

Davina, Reeta, Bronie and Tina shared none of my concerns and so positioned themselves comfortably in the concrete hut (which doubled as both an office and a café) to watch our training and our descent. Liz and I autographed various disclaimers, all of which seemed to sign our lives away. There were three pages to sign with lots and lots of legal clauses. However, it could all have been summed up in one sentence... *If you are daft enough to risk your life in this way then we are not daft enough to take the blame!*

I resigned myself to the fate ahead and slowly put on my jumpsuit. Liz and I spent what seemed ages learning how to tumble and roll. It was funny really - tumbling was something that I had done naturally on many occasions throughout my life and yet now I found it inexplicably hard to do. Fear appeared to have frozen all of my muscles. They no longer responded to my command; consequently, my tumbles resembled belly flops and my rolls were positively stationary. The terror that lay ahead of me dominated my thoughts and I found it impossible to concentrate.

After a last, quick dash to the toilet, Liz and I were strapped into our harnesses and stepped out of the building accompanied by Mike, our bronzed, blonde-haired instructor. The cool air hit my face, causing a wave of reality to flood my body. I felt an overwhelming need for reassurance and for a maternal smile. I looked back in search of my mum. She was engrossed in a conversation with Jimmy behind the desk. It seemed to involve her doing an aeroplane impression – with arms outstretched and her red fringed poncho dangling down to form wings! Jimmy roared with laughter and Davina went into a victory roll.

Finally, the moment came when we were put on board the aeroplane. With fear and trembling in my heart and ominous groanings in my stomach, I wished that I hadn't had bran for breakfast! The engines whirred and we started to bounce down the runway. Liz and Mike looked very relaxed and sat chatting away – an informal exchange of dazzling smiles and flirtatious banter. Their ease of interaction was surprising given the impending doom. All I was capable of was a silent scream. I appeared to have lost the ability to function normally - I became aware of my body creaking and groaning in its final protest about my situation. Individual organs and gases appeared to be trying to flee the scene. I looked out of the window. We had left the ground and were airborne. There was no going back now.

Fear overwhelmed me and my life went into slow motion. All I wanted now was to get this jump over with and return to normality. I counted as the clouds went by one by one and wondered how much longer it would be until we reached our destination. I was never quite sure what made one blue patch of sky different to another; they all looked the same to me, but clearly Mike and the pilot had a specific spot of blue in mind.

After what seemed an eternity in the air, the pilot shouted something to Mike, who promptly got up and opened the exit hatch of the aircraft.
"This is it girls! Who's first?" he asked with a smile. Liz motioned to me.
"Go on. It's your day," she said. I feigned a smile and attempted to step forward. My right leg failed me. No matter how much I tried to move it, my leg seemed stuck in its original position. I tried again and again, all to no avail. I guessed it was the fear rendering me motionless. Mike rushed forward to help me.
"Your leg's caught on the edge of the seat!" he said and leant down to release me. With a tug and a twang I felt the freedom to move again.
"Oh! Thanks," I said, disappointedly. Somehow I preferred it when my trousers did not want to leave the plane at least then I could have avoided my jump by joining them in a show of unity.
"Come on then. Here you go. On the count of three. One..." My head was facing out of the aircraft, but with the wind rushing past my ears I couldn't hear Mike properly. I turned my head to face him, lost my balance and yelped as I fell backwards out of the aircraft. Still, at least that way I got to see Liz jump out too.

The Hen Night

After expending all my efforts trying to turn myself over the right way, I immediately regretted it because I saw the ground approaching at an alarming rate. My silent scream from earlier finally found its voice. It was very loud! Fear gripped every part of me and, for the first time in my life, I had a sense of my own mortality. I wondered where I was going next - heaven or hell? The frivolity of my life could not help me now. I needed a spiritual safety net fast. With no time to think, I instinctively howled the international, emergency prayer:
"Ggggodddd heeeeeelp meeeeeee!"

Immediately, the static line engaged and my parachute released. All thoughts of death left me and my earthly perspective returned as I slowed right down. Survival seemed possible after all. Looking upwards I saw a reassuring sea of red and orange – my parachute. It was the sweetest sight I had ever seen. I started to smile and to relax into my gentle descent.

It is funny what you see when you are descending from the air. The silence of the approach means that everyone is blissfully unaware of your presence. I wondered where I would land… Maybe on some unsuspecting pedestrian? Or sunbather? I already knew from my experience in Germany that parachutists can turn up almost anywhere. As it was, I drifted towards the safety of a field of cows on the edge of town.

The closer I got to the ground, the more relieved I felt. Only a few feet to go and I would be safe again. This sense of peace soon left as I realised that the herd of cows below me had not moved. If I did not act quickly, I would find myself the unexpected bareback rider of a Friesian!

"Shoo! Shoo! Shoo!" I called, frantically waving my arms. Several of the cows looked up and then gradually sauntered away, still chewing the cud. It wasn't exactly the reaction I had looked for, but it was enough to produce a small gap for me to land in. I held my legs out beneath me and felt the impact of the ground. Step one... complete. I rolled out of the way of my parachute. Step two... complete. I had survived the fall of death! Relief overwhelmed me, causing every fibre in my body to shake. I stayed where I was, unaware of my surroundings as I recovered. I heard voices shouting, but it was background noise, lost in a haze of adrenalin. Even the smell of the cow pats did not bother me, although I recognised that they were very close. Too close?

I got up and started gathering my parachute. So much material. So much red. I heard a grunt and a puff. I looked up. To my left and my right was a sea of cows, all chewing lazily. However, straight ahead of me was a bull, complete with angry eyes, sharp horns and a ring through his nose. He looked at me and snorted. I looked at him and gulped. I looked down at the sea of red material trailing to my side. He looked too, scraping his hoof along the ground. That was the only signal I needed. My recovery could wait. Survival was at the top of my list again for the second time that day!

I cannot tell you what the bull did next because I was too busy running towards the fence. However, his breath was warm and his hooves were close! It is amazing the latent athletic potential that is released with a bull behind you... I reached the fence in less than three seconds and vaulted over it as best I could. Sadly I cannot say the same for the parachute, which hooked itself on to the fence post. Still in mid-flight, it caused me to recoil unexpectedly and belly flop to the ground (just as I had practised earlier). I felt a pain shoot through my ankle and adrenalin shoot through my heart. My mind escaped to its own recesses leaving my body behind.

"Laurie… Laurie…"
I came around slowly as reality started to merge with my mental fog. Gradually, I started to discern the familiar voices and faces of Liz and Mike.
"Are you okay?" Liz asked, looking worried (but amused by the scene).
"I'm fine! Don't fuss!" I replied defensively, lifting my face out of a cow pat.
"Okay then," she said, confused by my protestation, and took a step backwards. Mike was not so easily fobbed off.
"Are you sure you're okay? You're looking a bit pale."
"I'm fine!" I repeated, stubbornly. Pride normally comes before a fall, but in this case it came after.

Mike released me from my parachute and I tried to stand up. My foot gave way underneath me. He took one look at my ankle and grimaced, then got straight onto his radio.
"Jimmy. We've landed in the cow field. Come and get us but bring an ambulance. It's not just the fence post we've broken."

I sank back in defeat onto the soft ground and felt the crispness of the cow pat underneath me. My heart sank as did my pride, and I surrendered to the entirety of the situation. However, Liz tried to raise my spirits by engaging me in conversation.
"It's probably not that bad, Laurie; a sprain or something similar."

"Really?" I was heartened by this glimmer of hope. She looked at my ankle. "Actually, no. It's definitely broken!" she replied honestly. My heart returned to its former state of despair. She tried to cheer me up again. This time she used a different tack.
"Still, it could have been worse?"
"Could it? How?"
"Well you survived the jump didn't you? If you'd broken your ankle in the field with the bull who knows what would have happened. As it is, you escaped from the bull in one piece... Or rather... in two."

The ambulance crew arrived along with Jimmy and Davina. Liz withdrew into the background, leaving my mum to comfort me and to whisper sweet nonsense into my ear. As always she took centre stage, even repeating her aeroplane impression for the paramedics. They all laughed, and even I managed to squeeze out a chuckle. The combination of my mum and gas and air seemed to be working a treat. I was starting to relax again. Eventually I was bundled into the ambulance. Through the closing doors I saw Jimmy's van depart with Mike and Liz in the back. I watched as they laughed effortlessly and knew that it would be a while before I would join them again.

So that was my briefer-than-planned hen weekend – a morning slice of sheer terror served with an afternoon dose of hospital waiting room. Not exactly the concoction that Tina or I had hoped for. Still, it all made for an unforgettable weekend!

By the time I got back to the house, with my leg in plaster

and my perfect wedding day dreams in tatters, there was only one thing left to do... We all snuggled up on the sofa with a bottle of wine, a takeaway, some chocolate and a DVD. I looked around me and smiled. My ankle was unimportant; what mattered was that I was surrounded by my dearest friends and my mum. What could be more special? I had an overwhelming sense of their value and decided there and then never to let the busyness of life or marriage set our friendships adrift again.

Chapter 3

The Engagement

One year before...

One beautiful, August afternoon, Ben and I took a picnic into the hills. Up on that hill, the sky was crystal clear and we could see for miles. This was one of our favourite spots, a place where we would often come to survey our kingdom (as we liked to refer to it) and dream location - the pretty village of Lower Tweedle, nestled in the heart of a small patch of woodland in the midst of a rich, green, fertile valley. It was a world apart from the grey, industrial city on the other side of the hill, with its bleak, overdeveloped landscape and overpopulated housing. This secret slice of heaven was our aspiration; our spot; our kingdom; our dream.

"One day," Ben said, placing his arm gently around my shoulders. "One day, we'll live there."
"You think so?" I questioned, the doubt echoing through my words.
"Of course! Together we can achieve anything!"
"I'd like to think so, but it's so expensive. I can't help thinking that we'll always be stuck over there!" I pointed

A Rampage of Grace

to the other side of the hill.
"Trust me, Laurie! I shall get us our dream. Look!" he said, sweeping his fringe back over his head and puffing up his chest. "I can be a manager if I want to." His fringe fell defiantly back over his eyes and I fell into fits of giggles.
"Just not today, eh?" I chuckled.

We talked and laughed and laughed and cried until our sides hurt and our jaws ached. With my smile indelibly etched across my face by the laughter of the day and the joy of our souls, we collapsed back into the long grass. Wine glasses in hand and half-eaten sandwiches abandoned on the rug, we watched the cloud formations in the sky.

"It's so beautiful here," I whispered dreamily. Ben smiled.
"Certainly is."
"Look up there. That cloud looks like a shark. Can you see it?"
"Where?"
"Over there," I replied pointing. "You can just make out its teeth."
"Oh yeah!" he said with an impish look in his eye. "I see it... although to me it's more of an... iceberg... with great stalactites hanging off it." Ben looked at me smugly and grinned.
"Mmmmm. Okay then clever clogs, what do you make of that one?" I pointed to a small cloud with two tall peaks. Ben stroked his chin thoughtfully, clearly he was in one of his awkward moods.
"I'm sure that you would say that it looks like a rabbit, but to me it looks like... a wisdom tooth! Next?" I grunted in disapproval at his answer and pointed to another cloud formation. "A bit tougher...," he acknowledged, "but definitely an aboriginal didgeridoo."
"What! An aboriginal digeridoo?"

The Engagement

"Uh huh," he nodded with mock seriousness. I rolled my eyes.
"It looks like a stick!"
"To you maybe," winked Ben.
"Oh, I give up! Last one." I pointed to a great big, blob-like cloud, completely round, very lumpy and resembling a giant hairball. I was interested to see what interpretation Ben could conjure up this time.
"Mmmmm... Now let me think..." said Ben, slowly rising to his feet. "I think..." He took a small step backwards. "It looks like..." He took another step. "YOUR BACKSIDE!" With that he shot off across the hill.
"You cheeky swine!" I shouted running after him. Ben knew that he could easily outrun me, so he dodged behind a bush, in order to even up the game. His big arm grabbed me as I ran past and he pulled me towards him, held me tight and kissed my nose.
"I do love you, Laurie Booth. ALL of you... even the big bits!" I squirmed in his arms and turned my face away in protest.
"I'm not saying anything nice to you, Ben Driver, unless you take back your comment about my bottom. That cloud was VERY big and VERY lumpy!" Ben released his grip and hung his head in pretend shame, his foppish fringe hiding his huge grin.
"I'm sorry Laurie. Your bottom is not lumpy. There! Happy?" He looked up at me, smirking mischievously. I scowled at him jokingly.
"And?" I prompted.
"And what?" he replied with feigned innocence.
"You know very well. I'm waiting..." I tapped my foot on the ground and put on my best stern expression (which is very hard to do when you are trying to suppress laughter).
"Okay then... Your bottom is not as big as that cloud!" I could not help it any longer, I roared with laughter and so

did he. Stroking his fringe away from his eyes I observed, "You do make me laugh."
"I know!" he admitted proudly.

As he held me in his arms, gazing at me fondly, Ben developed a wistful expression.
"It's funny really…"
"What is?"
"How alike we are."
"What do you mean?"
"Well… No one else can make me laugh the way you do… and you often know what I'm…"
"Going to say?" I interrupted. Ben laughed.
"Exactly my point! It's as if you know how I think. Like we were carved from the same block. Like we were…" he hesitated.
"Made for each other?" I offered. He nodded.
"Yes. I reckon we were…"

Ben paused for a moment lost in a sea of deep thought. The reality of a bird cawing overhead cast him back onto my shore. His expression transformed instantly as a cheeky glint entered his eye.
"Your Majesty!" he exclaimed haughtily as he offered me his hand. "Shall we return to our royal picnic, before our subjects (the local wildlife) eat it all?"
"Such wise counsel!" I replied, offering him my hand as only royalty do. And so, as every good King and queen should, we walked serenely back across the hill to our rug. (Okay, so that is a bit of a lie. We did try walking majestically for all of 30 seconds until I disappeared down a rabbit hole dragging Ben down with me. However, the first version makes for a much more romantic memory.)

Black clouds started to loom in the sky above, thus

heralding the end of our 'royal' picnic. We took our cue and bundled everything back into our rucksacks and, hand in hand, meandered slowly back down the hill.

"Do you mind if we pop to the shop quickly, I just need to pick up some extra bits for dinner?" I asked.
"Eugh! More shopping?" Ben teased. I looked at him sternly and he capitulated with just a hint of sarcasm. "I'd love to!" he winked
"Thanks." I took his arm and we ambled towards the corner store, chatting easily about nothing in particular, immersed in each other's company. I looked up at Ben's face, admiring the strength of his jaw and the softness of his eyes. Suddenly his expression changed and he stopped dead in his tracks.
"Laurie, look!"
"What?"
"There! By the ice cream sign." I followed the direction of his finger and gasped.
"Ugh! But how?" There lying on the pavement were two pieces of a wooden chess set. A king and a queen, carved from the same block.

Ben and I stood rooted to the spot. Both staring at the pieces in awe. Both comprehending their significance. Both dumbstruck.

Ben was the first to break the silence.
"I guess they're for us!" he whispered, gently picking up the wooden pieces and placing them in his hands.
"Yeah! It's a sign if ever I saw one." I agreed.
"Or maybe it's the confirmation and courage that I needed…"

Without warning, on the pavement outside the Co-Op, Ben

A Rampage of Grace

dropped down onto one knee. "Laurie, will you be my queen? Will you marry me?" Tears welled up in my eyes, my heart pounded on its cage and fireworks went off in my stomach. I flung my arms around his neck.
"Yes, Ben! Yes! Nothing would make me happier or more proud than to marry you!"

So there we have it – our sign from heaven that our marriage was meant to be. Those two chess pieces became symbolic of our union. We mounted them proudly in a frame and, when we finally moved into our marital home, placed them above our fireplace as a constant reminder of our entwined destinies. We never considered the roles of the missing pieces or the dangers of the game. For us these two pieces were everything - they were our assurance of success.

Chapter 4

The Darkened Room

Two years on, we found ourselves in one of the most important waiting rooms of our lives. Filled with a waddle of women, all with varying degrees of bumps, this place held the key to unlocking the next step in our marriage. This was only our first appointment. We were just here to check that everything was okay and to find out when our little bundle was officially due (although we had our suspicions).

A door opened and a huge, pregnant lady emerged from a darkened room. Supported by her husband, she slowly walked John-Wayne-style across to the reception desk. I stared at her and wondered if I would look that awkward and ungainly in a few months. I decided not to go there; the thought was too distressing to contemplate! The sonographer appeared from the room a few minutes later.
"Laura Driver?" she called. Ben nudged me in the ribs.
"Here we go." He started to help me up.
"I don't need help yet, you know."
"Sorry!" he said. "It's instinct."

Instincts are funny underground creatures. They stay hidden for most of our lives and only surface when situations arise. Like moles, they are short-sighted and can, if we are not careful, leave piles of debris behind them. Ben's protective, paternal instinct had kicked in as soon as I had discovered that I was pregnant. It caused him to behave in all sorts of endearingly irrational ways. He allowed his instincts to overrule his common sense, consequently his perceptions and treatment of me had changed. He no longer noticed my robust, playful self but instead, through the fog-filled filter of protection, saw only fragility and danger. If I went to the supermarket he now came with me and walked ahead of the trolley to ensure that no-one crashed into me. If we walked through the town centre then he would hold his arms out to the side of me to make sure that I had enough space to walk without being jostled. Wherever possible he encouraged me back into the nesting position – constantly ushering me to sit down and rest.

"I'm not a bird you know... I don't have to sit on our baby until it hatches. It's inside me, and it's quite safe."

"I know," he apologised. "I just don't want anything to happen, that's all. It's so... precious. You're both so precious."

"I realise that. It's very sweet... if a little frustrating."

The sonographer, a small lady with rosy cheeks and shocking-pink hair, ushered us into her darkened room. After the usual introductions, she proceeded to ask a few basic questions.

"So, have you had any problems so far, or has it all been tickety boo?" she asked in a surprisingly squeaky voice.

"Quite normal, I think... I mean... I haven't done this

before, so I don't really know. I was hoping that you'd tell us."
"Absolutely!" she acknowledged shrilly. "Just one more question before we have a look... Do you have any idea when your baby is due?"
"25th September?" we suggested in unison. The sonographer smiled.
"Ah! Christmas! A time for celebration," she quipped. We nodded, slightly embarrassed. She chuckled. "You're the third one I've seen today! I'm expecting to see quite a few more over the next few weeks. Now let's have a look shall we?"

She spread some ice cold gel over my stomach and placed the scanner firmly on top. There was silence. A long silence. She scrutinised the screen. I craned my neck to catch a glimpse, but the angle of the monitor made it impossible, so instead I looked for clues in her facial expressions. She gave nothing away but simply pursed her lips, inhaled some air (it must have been helium because her voice went up another octave and became positively cartoonlike) and then turned to look at us.
"Okay. Erm..." she began and then coughed nervously. "Everything looks fine... HOWEVER..." She paused for dramatic effect and my heart stopped. Ben clutched my hand. "There is one thing that I need to tell you before I let you have a look for yourselves..." I swallowed hard and gripped Ben's hand even tighter, unsure of what was to follow. We stared at her intently... willing her to speak... to reveal her secret. Instead, she smiled gently, leant forward and whispered in her softest Minnie Mouse voice, "I can see TWO heartbeats." She let the revelation sink in before she spelt it out for us. "You're expecting twins." Ben and I stared at each other in disbelief and then started to laugh nervously. To be expecting one child had been a

surprise, but two... well that was a whole different level of anticipation!

The sonographer recognised our reactions; she had seen them so many times before in that small, darkened room. She sought to reassure us. To bring us back into the present.
"Don't worry about the practicalities for now; just enjoy looking at them today," she squeaked. With that she turned the screen towards us and showed us a snapshot of the beautiful things to come.

By the time I was 20 weeks pregnant I was enormous. Double the bundle of joy meant double the size. I started to suffer from bump envy whenever I attended the ante-natal clinics - I snarled at the other glamorous mums-to-be with their neat little bumps and growled at the slim-line scrummys who were still able to wear their own clothes at this half-way stage. For some months now I had been reliant on the sack-like contributions that they call *maternity wear*, copies of which could often be found in my local camping store. Still, I recognised that this unflattering pregnancy uniform was all part of the process of attrition of self that was preparing me for motherhood:

The first part of this process involved the transfer of ownership of my body – it seemed to have become public property. Random people, some of whom I had never met before, now found it perfectly acceptable to walk up to me and place their hands on my stomach. So long as they accompanied this action with the key phrase, *How beautiful!* or *When is it due?* then this seemed (at least to everybody else) to be a socially acceptable practice and one to which I was expected to submit.

The second part of the process had been the unrecognisable transformation of my reflection. My mind remembered my old svelte self (I purposely eliminated from my memory any lumps and bumps that may have disqualified me from that description), yet whenever I caught sight of myself in a shop window I was confronted with the image of a small elephant! Eventually I learnt not to look. Unlike me, Ben did not seem to mind this transformation and appeared to be rather fond of elephants, taking his position of Elephant Keeper very seriously!

The two elements of this process were clearly designed to desensitise me to my body and to numb me to my own self-image. The purpose? So that I would be unfazed by the birthing process – when, with my legs akimbo, strangers would be peering, prodding and poking where strangers ought not to be. Also so that when I did finally walk into town with my little children hanging off my limbs, pawing at my body and with baby sick covering my shoulder, I would not be shocked or even dismayed!

Eventually I conceded my expectations of all things thin and feminine and started to enjoy my new shape and size. I no longer noticed or fought against my pregnant waddle, (comfort was now my highest priority) and Ben learnt to adjust to my newfound wind problem (an unfortunate side-effect of twins – there was no longer enough room to carry *extras* on the inside of me, everything had to come out). I listened to the mid-wife's advice regarding a sensible diet and tried where possible to follow it. I increased my vegetable intake – gherkins became a staple feature of my diet, particularly at breakfast time – and introduced some additional protein sources – mostly in the form of pickled eggs. Occasionally though I lapsed into some of my former bad eating habits - consuming vast quantities of chocolate in front of the television. Well, nobody is perfect!

Chapter 5
Arrivals

On the 10th September 2001 the air was shattered by two piercing cries as Henry and Alfie entered this world - two slippery, slimy, purple beings, with screwed up faces, eyes tight shut and mouths open wide. Totally dependent. Totally helpless. Totally here!

As the umbilical cords were severed, my heart reached out to them both and forged an unbreakable, eternal connection. Mesmerised by their new-born beauty, I did not notice when responsibility snuck into the room and seated itself on my shoulders. My awareness of its weightiness would take a few days to reveal and a lifetime to unravel.

Love and joy had yet to enter my room. They would come later, in the comfort of my clean bed and in the peace of our own home, but first I needed to introduce myself to these two strangers. I needed to study their faces, their tiny fingers and toes, and to feel the softness of their new-born skin, untouched by the corruption of life - purity in its truest form. I smelt them both, inhaling their fragrance – the sweetest perfume ever created, straight off heaven's shelves.

A Rampage of Grace

The chief mid-wife shattered the moment by introducing practicality into the mix of emotions:
"Your sons are hungry. You need to feed them!" And so began the reality of twins...

People talk about the *patter of tiny feet*. However, when Henry and Alfie arrived into this world, there was no pattering, just pooing, screaming, weeing and feeding. An endless cycle. The only pattering sound was when I was not quick enough with the nappy and Alfie weed on the laminate floor (or even worse, on Henry's head).

The twins colluded in their requests and coincided in their dramas. If one screamed then they both screamed. If one was hungry then they were both hungry. By the end of the first week Ben and I were completely frazzled and totally worn out. We were novices and it showed! We needed help. We sent for my mum, Davina.

Davina arrived in a flurry - a whirlwind of colour, life, humour and experience. She came for a week and stayed three months; such was our need! In one fell swoop I had become both a parent and a dependent child.

"Oh sweetie, they're only crying. Don't let it worry you. It's what babies do. They're exercising their lungs. Look, I do it too." With that she let out an operatic warble, surprising everyone into silence, including the twins! Here, you grab Alfie and I'll grab Henry," Davina instructed picking the wrong child up in her arms.
"Mum, you've muddled them up again. This one's Henry."
"Oh dear! It's so tricky to tell. What we need is a system... I know! Why don't we always dress Alfie in

Arrivals

orange and Henry in purple, that way it'll be easy to tell who is who. It's either that or I write their initials on their feet in sharpie." I reeled in horror at the latter suggestion so deferred to the clothing option with some slight colour modifications.

"Colour coding's a good idea, but it'll have to be their socks that are colour coded and I think blue and red would be more appropriate colours." Davina looked disappointed at my moderation, so I tried to appease her. "They're the colours that I have in the draw." She shrugged and conceded.

"Very well. Oh! That reminds me... I haven't given you their presents yet. I bought them some gifts." She tottered out to the car and came back with bags in hand. I opened the first present tentatively. It was clothing and I dreaded the contents. I was right to be fearful. The paper fell open to reveal two bright orange sets of rainbow-adorned dungarees complete with hats."

"Oh Mum!" was all I could utter. She misinterpreted it as a sign of appreciation and, beaming like a Cheshire cat, handed me the next gift.

"It's for their room!" she announced proudly. I opened the parcel and saw a large orange plastic clock with bold Disney characters on it. "Every half hour it chimes, sings a song and the characters change," she explained. "It'll do them good to get used to noise; too many people pussy foot around their children. It's no good for them you know." Dismay filled my heart. Ben and I had spent hours painting and decorating the twins' nursery in soft pastel hues. Everything was co-ordinated and carefully chosen. This bright orange clock would be a carbuncle in its midst. "I've checked their room and know exactly where it can go. I'll pop it up for you later."

"Thanks." I mumbled insincerely.

"Now, let's try on these new outfits. I can't wait to see

them ..."

Davina was brilliant at hosting the onslaught of well-wishers who came to see our new arrivals. She reduced the pressure on me by producing endless plates of homemade biscuits and mugs of tea. When I was resting she would keep my guests riveted with her elaborate life-stories, engaging them for hours. The role suited her personality perfectly. She entertained my friends and I in turn got used to the additional guests that she brought to the house – the local milkman and fireman optimistically became frequent visitors around our kitchen table – although she had little time for her admirers because she was too busy delighting in her new grandchildren.

Davina took on the responsibility of the housework and meals, whilst I took on the practicalities of feeding, dressing and socialising Henry and Alfie. Ben easily stepped into the role of doting Dad, providing unlimited cuddles and nappy changes for our boys, when he was around. However, nowadays that was not much - his time was mostly spent at work. Whilst I felt the stress of the twins' daily needs, Ben felt the full burden of provision. We had taken the brave step for me to give up work and were now reliant solely on his income. We had calculated our finances carefully when we made the decision, but we never factored in the cost of the extra pressure on Ben. It meant that he needed to work harder and longer - his job opportunities flourished and his paternal opportunities declined. What we gained financially, we lost in time as a family.

Chapter 6

Moving In

Eighteen months later...

Hand-in-hand we stood mesmerised by the grubby, white building that was peeping out from under the overgrown ivy. I drew in a deep breath of delight.
"Is it really ours?" I asked in disbelief.
"Certainly is!" Ben acknowledged proudly as some moss slid off the roof and fell in front of us. "Don't you remember...? I promised that we'd achieve our dream."
"I know! Although, if I'm honest, I thought that was one promise that you wouldn't be able to keep."
"You should have known me better than that, Laurie... I've never let you down yet!" He kissed the top of my head and I nuzzled in tight. I looked up at his soft face and attempted to ruffle his short fringe.
"You sacrificed a lot for this," I teased.
"The fringe? It was nothing! Everyone has to grow up sometime! Anyway, short is the new long these days and managers need to keep up with the times. It's official - managers don't have floppy fringes. At least that's what I keep trying to tell Eddy in the office, but so far he and his fringe are not to be parted." I laughed. Eddy was the post-

room boy. It was typical of Ben to see and encourage the potential in everyone.

"He'll come round to the idea, eventually…" I said. "When he finds the motivation."

"Ready?" Ben asked. I nodded. He took the key and, brushing away the ivy, inserted it into the keyhole. Slowly and deliberately he opened the door to our new home, revealing the wide, bright hallway with shocking yellow walls. Turning around he beamed at me and then scooped me up into his arms to carry me across the threshold. "Mrs Driver, let me escort you safely into our new home. I now declare it officially ours!"

Ben deposited me in our new lounge which was a gaudy, blank, orange canvas on which to place our family mark.
"Have you got it?" I asked.
"What?" Ben asked cluelessly.
"The chess pieces!" I exclaimed.
"Of course!" he laughed, producing the frame. "Where would you like it, Your Majesty? Above the fireplace?"
"Definitely!"

Ben had only just finished mounting our frame onto the wall when the removals van pulled up outside and the moving in process began in earnest.

Five hours later, Davina arrived with the twins and Benson (our black, labradoodle puppy). Our family home in Lower Tweedle was finally complete.

Chapter 7

Decorative Delights

A few months later...

Ben appeared in the kitchen, looking gorgeous in his new blue suit. I smiled and felt warm inside as I looked at him. The aroma of his after-shave surrounded me, setting all my senses on fire.
"Looking good!" I whistled. He smiled.
"Thanks!"
"But seriously, how are you feeling about today?"
"A bit tense. There's a lot riding on this meeting. If it goes well then we'll all be in for a big bonus, but if..."
"Let's not do ifs. They've got you in the room. Of course it will go well!" Ben smiled, reassured by my confidence in him.

The connective moment was short-lived. A lump of porridge went flying through the air and landed on his shoulder. A direct hit! Ben glared. Alfie giggled. I grabbed the dish cloth.
"Can't you control these kids?" Ben snapped. It was a rhetorical question really. He knew the answer... No I could not!

"Sorry! I'm doing my best. Next time warn me when you're coming through and I'll remove any missiles." My attempt at humour failed, lost under the pressure of Ben's work.

I turned my efforts from humour to restoration and wiped him clean.
"There! Good as new. No-one would know." I playfully adjusted his tie and kissed him on the nose. He held me tight, so tight that I felt the tension of his meeting ahead. "Now hurry up, you don't want to be late. I still find it hard to believe that I'm married to a director! I'm so proud of you." Ben softened and smiled at my recognition and praise. He reached for his briefcase and gasped in Horror. Henry was sitting beside it, felt tips in hand.
"Daddy! I drawed rainbow!" he uttered in two year-old speak, pointing proudly to his picture on the side of Ben's briefcase. Ben glared at Henry, looked exasperated and left.

I looked at the twins with their innocent, little, toothy grins and assessed the devastation around me – porridge spots adorned every cupboard door and cave-like, felt tip drawings covered the floor. I made the only decision that a mother could -
"Come on then you two. Let's go into the lounge and play." Then with one final glance around the room I whispered. I'll sort this out later."

So we walked away from the bombsite and entered the restful peace of the lounge. Pulling their toy box into the centre of the floor, I started to take out their wooden train set. The twins helped by building their own little offshoots to the track and before long we had a huge, swirling rail network with lots of junctions, stations and crossings. I knew that the boys would play with this for hours. It was the only thing that would engage them for any length of time, so it was my secret weapon to gain a slot in the day for me.

I sat back on the sofa and mused over the twins' photograph over the fireplace. It was a large, framed, professional, photograph of a very cute looking Henry and Alfie on their second birthday. They were sitting back to back with broad grins and little tufts of fine, blonde hair, which I had gelled on the day, transforming them into miniature Jedwards. Ben and I were so proud of the photograph that we made it the centrepiece of our room. To make space for it, we consigned our framed chess pieces to a wall in the back room, an unwitting symbol of our changing priorities.

By the time Ben came home the place still looked like the scene of a nuclear disaster. All my good intentions of tidying the kitchen and house had gone to pot, due to a distressed phone call from my neighbour Marcie.

"Laurie, is that you? It's Marcie." She had sounded desperate.
"Are you okay?"
"Not even slightly! I've managed to lock myself out of the house and Josh is still inside. In fact, he's there at the back door right now, laughing! Can you bring my spare key please?"
"Sure thing!"
"Do hurry!" The line went dead.
"Alfie! Henry!" I yelled in my loudest fishwife voice. I had long since given up the practice of tracking down the twins, nowadays I chose shouting as my default option; that

way the twins would track me down. Unfortunately it made for a very noisy household. "Come on, we're going out!" I shouted.

Alfie appeared first. He poked his head around the corner but refused to follow with his body.
"Come on Alfie, we're in a hurry. I need to put your shoes on." I shot him my biggest smile of encouragement. It worked! He beamed back and tentatively placed a glistening white leg around the corner, closely followed by the rest of his white, nappy-cream-covered body! My smile slipped and so did his. All I could think was, *where's Henry?*
I ran upstairs to the bathroom just in time to catch Henry finishing the regrouting of the tiles… the floor-tiles! He stood up immediately and pointed proudly to his handiwork; his face and hands covered with the white, gloopy, nappy cream. My phone went again…
"It's Marcie. Where are you? Josh is opening all the kitchen cupboards and taking everything out."
"Okay. I'll be straight there." I reached over and rescued Henry from the sea of white; then carried him downstairs to meet his semi-naked partner in crime. Carrying Alfie was not an option – he was far too slippery. So instead I just put his shoes on and he squelched his way across the road to Marcie's.

"Here you go…" I said, wiping the nappy cream off the key as I handed it over. Marcie grabbed it gratefully, opened the front door and headed straight for the kitchen. She returned a couple of minutes later with a very tearful, Nutella-covered Josh.
"You might as well stay for coffee. Looks like all of our kids need a shower!" Marcie offered wearily.

So that's how it happened... Three showers, several cups of coffee and one afternoon later, I meandered back across the road to embark upon dinner. Yet more mess creation! By the time Ben got home, the twins were happy and settled but not the house. I had just embarked upon the task of scrubbing off Henry's cave-drawings from the floor when Ben's two polished shoes appeared beneath my nose. I grimaced and a wave of failure swept over me as I realised that I had fallen very short of the standard of a perfect wife. I stood up and looked him in the eye, but I was not met with disappointment, just a great big smile.
"By the looks of things my news has come at just the right time..." I looked at him quizzically.
"What news? Did the meeting go well?"
"Very well! I'll tell you about that later. But that's not the news." I was intrigued. "I've drafted you in some help." This time it was a tsunami of failure that swept over me, washing me aground.
"But I don't need any help! I'm fine!" I protested.
"Really?" he said, gesturing around the room, but smiling none-the-less. I giggled.
"Well, maybe I could do with a little help."
"That's what I thought. It would be nice if you were able to concentrate on the twins without having to juggle all the clearing up too." Now I was interested...
"So what are you proposing?"
"An au pair. Danny at work told me about his sister, Kelly. She's an au pair and she is looking for somewhere to work. She had to leave her last employer quite quickly... Something about the wife having a temper... I'm not really sure of the details, but anyway, she's desperate for work and I figured we were... um.... desperate!" I scowled at this last allegation (albeit that I knew it was true).
"So, how much will it cost us?"
"£100 per week and you get your sanity back..." Ben knew

not to push me any more at this point, he had long since learned how to manipulate my stubborn streak. "Anyway, it's just an idea. I'll leave it with you…" However, he did not need to leave it with me, I already knew the answer – things were not working out. Our twins were quite literally double trouble and often made me feel like half a mother and even less of a wife. This was the lifeline that I craved.

"When can she start?" I asked enthusiastically.
"Tomorrow, if you want." Relief rapidly replaced failure and I settled back against the kitchen cupboards, surveying the scene of Armageddon. I winced as I considered the mammoth cleaning task ahead of me.
"Are you sure she can't start now?" I quipped!

Kelly arrived just in the nick of time. After two years of coping with Henry and Alfie on my own, I had reached the point of exhaustion. With a constant cycle of entertaining the twins, washing, cleaning, clearing up and cooking, my own life had been overtaken, my identity evaporated and my friends forgotten. Coffee mornings, whilst a welcome break, often proved to be a source of endless spillages and mess. Life with Ben had degenerated too - our only free hour to spend together each evening was often spent with me half-asleep. At last we would be able to redress the balance.

Kelly turned up at our door with suitcase in hand at 11am. She was a pretty girl with jet-black hair and petite features. There was something delicate about both her frame and her disposition. I wondered how she would cope with our twins! Still, for now I did not care. She was my hero and I was just grateful for her arrival!

"Come in!" I said with gusto. "I'm Laurie, Ben's wife." Bustling her in the door, I tripped over my own enthusiasm. "So where would you like to start? Coffee? Meeting the twins? A tour of the house?" She looked overwhelmed at my ebullience. "Sorry! I'm just a bit excited about you coming to stay." With that, Kelly seemed to relax a little. "Tell you what... just leave your case there and come and meet the boys. They're out in the garden painting (it's the safest place, that way only the grass ends up multi-coloured)." Kelly giggled.

I poured us all a drink and called the twins inside where we all sat down together at the kitchen table.
"So, Kelly, tell me a bit about yourself. I mean, all I know about you is that you are Danny's sister and come highly recommended."
"It's hard to know where to start," she replied softly. "I've always loved kids, I've had to because I'm the middle one of nine."
"NINE!"
"Everyone says that! Of course, I've never known any different. It just means that I'm quite used to little ones and also to a bustling family life."
"I should think you are quite used to cleaning too!"
"Funnily enough, my mum chose to do all that herself." I felt somewhat belittled by Kelly's mum. Not only had she given birth to nine children (a mammoth feat in itself) but she had also coped all on her own with the housework too.
"Did she have any help?" I asked feebly.
"Only my Dad... Oh! and my Gran. She lived with us up until last year, when she went into a home." Kelly's mum sounded far too perfect and capable for my liking so I

A Rampage of Grace

decided to change the subject for the sake of my own self-esteem.

"So what about you? You're 24?" Kelly nodded. "How long have you been au pairing?"
"Just for the last two years."
"So what happened at the last house? Why did you leave? Ben wasn't sure." Kelly's whole demeanour changed at my frank questioning, her eyes widened and her porcelain complexion went china white. For the first time, I noticed the faded bruising around her eye. "Oh my goodness! Whatever happened to your eye?" Kelly looked mortified at my discovery.
"It was just... It was just... She..." she struggled to find the words and hung her head low in shame.
"Did your last employer do that to you?" I asked, guessing the truth behind her departure. She nodded her head and then dissolved into a torrent of tears, occasionally mumbling some incoherent explanations.
"They were so horrible to me...! So horrible...! It wasn't my fault..." but it was difficult to establish anything from between the snivels, so I decided to drop the whole subject and focus on pastures new.
"Shhhhh! Don't worry! You're safe here. We won't be horrible to you, I promise. We're far too grateful for that!" I handed her a tissue to blow her nose. "We're messy, but not horrible." Kelly giggled at this and blew her nose again, for the last time.

"Right! Let's show you around. Alfie, Henry, you can go back to your painting." They beamed smiles of contentment and shot back outside, standing on either side of their easel, dressed only in vests and nappies. For the next five minutes I took Kelly on a tour of our less-than-substantial house, ending up at the spare room that was to be hers for the months ahead. I left her unpacking and wandered slowly downstairs to join the twins. As I walked I mused about the pressure that was about to leave my shoulders. I felt warmly optimistic inside, but like most optimism, it was cut short before it bore any fruit

Stepping outside onto the patio, my joy plummeted to the floor as I found a small pile of vests and nappies. I swallowed hard. This could only mean one thing… body painting!

With fear and trepidation I scanned the garden for evidence of the crime and immediately found two green-and-blue boys standing proudly on my lawn. They would have reminded me of the warriors from *Braveheart* had it not been for the thoroughness of their painted bodies and the inclusion of their painted blue willies! The only natural colour still remaining for them both was the colour of their blue eyes and white teeth – which were currently on display due to their big, toothy grins. Even their curly, blonde hair was interspersed with seaweed-like, wavy streaks of green.
"Look!" they said in unison, with arms out wide.
"What am I to do with you both?" I laughed and hugged them both tight (after all, it was now Kelly's job to do the washing!).

Chapter 8

Relief and Escape

Kelly slotted in well to our household. Her pleasant, easy-going manner suited our chaotic lifestyles. She giggled at my mishaps and mopped up my mistakes. Unfazed by the frequent, sticky deposits that appeared around the house courtesy of Henry and Alfie, she cleaned, washed and ironed herself into my affections. Finally under this newfound routine, we started to function properly as a family and each night Ben returned to a more peaceful home. What Ben and I sacrificed in privacy to incorporate Kelly into our family we recouped in sanity and cleanliness. It was a small price to pay.

I struggled to relate to Kelly on a close friendship basis because she was far too emotional for me. Her bottom lip was in an almost permanent state of trembling whenever music played or she was left alone. Solitude, it appeared, was her enemy and chaotic household her friend. Her fragility concerned me, a legacy from her previous employers it seemed, although the details of prior events were still sketchy and as yet unspoken. She sought solace in Ben and related to him as if he were an older brother; constantly drawing on his strength and stability. Ours was

A Rampage of Grace

a more practical, working relationship so I never did fathom the full extent of her angst but merely gleaned the snippets that Ben imparted to me at bedtime. He spent time affirming her as a person and resetting her eyes on the future. I smiled as I watched him minister to her needs, and remembered the many occasions when Ben had ministered to my brokenness, thus establishing himself in the position of *Best Friend* and ultimately *Husband*.

Slowly, slowly over the months Ben's tender, protective approach succeeded with Kelly. Her constant lip trembling turned to an infrequent quivering, and finally to an occasional wobble. Her mouth and emotions were no longer being tossed to-and-fro on the rough seas of past experience but were now firmly docked in the harbour of love and acceptance.

Henry and Alfie benefitted from the stability too. Their toddler graffiti had flourished in this calmer atmosphere, with plenty of bright, crayon drawings depicting happy family scenes, rainbows and rabbits. Unfortunately their loving portrait of Mummy and Daddy naked in bed did not scrub off the gaudy, orange living room wall because on that day they had happened upon my permanent marker set. Still, at least we got to decorate the lounge six months ahead of schedule!

Occasionally Ben and I managed a night out together alone. We intended it to be a weekly event, but work commitments dictated otherwise. Monthly or quarterly proved more achievable.
"This feels strange." I commented, on our first solitary, adult encounter.
"What does?"
"Being out alone. I'm so used to having Henry, Alfie or

Kelly around."

"I know what you mean. There is no you and me anymore." His wistful tone and piercing words betrayed the regret hidden in his heart.

"It feels like years since we've done this," I mused.

"That's because it is!"

"Really?" I chewed on my lip as that realisation sank in. Time, it seemed, had outwitted us and escaped with our personal relationship.

"So where shall we go?" Ben asked, bringing a healthy dose of reality to our conversation. We had been so excited at the prospect of our time alone that neither of us had thought to plan it. With so many choices available to us, we failed to think of any.

"Ummm. The pub?" I offered eventually.

"Okay. *The Emerald Crown* it is. We had some good times there."

"Yes we did!" I giggled.

Sitting back in the car seat I reminisced about the times we had spent snuggled up in the recesses of the snug at *The Emerald Crown*. The coolness of the flagstone floor and the warmth of the crackling fire had provided the perfect backdrop for our romantic encounters. We had exchanged many secrets in the quietness of that pub with only the chinking of glasses and sound of footsteps on the stone floor to offset the eavesdroppers. I looked forward to rekindling some of our own embers in that place this night.

"Oh no!" Ben groaned as we pulled into the car park.

"What's wrong?" I asked as I dreamily opened my eyes.

"It's packed! They must have a party on or something." My romantic expectations evaporated, as did Ben's. He hesitated, unsure of what lay ahead.

"Let's give it a go anyway... For old times' sake," I

suggested.
"Sure," was his unconvinced reply.

Tentatively we held hands as we approached the familiar wooden door. However, even as we stood on the other side we could hear the music blaring from within. Suddenly the door flew open as a young lad and his friends were deposited into the car park by two big, burly bouncers dressed in black. They looked us up and down.
"Coming in?" they grunted through grizzled mouths. I looked at them, then looked inside. I saw the beer-stained carpet on the former flagstone floor, spotted the gigantic, gaming machines standing in the recesses of the snug and watched the herds of youngsters drinking, texting and bellowing. Clearly this pub had undergone an 'improvement' program since we last frequented it!
"No thanks! I think we've come to the wrong place," I replied.
"Suit yourselves!" retorted the bouncer, clanging the door shut in our faces.
Ben and I looked at each other in dismay and disbelief.
"I guess that's progress for you!" he quipped sarcastically.
"I guess so… Where to now?"

Eventually, we achieved our goal that night of a romantic night for two – snuggled up on a park bench at the top of the town, sharing a kebab, watching the world go by. It wasn't exactly the date night we had envisioned, but then again this was only the first oiling of our rather rusty romance.

Chapter 9

Expect the Unexpected

The call came from nowhere, one Friday night:
"Hello Darling."
"Hi, Mum!"
"How are you and my boys doing?"
"We're all fine thanks."
"Fine? Are you sure? I bet you could do with a bit of R and R? A nice holiday? Somewhere hot?"
"What are you getting at, Mum?"
"Your Great Aunt Lesley has leant me the keys to her villa in Southern Italy and I wondered if you and the boys wanted to come over and stay for three weeks."
"Three weeks! Are you serious?" my heart leapt at the prospect of such an escape. I knew Aunt Lesley very well and her taste in property was quite simply luxurious and show-stopping. I had heard about her house in Italy, but had never been invited (apparently I was such a nasty, sticky child that she had always insisted on meeting me on neutral ground). Apparently her house had its own private full length swimming pool, tennis court and sauna. This was one invitation that I was not going to turn down. "Of course I want to come! When?"
"Monday."

"What, this Monday?"
"Yep!"
"But that's too soon!" I responded, panicking.
"Why is it too soon?" asked Davina. I was silent as I tried to formulate my reply. It was not really too soon, it was just that it was a shock and I felt like I needed time to prepare and plan. Davina anticipated my resistance and pressed in for the kill.
"Go on… live dangerously for once, Laurie. All you need is a few clothes and some armbands for the boys. You don't need any time to prepare for that, now do you? Just say yes. You know you want to." She was right, I did want to. I inhaled deeply and stepped into the unfamiliar realm of spontaneity.
"Yes! We'd love to."
"Brilliant! Right, I'll go and book the flights now and call you back to arrange timings. You go off and tell Ben."

Ben! Oh my goodness, I had not even considered him in my decision. I had just assumed… A river of panic and guilt coursed through my veins, I started to drown in a flood of worry. He had become so distant recently, bogged down in the quagmire of work. Surely I should be here to support him through this difficult time? But what if it was better for us to be away and him to have peace and quiet? Or maybe he will not want us to be away for so long? Will he cope…? I dismounted the Ferris wheel of arguments and picked up the phone to call him at work

I should not have worried. Ben was instantly delighted for me and the boys.
"Of course you should go! I'm happy for you," he added reassuringly.
"Thanks. Maybe next time we'll go together as a family (if we behave ourselves this time!)." Ben chuckled.

"Good luck with that one!" he retorted. I ignored his comment and plodded on with the practicalities.
"And you're sure that you'll be alright?"
"Definitely! I'm a big boy now, Laurie. I'll be at work most of the time and Kelly will cook for me so what's to worry about?." I heard his boss in the background. "Listen I've got to go. I'll see you later."
"Okay. Love you!" I uttered, but he was gone.

A few days later, I sat back in my aircraft seat, with soft music piping into my ears, courtesy of the no-longer-free headphones. Alfie sat beside me zapping aliens on his television monitor whilst Henry quietly dozed across my lap. All things considered, the journey had been a lot less stressful than I had predicted. Both of the boys had enjoyed pulling their own suitcases at the airport, (only knocking into a few people) and whenever they had looked bored I got them to rummage through my handbag for something nice to eat. This distraction technique had seemed effective (albeit not one recommended by most parenting manuals), so I stuck with it as a strategy until we were successfully on board.

I switched over to the film selection on my television screen and was soon engrossed in the romcom of the year *A Rampage of Chocolate 2*. Ben and I had intended to see it together, but as per most of our intentions, it had never come to pass due to the busyness of our lives.

I was totally immersed in thoughts of romance and chocolate when the air hostess appeared.
"May I put your trays down, I'm about to serve lunch?" I nodded. She leant across me and, with lightning speed and

the dexterity of a spinning spider, released each of our trays. Then she was gone, leaving a thick trail of cloying perfume behind her. The clatter of the trays woke Henry up with a start. He opened his eyes blearily and then started to twitch his nose.
"What's that funny smell, Mummy?"
"It's the air hostess darling. It's her perfume."
"I don't like it. I prefer how you smell, Mummy," he said, nuzzling into my neck. Just then the air hostess returned and deposited three foul smelling trays of food in front of us.
"Yuk! That smells bad too!" Declared Henry in his loud four-year-old voice.
"Does something else smell?" the air hostess started to enquire. I quickly blocked Henry off with my body and sent her away with a hasty,
"No! No smells here! You're fine! We're all fine! Thank you!"

We removed the lids from each of our trays and revealed a congealed substance that masqueraded as *Boeuf Bourguignon*. The boys looked at me in horror, their little eyes pleading with me for mercy. I decided not to fight the battle.
"Just eat your roll and your cheese, and then you can have the pudding." They smiled gratefully and tucked in. However, more disappointment followed when they opened the dessert to reveal a healthy (if a little tired) fruit salad.
"Oh!" sighed Alfie, pushing a small mandarin segment around the plastic tub. "I'm full."
"I don't blame you. Have some of your drink. I got you lemonade." His face beamed as I handed him the plastic glass full of bubbles. Unfortunately as the first air-filled bubble hit his mouth the aeroplane unexpectedly hit an air pocket and dropped dramatically. Alfie's glass flew out of

Expect the Unexpected

his hand and cold lemonade showered down drenching both of us.

Henry, who had seen it all, but experienced none of the wetness, giggled. Alfie on the other hand howled, so I dragged him off to the toilet to get dried off, leaving Henry to fend for himself for two minutes…

Ten minutes and one long queue later, Alfie and I returned to our seats to a very chocolatey Henry.
"What have you been eating?" I enquired.
"Nothing!" lied Henry, staring at the ground.
"Your mouth is covered in chocolate, Henry, what…" Just then I spotted an empty chocolate mousse container under his chair. I picked it up and matched the contents to the brown smears around his mouth. "Where did you get this, Henry?" He said nothing and shuffled his feet on the ground nervously.

All was revealed a moment later in a heated conversation on the other side of the blue curtain dividing us from first class.
"It was here I tell you! I left my pudding here!"
"I'm so sorry sir!" I could hear the exasperated air hostess replying. "I just don't know what's happened to it! Let me get you another one, sir." With that the curtain flew back as the air hostess marched through on her mission to replace the missing mousse. Quickly, I stuffed the empty pudding pot in the seat pocket in front of me. The air hostess glanced towards us and narrowed her eyes as she caught sight of Henry's guilty expression and chocolatey mouth. I smiled broadly with the hope of deflecting her suspicion.
"Everything okay?" I asked her brazenly.
"Hmmm," she replied marching off at full pace. I turned

and glared at Henry. He assumed a quiet and angelic pose in his seat; the seat where he remained on house-arrest for the remainder of the flight.

"Cooee! Over here!" shouted Davina frantically waving her arms and a bunch of multi-coloured balloons. Surrounded by several sombre-faced chauffeurs, all dressed in grey and black, her shock of colour and high-pitched calls made her as prominent as a parrot in a pigeon coop. Her orange and green striped kaftan flapped wildly, engulfing a little boy who mistook her for a balloon salesman. I blushed with embarrassment, but my boys ran forward with squeals of delight.
"Nanny!"
With hugs of joy they embraced each other warmly and then with a hug of motherly love she held me tight. My aircraft ordeal was officially over; our holiday had begun.

"Come over here and meet Carlos. He's Aunt Leslie's chauffeur and odd-job man. He's very handsome and I do believe he has a crush on me."
"Oh Mum, stop it! You believe that everyone has a crush on you."
"Well I'm just saying how it is. You can judge for yourself," Davina replied unashamedly.

We bundled the cases into the boot and the boys into the back. I nudged in beside them whilst Davina plopped herself next to Carlos in the luxurious front seat.
"Tally ho!" she yelled, patting Carlos on the knee. Smiling, he put his cap on and we set off on the ten-minute drive to the villa.
"Oh look!" I kept saying, pointing at various things Italian

Expect the Unexpected

out of the window. The boys did not even look up, preferring instead to wrestle each other in the back of the car. Cultural differences it seems are wasted on four year-olds. However, the grandeur of Aunt Leslie's estate was not wasted on anyone. We all gasped as we sat watching the seven-foot high automatic gates slowly part to allow us entry. We espied for the first time the cypress-lined driveway, which snaked its way through ornate Tuscan gardens, until it reached the marble pillars that defined the entrance to the house.
"Wow!" I exclaimed. "This is seriously nice!"
"Oh darling, this is nothing! Just wait until you see inside."

Carlos stopped the car outside the front door. Davina teetered out, on her favourite platform heels.
"Come along boys! I'll show you which room's yours. You're right next door to me and I've bought you both some new clothes. They're on your beds."
"Woo hoo!" shouted the boys in delight as they ran after her.

I listened as the clatter of their feet on the marble floors and their squeals of excitement disappeared down the marble corridors into the depths of the house. Enjoying the warmth of the sun on my face and the chorus of the cicadas in the garden, I stood for a moment, closed my eyes and smiled. A cloak of peace enveloped me covering the weariness of my day.

"Ciao Signora," said Carlos, driving away to park the car.
"Ciao," I responded dreamily.

Chapter 10
Family Values

Our days in Italy passed easily, as we quickly embraced the laid-back lifestyle. The twins were an instant hit with the locals and had permanent dimples on their cheeks from the constant pinching. Children were warmly welcomed everywhere, particularly the blonde-haired, blue-eyed variety, so I felt free to release the twins into the fullness of their true personalities which in turn released me into mine. Laurie the Sergeant Major was slowly replaced by Laurie the Encourager.

Henry and Alfie revelled in the affection that they received everywhere and started to develop confident swaggers. They waved and smiled at every local girl as they passed, thus ensuring that they received positive attention from every female generation. This attention was never more evident than on market days when they would return with armfuls of free gifts - succulent fruit and sugary sweets from the many stall-holders.

Daily we ate in the local restaurants. The twins' messy, public displays of spaghetti-eating became a source of fame and entertainment amongst the locals. The boys reveled in their notoriety whilst I carefully chose cleaner pasta options for myself. Carlos introduced us to his extensive family, so we spent many evenings seated at tables in the market square watching all the children play happily together. I smiled as I started to appreciate the true concept of community and family. Davina smiled as she started to appreciate Luigi the waiter!

I relayed our escapades to Ben daily on the phone, but I could never quite portray the essence of our experience.
"Oh Ben, it's so beautiful here. I really wish you could come out and join us. It's just not the same without you." I heard a distracted grunt from the other end of the line. I ignored him and continued on optimistically. "I've discovered something here that we've lost sight of."
"Really? What?"
"Us. Who we are. What's important."
"Hmmm. I'm pleased," was his lack-lustre response. He changed the subject. "I really must go now. This proposal needs to be in front of the board by Friday. The profitability of the whole company rests upon it. Glad you're having fun though." I sensed his remoteness and distraction, so I tried to draw him in close.
"Okay then. I'll call you tomorrow. But remember this… That company is really lucky to have someone as great as you working for them. You are a man of integrity, honour and intellect; a rare breed." Ben paused as he silently internalised my affirmation. He seemed uncomfortable in the presence of such praise.
"Thanks. Errr, I really *do* need to go. Sorry, Laurie!"
"Sure. I understand. I love you!" I said with every fibre of my being.
"What?" he asked, distracted by someone in the background.
"I said – I love you!"

"Yeah. Love you too," came the distant reply.

My daily phone calls to Ben got shorter and shorter as the call of his deadlines and workload increased. I was too far away to help him through this season of pressure and I felt guilty as he moved into winter without me to sweep up his leaves. His isolation was deafening and exposed the weaknesses that were there. I determined to invest in our marriage upon our return and now realised that if I wanted to see snowdrops in spring again then I would have to plant the seeds first.

Chapter 11

DIY and Danger

Of course the holiday was not without its dramas, but I think that the mansion survived our presence quite well and was left reasonably intact upon our departure. That was amazing really given Alfie's new found fondness for DIY…

"Look at me!" squealed Alfie in excitement. I turned around to see him standing there wearing an oversized hard hat and a tool-belt laden with screwdrivers and a measuring tape. "I'm *Bob the Builder!*" he exclaimed, puffing out his chest with pride. I chuckled to myself, rearranged his tool-belt and lifted his hat from over his eyes.
"I guess you are," I said kissing his forehead tenderly.
"Carlos says I can help him today. We're going to build a kitchen and a garage!"
"No, no! We are MENDING the kitchen and garage. They are already built Signor Alfie."
"Is that okay, Mummy?"
"Sure. Run along. Oh! And make sure that you don't get in Carlos's way."

"I won't!" came the instantly-forgotten reassurance.
I headed down to the poolside where Davina was looking after Henry and entertaining Luigi, the waiter. I arrived to find her reading a book, Luigi sunbathing and Henry splashing merrily in the shallow end of the pool. His vibrant arm bands provided a dazzling display of colour above the mellow blue canvas of the pool. All was calm.

I sat for a while and soaked in the sun and ambience of the lazy Italian day. All thoughts of England and Ben melted away, leaving only the peace and the prospect of lunch.
"Come and play Mummy!" beckoned Henry.
"Why not!" I replied. "You'd better watch out! The crocodile's coming to get you!" Henry squealed in delight and anticipation. Davina sat forward to watch the spectacle. Menacingly I approached the diving board. Henry giggled. I stood on the end of the flexible plank and made giant snapping motions with my arms. "Ready? I'm coming to get you! One... Two... Three!" I launched myself into the air, arms outstretched. With one final roar I entered the water with the full weight and force of an attacking crocodile. I felt the water rushing past my face, my shoulders, my arms, my waist, my... My bikini bottoms! I threw my arms back quickly, but it was too late to catch them. The force of the water had propelled them back to the deep end of the pool. The crocodile within disappeared instantly, replaced by the great white whale without!

Laughing heartily, Davina recovered my bikini briefs for me within seconds, but my dignity took longer to return, so I avoided adult contact and escaped to the world of childish imagination by playing with Henry. After an hour of frolicking, my dignity, pride and bikini were intact and hunger pangs were calling.

"Lunch anyone?"

"Yes please!" came three replies.

"Mum, can you watch Henry for me please, while I make lunch and find Alfie (assuming the kitchen's still standing that is!)." She nodded, waved one hand in affirmation and then returned to her book.

I did not have to look far to find Alfie. He was sitting on the side in the kitchen chatting away whilst Carlos wrestled with some plumbing under the sink.

"Lunchtime, mister," I declared, removing him from the side and transferring him to the safety of a chair.

"Thanks, Carlos. Has he been any trouble?"

"No trouble. He was a good little helper. We worked together for a short time and then he went off with a screwdriver and fixed things." Carlos removed Alfie's hard hat and ruffled his blonde hair. "He'll be a good little builder one day." Alfie smiled proudly. Carlos smiled affectionately. I smiled gratefully. I looked with thanks and admiration at the man who had reached out to my son and affirmed him. To the man who had taken time out of his busy schedule to notice and include a four year-old boy. To the man whose priorities were formed by family not finance.

Carlos left his tools and the kitchen, providing me with the time and space to muse upon these things, whilst I split and buttered the crusty loaf for lunch. After an industrious ten minutes our banquet was ready! Using an array of spectacular meats, fruits and cheeses, Alfie and I prepared a platter worthy of royalty. With full recognition of our own craftsmanship, we carried the salver proudly to the poolside. Davina looked up lazily from her book.

"That was quick!" she observed then instantly settled back down again.

"Was Henry okay?" I asked.
"He was fine! No trouble at all! You worry too much. He's a wonderful little lad, aren't you Henry?" I smiled to myself and continued to arrange the lunch out on the table.

Out of the corner of my eye I spotted Carlos at the other end of the veranda, standing in the sun, his T-shirt and trousers soaking wet.
"Why is Carlos dripping wet, Mum?"
"Is he? Really?" She peered over her book at the handsome Italian drying in the sun. "Oh! Ermm… I'm not sure? Maybe he went for a swim." I raised an eyebrow at her.
"In his clothes?"
"Well you never know. We are in Italy. Things are different over here."

I was not so easily convinced and decided to extricate the truth from Henry. The one thing that is assured about every four year-old is that they never miss a thing. I had fallen prey to Henry's observant eye on many a sorry occasion.
"Henry?"
"Mummy! You're back! Can we play crocodiles again?" he asked excitedly. I gulped at the prospect and changed the subject very fast.
"Maybe. After lunch perhaps? Henry, do you know why Carlos is wet?"
"Yes. Coz he came and got me?"
"He came and got you?"
"Yes."
"From the water?"
"Yes." My frustration started to build at Henry's one-worded four year-old-style answers. I needed an explanation not a guessing game. I changed my tack.
"Why did he need to get you from the water?" It worked.

DIY and Danger

Henry beamed and proceeded to provide me with the detailed answer that I had been looking for complete with re-enactment.
"I was being a crocodile. Look!" He proceeded to show me his giant snapping motion. Unfortunately his armbands kept rebounding off each other, making it a difficult manoeuvre to achieve. "I walked along the bouncy plank just like you. It was very high, but I was very brave because I was a crocodile and crocodiles are very brave, aren't they Mummy?"
"Yes, I guess they are," I replied weakly, realising where this tale was heading.
"I jumped into the water just like this." He bounded around the pool in a Tigger-like demonstration, giggling and smiling, while I waited frustratedly for the end of his saga.
"So what happened next, Henry?"
"What? Oh! My armbands came off." My heart pounded as I pictured the scene in my head, my mouth went dry at the thoughts that swamped me. "I couldn't swim without them and I couldn't get to the side, so Carlos jumped in and got me."
"Right. I see. And... um... are you okay?" I asked tentatively.
"Yes! Why?"
"No reason." I lied.

I stood for a second calmly contemplating the situation whilst paling at the thought of Henry's near-drowning experience. However, he continued to splash about in the pool, blissfully unaware of the danger that he had faced and the debt that he owed to Carlos. Suddenly a question popped into my mind.
"Where exactly was Nanny when Carlos was rescuing you?"
"Over there," he said, pointing to her sunbed. "She was

reading her book."

"And Luigi?" Henry wrinkled his nose as he thought about that one. He shrugged his shoulders. I looked over at the sunbeds and realised that Luigi had not stirred since I first went down to the pool some two hours ago.

Oblivious to the life-threatening nature of this event, Henry cheerfully carried on playing in the pool.

"Carlos is a very good swimmer, Mummy; maybe he can play crocodiles with us this afternoon."

"Maybe," I said, distractedly looking over my shoulder at Davina, who was beside the food, flirting with an awakened Luigi. I felt a surge of anger and approached the table. Davina was in the middle of recounting and re-enacting her life history to him whilst giggling coquettishly.

"Mother. I'd like a word please," I demanded icily.

"Mother eh? Oh dear, I must be in trouble!" She winked at Luigi and turned to face me. She saw the tears and anger in my eyes. Her giggle disappeared. I had her full attention

A few home truths and a short lesson on responsible parenting later, we all sat down to a tense but leisurely lunch.

"Let's head off into town this afternoon." Davina suggested. "We can have a hot chocolate in the square and watch as the children play. I promise that I won't take my eyes off them, not even for one minute…" I hesitated, still annoyed from the morning. "My treat?" she offered penitently.

"Go on then!" I replied, succumbing to my mother's charm and the prospect of one of the best hot chocolates in Italy. She beamed at me.

DIY and Danger

"I knew that you couldn't stay angry with me forever! I really am very sorry. It will never happen again. I'll go and get the boys dried and changed while you relax. It's the least I can do."

Wistfully I watched from the veranda as Davina disappeared off with a boy in each hand. Still suffering the after-effects from the eventful morning, I approached a somewhat dryer Carlos, who had his back to me.
"Carlos?" I spoke gently; even so I startled him. He turned around, saw me and smiled.
"Si Signora?"
"I just want to say thank you. You saved Henry's life today. I can never repay you."
"It's nothing. I am just glad that I was there. I have a young son too and I know that they can get into trouble very easily." His brown eyes looked into mine and he smiled soothingly. He took my hand and cupped it in his. "We all need rescuing sometimes," he whispered.
"Yes. Yes, I guess we do." He held my hand for a few seconds more, just long enough to connect with my heart. Then he released it leaving me to ponder alone as he left for the rest of the afternoon.

I felt a surge. A quickening of my pulse. A racing of my heart. A tingling of my skin. An excitement. For a moment there I had felt like a princess… rescued and held. For a moment I had felt… I had felt…
"Lust!" came the small, still quiet voice of my conscience, pinpointing the emotion. Then it added a wisdom that shook me to the core. "You felt, the first step of adultery."

The reality hit me and shook me to my senses. I felt sick to my stomach. I had been so easily led, so easily duped. By what? A simple surge of electrical emotion! Was it really that easy to step onto that path? Was I really so fickle? I had always considered myself to be a woman of integrity. Grounded. I had valued Carlos's family focus, his priorities. I had admired him as a family man, a loving husband. Yet in one split second, because of my desire to be rescued, my concept of him had transformed into something else.

I realised that on this holiday I had been blinded by my focus on myself and forgotten the importance of my marriage and the qualities of the man I had married. I fixed my thoughts on Ben and remembered my commitment to him. I had promised to support him, not discard him; to love him, not replace him. He may not be perfect but neither was I. A wave of happy memories flooded my mind. I focused on them and on his endearing qualities. Lust left. I felt a stirring in my heart. It was not fleeting like the electrical pulse of lust but pure, warm and long-lasting - the embers of love rekindled in my heart. I realised that we had become lazy towards each other, reliant on our past with no effort in the present. Like our chess pieces our union had been consigned to the back room and yet we had expected it to thrive. I resolved to transform my focus upon my return.

Returning to the poolside I settled myself on a recliner. The turbulence of the day dissipated as I drifted off to sleep in the reassuring warmth of the sun.

I was woken with a start.
"We're ready, Mummy!"
"What?"
"We're ready, Mummy" repeated Alfie. I peered out

through blurry, sleepy eyes.
"There we go! Two boys, dried, changed and not a catastrophe in sight!" Davina declared proudly, her parenting credentials redeemed. I begged to differ... She had clothed my children in orange and purple lederhosen!
"Are those their new outfits?" I asked, hoping desperately that they were only borrowed.
"Yes!" she beamed. "I bought them for the twins when I was in Freiberg. I found a shop that specialised in recycled materials. Aren't they gorgeous?"
"The boys will certainly stand out in them!" Davina beamed again as she mistakenly received a compliment. I clutched at straws in a bid to change their attire. "Are you sure they're practical for out and about? I mean, they don't look very comfortable to me. Possibly a bit too hot as well?"
"Nonsense! They're perfect aren't they boys?" The twins nodded and took my mum's hand as they headed for the front door.

"What's this?" asked Henry stopping to pick something up from the marble floor in the main hallway.
"It's a screw... Not sure what off though... Maybe one of your toys?" I surmised.
"Don't worry Mummy I'll fix it for you!" grinned Alfie. "I fixed lots of things this morning."
"Thank you darling! I'm sure you did."
Davina headed out towards the car first, closely followed by her two multi-coloured partners in crime. I gently tugged the ornate wooden door closed and listened to the familiar convent-door-style *clang* that resonated around the hallway, closely followed by an unfamiliar metal-on-marble *clunk*. My heart sank as the door handle came off in my hand and I realised that it had dropped off on the other side. "I think I know where that screw came from, Henry!" I

announced feebly.

The others came to look.

"The door handle's dropped off." I explained, stating the obvious.

"But how Mummy?" asked an indignant Alfie. "I fixed it this morning!" It took me a few seconds to digest his statement before understanding the implications of what he had just said. My heart sank even further.

"How exactly did you *fix it*?" I asked as calmly as possible, feeling the annoyance that was rising inside of me.

"There was a big screw sticking out of the side of the turny thing."

"You mean the handle? This?" I asked holding out the disconnected example in my hand.

"Yes! The handle!" he agreed. "I tried to screw it in, but it was too strong for me. Then I found a little screw on the floor in the corner. So I took the big screw out and put the little screw in. It fitted perfectly!" He explained, beaming with pride.

With Carlos away, every door in the house locked and every window closed, the horror of Alfie's confession took seconds to process but substantially longer to rectify! Still, at least Aunt Leslie would never find out, so I still lived in hope of a return visit.

Chapter 12

Return to Normality

The flight home was a less stressful affair than the one going. Thankfully, there was no danger of a repeat of the chocolate mousse incident because the boys, exhausted after three weeks of swimming and sun, slept the whole way. I tried to seize the opportunity to relax, but the cacophony of baby cries, voices and hostess bells that filled the cabin meant it was a fruitless exercise. Eventually I retreated to the peace of the classical music channel and thoughts of Ben.

This holiday had provided me with more than just a relaxing break. It had shown me marital insights and wisdom which I had previously overlooked. Our focus had always been on earning money and achieving a good standard of living for us as a family – a nice home, decent car, designer dog, and wide range of stimulating activities for the twins – but in doing so we had lost sight of our priorities and lost our sense of family. We had surrendered ourselves and our values to the pursuit of money. I realised that laughter and fun had all but disappeared from our existence. We had grown stale, and like all stale things we were in danger of being tossed to the birds.

Fortunately, with this revelation had come a vision - new ideas and new plans. They were bursting inside of me, inspired by my observations of the market square and of the families that I had been privileged enough to meet. I had discovered ways to get us all back on track; to secure time for each other; to have fun and reconnect. I could not wait to tell Ben. He would be home at 7pm. It seemed so long...

Waving at Marcie as she observed us from behind her curtain, I slipped the key into our front door, opened it and smiled. I inhaled the familiar surroundings and smells. We were home at last. Benson caught wind of our arrival and with tail wagging furiously came running to greet us. In his haste his paws slipped on the smooth, wooden floor and he ended up a tangled, black, furry mess of legs at our feet. The boys dived on top of him, hugging and rubbing his shaggy, black fur, clearly glad to be reunited with their four-legged friend. Benson licked Henry's ear and Alfie's hand. Obviously the affection was reciprocal.

"Let's bake a cake for Daddy, for when he gets back." I suggested to the boys.
"Yes, let's!" they agreed, jumping up and down.
"Henry, you put your teddy up in your room and then wash your hands. Alfie, you come with me." Henry wrinkled his nose and then skipped off excitedly, his bedraggled, but-well-loved teddy bumping along the floor behind him. I took Alfie and ran a sink full of water for him in the basin, then we headed into the kitchen.

Kelly was standing at the sink, preparing vegetables.
"Hello, Laurie," she said, smiling awkwardly. "Welcome

back." Her words were straightforward but there was a tension in her voice. She had clearly enjoyed ruling the roost and found the demotion of my return hard to bear. Just then, Alfie came into the kitchen and spotted her.
"Kelly!" he screamed, leaping forward to hug her; latching onto her leg and squeezing as hard as he could.
"Careful! I do break you know," she laughed, pinching him on the nose. Normality had resumed.

"Ta da!" we chorused as Ben walked in the door. "Welcome home!" The kids held up their valiant attempt at a chocolate fudge cake – a demi-risen sponge with chocolate frosting slopping everywhere. We had created a formal greeting line for Ben's return, but we soon broke ranks to grab him and hold him. Alfie placed the cake on the bottom step to free up his arms so that he could attach himself firmly to his dad's leg. We smothered Ben with hugs and kisses as he stood still, overpowered by the love of his family. He smiled tearfully and bent down to look Henry and Alfie in the eye.
"Boy have I missed you guys!" He hugged them tight. A gigantic, safe, Daddy hug that only a true father can give. A reassuring hug that says a thousand words but utters none. The hug lasted minutes, but its memory lasted all week. The boys went all gooey and floppy in response. Both started vying for his attention. I waited my turn, allowing the boys time to bond with their father first.

"Hello stranger," I whispered huskily. "Long time no see." I gazed into his eyes, but was met by stone. Clearly the birds had already started to peck away at the staleness of his heart. My heart yelped at his coldness, but I refused to submit to discouragement. I already knew that we needed to rekindle our embers; neither of us had tended them and they were almost out. I kissed him tenderly on his cheek. A kiss that said *do not worry because I'll meet you where you're at*. A kiss that expected nothing in return. The first kiss of a new beginning.

I gazed into his eyes again, to see if there was a softening, but I saw only… only… horror!
"No!" Alfie screamed. I spun round. Just in time to see Benson, the dog, demolish the last piece of chocolate cake!

Chapter 13
Old Habits

"**O**hhh!" groaned Kelly, clutching her stomach. "I'm sorry, Laurie… I don't think I can help you today… I…" She never got to finish her sentence. She just had time to cover her mouth and run to the toilet. The volume of her vomiting echoed through the corridor, forcing me to turn the music up in the kitchen. I looked up at the clock. It was only five to eight. Sighing, I abandoned the comforting peace of my early morning cup of tea, shifted into practical mode and headed towards the dreaded corner cupboard.

Kneeling on the floor, I stretched my arm in as far as I could, squished my face against the wall and rummaged blindly at the back of the overcrowded repository. After much prodding and poking, I finally located what I was after, withdrew my arm, released my face and closed the door quickly so as to curb the landslide of Tupperware that had been set in motion by my rummaging. I set off to tend to Kelly.
"Sick bowl?" I offered kindly, handing her the plastic mixing bowl that we reserved for just these occasions. "Is there anything I can do? Anything you need?" Kelly shook

her head, her face ashen white. "Right! Off to bed with you. I'll check on you in a while." She nodded meekly and headed to her room, bowl in hand.

Ben emerged from our bedroom dressed only in his stripy blue pyjama bottoms. He ruffled his hair in a sleepy daze. I gazed at him and smiled. I loved his appearance in the mornings – all crumpled and dishevelled, innocent and reachable. It was such a stark contrast from his crisp, untouchable, business persona.
"What time is it?" he asked yawning.
"It's eight o'clock. You can go back to bed if you want. The twins are happy playing downstairs and we haven't got anything planned for today."
"Mmmm…" he mused thoughtfully, ruffling his hair yet again. "Tempting… but I think I'll go and hang out with the boys for a bit."

I waited expectantly for him to amble up to me on his way to the stairs, hold me in his arms and kiss me gently on the lips, but this time he just ambled past, oblivious to my presence. Rubbing the sleep away from his eyes and yawning heavily, he held on tightly to the bannister as he descended down the stairs. Ben had been working so hard of recent and was clearly still tired. Wistfully I stood there remembering the many times on a weekend that he had kissed me in the corridor, said something affirming like *Good morning, Mrs Driver!* or *Good morning, my gorgeous wife*, winked and then sauntered away to begin his day. It was always a brief exchange, but to me it was always an intimate moment of marriage that left me blushing and tingling with delight. A moment that reminded me how much I loved my husband.

To the sound of the boys playing and Kelly vomiting, I

Old Habits

wandered into the twins' bedroom to bring order out of chaos. I drew the curtains and picked up all their clothes. As the sunlight filtered in, I surveyed the scene; there were toys everywhere! I started by lifting up Benny, Alfie's favourite teddy, only to find a biscuit mashed into the carpet. I growled in annoyance and picked up the lorry depot, only to reveal a milk spillage and a half-eaten dog chew. I could feel my frustration rising but kept my emotions safely bolted in. At least that was until... I looked up to see a rather smudged, brown rabbit drawn on the wardrobe door. I knew instantly that it was Alfie's handiwork (he had signed it).
"Alfie!" I shouted. "Come here at once!" My emotions had escaped and were gathering pace.

Two minutes later a wide-eyed Alfie appeared at the door.
"Yes Mum?" I pointed at his masterpiece and he beamed.
"It's a rabbit! His name's Rory!" he announced with pride. My heart sank at his lack of understanding. We had had this conversation so many times before.
"I know it's a rabbit, but what've I said about drawing on the furniture?" He wrinkled his nose and shuffled his feet, tears welling up in his eyes.
"But I thought it would look nice there, Mummy. He's a nice rabbit and I...."
"Mummy, quick! Daddy's been sick!" interrupted a breathless Henry. I abandoned my inquisition and shot down the stairs as fast as I could, only to see the large soles of Ben's feet poking out from the toilet door.
"Bowl, Mummy?" asked Henry.
"Bowl, Henry!" I confirmed.

"Mummy! Daddy's calling you!" shouted Henry from the

lounge. I abandoned the potatoes and ran upstairs. A rather feverish Ben lifted his head off the pillow and smiled weakly.
"Could you get me some water please, darling? I'm so thirsty. And if you'd empty the bowl too, that would be really helpful."
"Of course I will," I replied. He smiled gratefully and then rolled over to sleep.

I grabbed the offending bowl, holding it at arm's length. Walking smoothly and carefully, so as not to create a tidal wave, I proceeded to the nearest bathroom and disposed of its contents. Five minutes later, I returned to the bedroom with a glass of water and an empty bowl. Ben was already asleep. I set the water down beside him and gently caressed his cheek.
"Sleep well my darling," I whispered. Just then a very grey Kelly appeared at her bedroom door.
"Laurie!"
"Yes."
"I'm so sorry... I've been sick all over the bed."

And so the day continued - an endless cycle of washing, cleaning, fetching and carrying. The twins, whilst perfectly healthy, placed their own demands on my time and day:
"Mum! Henry hit me..."
"Mum! Alfie snatched..."
"I'm hungry..."
"Can't we play something else?"

I found myself in desperate need of peace; a little me time. The kids were engrossed with their trains in the lounge, so I escaped into the kitchen, switched on the kettle and made a cup of tea. I opened up the cupboard door and picked up my hidden packet of chocolate buttons. Surprised at the lightness of the pack, I peered inside. There were only two left.

"Hmmm, Ben!" I muttered accusingly. The rustle of the packet clearly alerted the twins' chocolate-radar because within seconds they both appeared expectantly, with hands outstretched. I looked at the packet and looked at the boys. They smiled sweetly. Reluctantly I handed over my last two buttons.

"Thanks Mum!" they chorused and ran off. I reached for my back-up plan and checked out the biscuit tin instead. It was empty.

"Grrr." I rummaged through the cupboards but there was nothing there to satisfy my desire. Finally I resorted to a spoonful of chocolate spread and a handful of chocolate sprinkles. Desperate times required desperate measures!

Chapter 14

The Red Rose

Since returning, things had become strained between Ben and I; our familiarity and easiness had evaporated. We had become strangers, coexisting in the same home. No matter how hard I worked at tenderising his heart towards me, I could not break the stone that surrounded it. I needed a hammer that would shatter rock. For his part, he avoided me by spending all his time immersed in his work or playing with the boys. The tension seemed to be heightened whenever Kelly was present in the room because there was friction between the two of them.
"What on earth happened between you two when I was away?" I asked after a few days. "The tension in this room is tangible!" I did not intend to be inflammatory, I just wanted to understand. Neither of them responded. Kelly chewed on her bottom lip and Ben glowered at me. I realised that I had hit a nerve. The silence was deafening.
"Well?" I asked more gently, trying to encourage a response. Ben's jaw tightened visibly, his bluebell eyes withered in a haze of anger.
"I don't know what you mean, Laurie. There's nothing wrong."
"Okay." I replied, retreating to safer territory. "It's obvious

to me that you two have fallen out, so I'd appreciate it if you would sort out your differences because this used to be a happy home." Kelly's lip trembled violently and she ran out of the room. Ben looked even more thunderous.
"How could you, Laurie? After all she's been through!"
"What have I done?" I asked innocently. "I was only trying to get rid of the bad atmosphere in here. That's all. I just don't understand what's happened. We used to be so good together."
"If there's a bad atmosphere, then it's not Kelly who's causing it," replied Ben accusingly.
"Me? You're saying it's me?" I asked incredulously.
"Well, let's put it this way... Things were fine while you were away." With that he stormed out. An unfamiliar Ben in an unfamiliar mood. I had only been away three weeks, but in that time so much had changed.

The next morning, when Ben was at work, there came a knock at the door. It was Marcie. As usual, she surrounded herself with an air of superiority, but this time she also appeared unusually anxious and jittery.
"Are you alright?" I asked.
"Yeah, I'm fine. Can I come in?"
"Of course!"
"Thanks." Marcie crossed my threshold tentatively, almost reluctantly, her head bowed dramatically towards the floor. Realising that something was dreadfully wrong, I did the only thing I could... I put the kettle on.

"Come and sit down," I said, ushering her into the kitchen and patting a seat. I grabbed the biscuit tin and brought two coffees across to the table. "Now, are you going to tell me what's wrong or do I have to drag it out of you?" She

smiled half-heartedly and then looked furtively over her shoulder.
"Where's Kelly?" she whispered.
"She's out shopping? Why?" There was silence. Marcie wrung her hands. My skin started to go cold and clammy. "Marcie, what's wrong?" I asked firmly, panic rising in my voice. She looked at me sorrowfully and then spoke the words that I shall never forget.
"It's Ben. Ben and Kelly." She did not need to say any more; suddenly everything started to make sense. I sat back in my chair, shocked. My mouth dropped open and my heart ripped in two.

Marcie, who reveled in gossip and drama with no concern for the impact on others, instantly shed her sorrowful façade and then proceeded to regale me with every sordid detail that she knew. She included every one of her curtain-twitching observations – the hugs, the laughter, the stolen kisses, the single red rose. She spared me nothing. I sat powerless. Rooted to my chair in despair, unable to turn back the tide of heart-breaking images that cascaded my way.
"I didn't want to be the one to tell you," she lied. "I'm so sorry." Then, with her marriage-demolition grenade released, she set about annihilating a bourbon biscuit and watched for my reaction.

Everything faded into the background as my body and mind absorbed Ben's betrayal. Half of me wanted to defend the man I loved, to scream out that this could never be true. A cacophony of thoughts rampaged through my mind, seeking a voice: *He would never do this*; *He's a faithful man*; *He loves me and the boys too much*, but I kept silent because I knew in my heart that what Marcie had said was true. The Ben that I knew was no longer present. His softness had departed and the stone man that was left was capable of anything. A sea of questions deluged my mind - *How? Why? When? Did he ever care?* - followed by a gut-wrenching churning of my stomach and senses. I felt sick. I felt numb. I…

"Laurie! Laurie! Are you okay?" I stared up hazily, from the floor, my vision blurred.
"Marcie?" I mumbled feebly, recognising the voice.
"Yes, it's me. You fainted. I'm so sorry! I'd never have told you if I'd known…"
"Told me?" and then I remembered. My gut tightened, my heart screamed and I rolled over into a tight, safe ball, weeping uncontrollably.

Marcie crept out of the room silently. She left me alone to wallow in the sea of despair, surrounded by the pieces of my shattered world.

After what seemed like an eternity, I wiped my eyes and hauled myself off the kitchen floor. My body felt heavy and dead. My senses had shut down. I was numb and in shock. I had but one goal in mind – to seek out the truth. I focused on the task ahead and slowly climbed the stairs, like a prisoner approaching the execution chamber. I held my breath in dread, steeled myself and headed for Kelly's room. For the first time in two years, I let myself in without permission or forewarning. It was necessary in order to be able to unfold the secrets of this dragon's lair. I shut my eyes as I opened the door, braced myself and stepped inside. I knew it was wrong. I knew it was unwise. I also knew that it was unavoidable if I was ever to know the truth.

I cast my eyes around the room. It was so neat and tidy, so beautifully laid out, so unassuming in its appearance. Matching pink accessories adorned the surfaces and bed - an array of hearts and flowers. Everything was co-ordinated and meticulously planned and positioned. Nothing was out of line. It all seemed so innocent, with one notable exception... the single red rose that stood in a vase beside her bed.

I swallowed hard as I approached this beautiful, fragrant rose. To me it was the ugliest thing that I had ever seen because it symbolised the ultimate betrayal – a betrayal of trust, of love and of covenant vows. I sat down on the bed beside it and touched the polluted petals. They felt soft, velvety and fragile. Tears streamed down my face. I sat bereft.

A card! Where was the card? Ben always gave a card with his flowers. I started to search, first on the side, then in her drawers. I did not have to hunt for long. It was at the top of the first drawer inside her nightly reading book. I picked up the white envelope with Ben's familiar handwriting, only this time it was not my name that was written upon it. Trembling, I pulled the card out and held it in my hands. I inhaled courage and then opened it. It simply read:

To my love!

Ben

xxx

"What the hell do you think you're doing?" Kelly barked at me angrily. I jumped, startled by her presence. I had not heard her return. I looked at her with tear-flooded eyes.

A Rampage of Grace

Saying nothing, I held out the card in my hand. Horror overwhelmed her and the colour drained from her face. Her bravado fled when faced with my shattered heart. She hung her head in shame. There was silence.

Time froze as I sat there on the bed, lost in a sea of numbness. Kelly spoke first.
"What do we do now?" No apology, just practicality. I steeled myself and calmed my emotions. Anger had not yet arrived. I could still control myself.
"I am going to go and pick up the twins from school. I want you to be gone by the time I get home." There was no room for debate or negotiation, my icy words were crystal clear. She nodded compliantly. I left. This door was now closed.

Ben was late arriving home. Two hours late. There was no phone call. No explanation. The boys were already in bed, sleeping soundly, blissfully unaware of the crumbling family walls that surrounded them. I heard the key in the lock. I sat in the kitchen waiting, my heart beating violently inside. Finally, Ben sheepishly entered the room. He could not look me in the eye.
"I take it that Kelly's spoken to you?" I asked calmly. He nodded then stood in silence, waiting for the axe to fall. There was no outburst. I just sat on the unfamiliar seat of betrayal and waited upon his next move. Eventually he spoke.
"I'm sorry, Laurie! I'm really sorry." Tears started to flood down his cheeks, humility and tenderness started to return. "I never meant for this to happen."
"I know." My heart reached out to him in his moment of vulnerability. Glimmers of the old Ben resurfaced. I patted

the seat beside me. He came and sat down. I could feel the warmth from his body and the connection between us as he sat close; it melted my resolve, my icy wall. I started to sob.
"How? How did this happen?" I spluttered.
"I don't know. I just don't know…" He paused for a bit, revisiting his journey to destruction. "I just couldn't get her out of my mind. I tried, but I couldn't do it. I thought if I stayed longer at work that would help, but that only made it worse because then we drifted apart too. In the end, I thought…" he hesitated, checking to see whether he should continue. I nodded. "In the end, I thought that if I slept with her and went out with her for a while then I would get her out of my system. That way you and I could just carry on and you would never know. You'd never get hurt and I'd still have you and the boys." I looked at him, incredulous that he could have been deceived by such a foolish plan. He placed his head in his hands and wept. We sat in silence again.

"How do you feel now?" I asked.
"I love her and feel joined to her… Like she's inside of me… Like I can't give her up!" I paused for a moment while I ingested his words.
"Do you want to give her up?" I asked. Ashamed, Ben turned his head away from me and shook his head.
"No. I don't."
"I see."

We sat in silence for ages as I embraced the hopelessness of our situation, then I steeled myself. My thoughts were chaotic and many, but my words were calm and few. I detached myself from all emotion, drew strength from within and issued my instructions.
"Then you must leave." Ben whimpered at these words but

nodded in agreement. He understood. Bowing his head, he went upstairs to pack and to spend his final night in the spare room.

I wanted to be held that night, to feel safe, to feel loved, but that option had evaporated without warning. I had gone from stability to nothingness in one afternoon; my solid foundations unexpectedly shattered, reduced to debris by a maelstrom of lust. Nothing felt secure or trustworthy anymore. I found myself standing on air, lost in no-man's land, alone and totally afraid. The coldness of the sheet and the emptiness of the bed made my insides heave with pain. My body convulsed as a dam of tears burst free, soaking my pillow and washing me into an exhausted sleep.

Henry, Alfie and I watched the next morning as Ben placed his belongings into his car. The twins clung to his legs and begged him not to leave, but without a word, he peeled them off and placed them in my arms. Ben steeled himself and forced a smile, a semblance of strength betrayed only by the torment in his eyes.
"I'll see you two on Thursday. That's going to be our special day together. Just you and me!" Unpacified by this hollow encouragement, the boys continued to wail. Ben looked at me with doleful eyes, filled with sorrow at the carnage that he was leaving in his wake. Then, with a turn of the key, he started his engine and set off in pursuit of his own desires.

Alfie and Henry turned to me, bereft. Their father had gone; all his things had gone, but they could not understand why. All they knew was that he was not coming back and that he would not live here anymore. They had trusted him to stay. They had trusted him to be there. They had entrusted themselves to him, without reservation and without question, but now he was gone.

"But he promised he would never leave! He said he'd always be here! He promised!" wailed Henry. Alfie nodded and sobbed, choking on his own tears, unable to speak, his four year-old heart broken in two, shattered by the father he adored and trusted.

The twins' lives had been so simple before, with no reason to ever question their basic security or their home, but now that their cornerstone had left confusion reigned, filling their minds with anxiety-laden questions. They looked up at me with tear-filled eyes, searching for stability, comfort and headship. I understood exactly how they felt because I craved the same, only I did not have the luxury of being able to let that show. Right now they needed me to appear strong. So I lay aside my own feelings and fears and wrapped my arms around them. Holding them tight. Easing their pain. Soothing their sorrows.

As I held the innocence of my children, I felt anger rise within me. I put up no resistance. I let it flow freely. Unforgiveness knocked at my heart. I opened the door and welcomed it in.

Chapter 15

The Rucksacks

"You're joking right?" exclaimed Marcie as the waitress arrived with a platter of ribs. "He seriously expects you to run around sorting out his mess, while he swans around with Kelly living the high life? Make him suffer for a change! Let him sort it out himself!" She ripped off her first rib, voraciously tearing the flesh from the bone.
"Yeah, you're right!" I agreed, reaching for my steak knife. "It isn't fair! I've done enough! He can do it himself!" I felt my indignation rising and self-justification settling into place. Marcie's words strengthened my resolve. I felt their fuel and decided to fight for justice and my pound of flesh. I severed off a chunk of rare steak, chewing aggressively; a fusion of blood and thought as I cogitated over Ben's offences.
"She's right, Laurie. You should be angry, not nice, at a time like this. Ben deserves all he gets. He's wronged you and you're letting him off lightly!" Petra, the professional neighbourhood divorcee, offered convincingly.
"You deserve better than him!" spat Marcie loyally. I nodded smugly in agreement and stabbed another piece of steak.

A Rampage of Grace

We spent the rest of the evening chewing meat, chewing Ben and spewing venom. With every wrong-doing I shared, my friends showed their loyalty and jumped to my defence. There was no jury required. We found Ben guilty on every charge and sentenced him accordingly. That night I went to bed full of power and self-righteousness. I was the victim here and a price needed to be paid. I just needed to decide what that price looked like to me. With thoughts of revenge and retribution I settled down to a bitter, restless sleep.

Ben came around the next day to collect Henry and Alfie. I felt the pang inside me at the forthcoming separation from my sons, closely followed by the poison of unforgiveness towards Ben. The lightness and indifference of Ben's manner stoked the raging furnace within me.
"So are you happy now? Have you finally got what YOU wanted?" I blurted out. (I no longer had any self-control around him). Ben wilted at my words. We had been here so many times before. It was a circular pattern that always culminated in me crying and him leaving. He was no longer shocked at my poisonous outbursts but instead was wearied by the barrage of my constant accusations.
"I'm getting there..." he replied, adding gently, "You know that I never meant to hurt you or the boys..." He paused for a moment and cast his eyes to the ground, shuffling uneasily. "I'm just sorry that it worked out this way. I know that I've messed up but let's just sort this mess out so that we can all move on."
"Oh, how very convenient! You'd like that wouldn't you?" I snapped acrimoniously, ignoring his honest appeal. "Well, Mr Lover Man, I'm afraid this isn't going to be the nice, neatly-wrapped package that you want. The fact is

that you've destroyed our lives, and for what? For K-E-L-L-Y?" (I was no longer able to pronounce her name with any civility, so instead I added a well-practised sarcastic emphasis and rolling of eyes). "Did you ever really care about us?" Ben hung his head again and gave no answer. There was no answer to give. He had made a mistake and fallen into the age-old trap of adultery. The facts were undeniable. Over the last three months, Ben had tried reassuring me of his feelings towards me and the boys. However, it never changed the outcome; he still went home to Kelly, leaving me with a gaping wound in my heart, infected by the flies of bitterness and offence.

Ben decided not to engage in any more fruitless discussions. He chose instead to ignore my question and side-step my gauntlet.
"I'll bring them back at five," he stated firmly. "Henry! Alfie! Come on! It's time to go!"

I heard the television switch off in the lounge and the stampede of little feet down the corridor as my bundle of boys rushed into the kitchen to join their father.
"Bye, Mum!" squealed Alfie, grabbing his coat and planting a soggy kiss on my cheek.
"Bye, Mum! See you later!" stated Henry confidently with a cheeky wink. He took Ben's hand. I watched silently, bravely smiling and waving as they disappeared out of view. The familiar warmth on my cheek began within seconds as my tears began to flow. A wail of devastation and separation erupted from my mouth. I collapsed into a heap on the floor. The circular pattern was complete.

Five o'clock came and went. I paced up and down the

kitchen floor. No car. No boys. Just silence. Five past, nothing. Ten past, nothing. The tension of waiting and the stillness of the house were noisy in my head. Eventually, the silence was broken by the frantic hammering of little fists on the front door. My boys were home! I flung it open and the twins charged in, filled with energy and enthusiasm. They had clearly enjoyed themselves with their dad. Ben stayed in the safety of his car and waved. Then, with a final turn of his engine, he drove away.

Before the front door was even closed, the twins started to recount their time with Daddy.
"It was so cool!"
"Yeah, sooooo cool!"
"We went bowling and I won!" bragged Alfie.
"Yeah! But Daddy didn't help me. I rolled the balls myself!" defended Henry.
"So did I! Daddy only helped me once," protested Alfie.
"Liar! He helped you loads of times," responded Henry accusingly, his voice and fists rising.
"Did not!"
"Did too!"
"Did not!"
"Did ...." I smiled to myself. With a squeal of voices, a scramble of words, a flurry of fists and a stamping of feet, normality had resumed.

By the time I tucked the children up into bed that night, I was emotionally exhausted. I plodded downstairs and slumped into an armchair in front of the television. Flicking through the channels, I found nothing but romance or murder. I was not in the mood for either, so I retreated to the comfort of my bed with a hot chocolate and a good book.

Summoning all my effort, I tried hard to focus on reading my book, but the weight of the day, the argument with Ben and the words of my friends from the previous evening provided a constant distraction. My thoughts constantly diverted to the bitterness and despair of my current situation. Like a cracked record, events and conversations replayed endlessly in my head. All the time, the war in my heart raged fiercely. Where had my peace gone? What about the gentleness and kindness that I used to dish out in great quantities? It had all evaporated, snuffed out by the immorality and injustice of life.

I abandoned my book to the bedside table and settled down to sleep and to dream….

Stepping forth into the ornate, marble dance hall with its towering pillars and gold leaf detail, I was impressed by its stature and magnificence. I looked around at the elaborately decorated tables, their crisp, white linen cloths stopping just short of the floor and their floral centrepieces towering upwards from large trumpet vases. The room started to fill with men and woman all bedecked in their finest garments. I marvelled at the array of glittering dresses and fabulous hairstyles. Never before had I seen or experienced such elegance and finery. An Arab sheikh swept into the room accompanied by an entourage of bodyguards and his beautiful wife by his side. Her necklace glinted in the light of the chandelier and I gasped at the splendour of the diamonds and rubies around her neck.

More and more dignitaries filed into the room, each one announced by name at the door:
"His Royal Highness….. The Duke and Duchess….. Lord and Lady…." The list of titles was impressive although eventually interspersed with some normality: "Monsieur Francois Courbet and Madame Lilly Courbet; Mr Terence Longbottom and Ms Jeanette Francis; Herr Hugo Kohl…." My mind wandered, numbed by the monotony of the voice and the sea of names. I focused instead on the detail of the stunning dresses, the ornate headwear and exquisite jewellery. I was mesmerised, blissfully unaware of the announcements. Until… "Mr Benjamin Driver and Ms Kelly Eccles." My ear heard it, my brain processed it and with the reflex of a cobra my head snapped around in time to see it - Ben and Kelly entering the room. With dazzling smiles, designer dinner suit and daring red dress they stepped forth into the splendid surroundings. My heart burned with jealousy and betrayal. Why did they get to enjoy such a magnificent occasion? This was not fair! I wanted to shout to everyone present, to warn them that Ben and Kelly were fraudsters and not to be tricked by their outward appearances, but I was merely an observer in this dream and could only watch as the two of them headed towards their allocated table of opulence.

As they proceeded down the aisles, they ricocheted off each other. It made no sense. There was plenty of space for them both and yet they seemed cramped; their elegance marred by some hidden force. Fascinated, I forgot my protestations and watched as they progressed towards me. Their clothes were impeccable but their demeanour ungainly. I was both intrigued and bemused. Finally they drew close enough for me to see the cause… They were both wearing rucksacks! Unbelievably, Kelly had accessorized her delicate, red silk dress with a tatty, gold-coloured rucksack, whilst Ben, in his smart, black dinner suit, carried a dirty, brown one. What was even more amazing was that neither of them seemed aware of the load they were carrying nor of the green straps that held them tight.

I started to laugh.
"They look ridiculous!" I smirked, but nobody else seemed to notice or care and anyway, no-one in this dream could hear me. The two of them sat down at the table in front of me and Ben leant over to kiss Kelly on her cheek. As he did so, his rucksack moved slightly, knocking his head so that the tenderness was lost.

I watched them for a while with a mixture of emotions. I was seething at their stolen opportunity to enjoy such an event together, and yet I was enjoying the ridiculous appearance of their ungainly rucksacks. I was curious to know why they were wearing them and equally why no one else thought it was strange.
"What are those rucksacks?" I thought out loud.
"They are *Guilt* and *Shame*," came the reply. I was startled by the voice, yet comforted by its familiarity. I had heard it first a long time ago, in a church, at a wedding. It was a voice that had guided me into a truth that had set me free… free from the bondage of self-loathing. I turned around but could see no one.

Ben and Kelly got up to dance, their oversized rucksacks wobbling uncomfortably from side to side. Every time their rucksacks moved their faces changed - their smiles disappeared. It was subtle and fleeting, but nonetheless there.

Our old friend, Tim, suddenly appeared in the room,

looking handsome in his dinner attire. He approached Ben and slapped him on the back (his hand passing right through the rucksack of shame, for it was not his).

"Hello old boy! Ben isn't it?"

"Yeah," acknowledged Ben. His rucksack started to vibrate and grow, it was clear that he was finding it difficult to maintain a semblance of normality when confronted with the past.

"How long's it been? Eight... ten years?" continued Tim, oblivious to Ben's plight.

"I-I-I guess so."

"So how's Laurie these days?" Tim asked innocently. Like a giant airbag, Ben's rucksack moved instantly from his back to his front, separating him from Kelly and from Tim.

"She's fine," he replied meekly.

"Great! We must catch up together one of these days," suggested Tim and wandered off.

Tim may have left, but the impact of their conversation on the size and position of Ben's rucksack remained. Ben tried to dance with Kelly again, but no matter how hard he tried, his rucksack got in the way and freedom eluded him.

"Serves him right!" I snorted judgementally.

"Come with me" whispered the voice gently. "I have something to show you." I was intrigued and wondered what it could be. Instantly I found myself out in the main street. There were neon lights everywhere and the noise was deafening. I felt myself drawn to a giant mirrored wall. "Now take a look at yourself, I have a surprise for you," instructed the voice. I felt a bubble of excitement rise within. Thoughts of Cinderella's transformation flitted through my mind. Would I too find myself wearing a beautiful ball gown? Would I be able to go to that amazing function as well? To be the belle of the ball and belittle

Kelly in what should have been her finest hour? The very thought of such a sweet revenge made me tingle all over, so I braced myself for the surprise ahead and looked into the mirror.

I gasped in horror and screamed.
"Nooooooo! It can't be! What have I done? Why am I wearing one?" I wept as I stared at my reflection and saw for the first time the giant, green rucksack burdening my back.

"Why is mine bigger than theirs?" I exclaimed. "Why? I don't deserve it! They're the ones who deserve the punishment, they…" I slipped into an all-too-familiar tirade of their offences. With every judgement I released, my rucksack grew bigger and bigger until I eventually silenced my poisonous tongue. "What is this? What is this rucksack?" I wailed.
"It is *Unforgiveness*," the voice replied calmly. I baulked at the answer and stared at the rucksack.
"But why is it growing?"
"Because you keep filling it - with bitterness, anger, hatred, envy, accusation and jealousy." I wriggled under the weight of the load and was suddenly aware of the rigidity of the straps holding it on. I tried to adjust them, but they would not budge.
"Why are the straps so stiff?" I complained.
"They are straps of *Pride*. All rucksacks are attached that way," came the matter-of-fact reply.

Instantly, I found myself back in the restaurant with my friends. Only this time I was observing and this time I could see the rucksack. I watched it grow bigger with every sentence we spoke against Ben. The misguided loyalty of my friends that evening had fuelled unforgiveness in my heart and unwittingly increased the burden I was carrying. I stood and watched as the evening replayed and the accusations flew, understanding for the first time the true dynamics of the situation.

I found myself back in front of the mirror. Horrified. Weeping.
"Will you take it from me please?" I begged.
"I cannot take it from you. You will have to lay it down yourself."
"But how do I do that?" I asked plaintively.
"You must forgive Ben and Kelly." As the voice uttered those words, I felt outrage overwhelm me.
"Forgive them? Forgive them? How can you suggest such a thing? After what they've done to me and the boys?"
"Then you must carry the burden. However, you need to know that very soon this rucksack will become so heavy that it will start to affect your bones and the pain that you feel now will extend beyond your heart. It's your choice. It will always be your choice."
"But it's not my choice! None of this was my choice! It's their choices that are causing this problem!" I spluttered.
"When THEY come and apologise…. When THEY treat me fairly…. THEN I'll forgive them."
"But what if they don't do those things? Are you willing to sacrifice your freedom, your strength and your bones and carry this burden to the end?" I could hear the wisdom in the voice, but my desire for justice overruled it.
"Why should they get off scot free?" I retorted bitterly, tears of indignation and despair streaming down my face.
"They won't. They have their own burdens to carry and their own choices to make."

The neon lights were magnified through my tears. Their constant flashing interfered with my thoughts. The noise of

the passing pedestrians and the roaring of car engines overpowered my own voice in my head. I was no longer able to think or function in this busy place and I was tired of the weight of my rucksack. I needed to rest.
"Let me show you one last thing," the voice coaxed gently. I shrugged my shoulders reluctantly and agreed to his request.

He led me to an open doorway. Through it I could see majestic, snow-capped mountains, lush, green pastures and a sparkling, babbling brook. Even from where I was standing I felt the freshness of the air, sensed the peacefulness of the place and experienced hope in my heart.
"Where is this?" I enquired.
"It is your hope and your future. My plan for you." My heart leapt at these words, at the thought of the peace and joy on offer.
"May I enter?" I asked.
"Whenever you are ready."

Eagerly, I started to step through the doorway, but immediately got stuck in the frame, wedged by my rucksack. I tried again, this time sideways, but again the rucksack was too big and bulky. I could not fit through the door frame. I started to weep. This was all that I desired and yet I could not reach it. Was my flame of hope to be extinguished yet again? The voice offered me one final piece of advice.
"You will need to lay your rucksack down here at my feet if you want to step into the fullness of the future that I have for you."

I awoke with a start and immediately checked my back with

my hands. There was no sign of a rucksack! I rolled my shoulders forward. There were no stiff straps. I smiled with relief and relaxed back into my soft pillow, replaying the dream in my head. Replaying truth.

As the images of Ben and Kelly together flitted across my mind, my heart seared yet again with heaviness and bitterness. It was then that I realised the truth: I was carrying a rucksack. A rucksack of unforgiveness. A rucksack strapped to my heart.

I knew that I had a choice to make.

Chapter 16

An Unfortunate Introduction

"Now hurry up you two or you'll be late for school!" I bellowed.

With a clatter of tiny feet and a sea of cheeky grins, the twins bundled down the stairs, ricocheting off the bannisters as they made their descent.
"Ready, Mum!"
"Ready, Mum!"
"Great! Here's your bags, now out you go. Nanny's arriving this afternoon so I've got lots to do. We need to hurry!"
Sensing my all-too-familiar morning maelstrom of emotion, Henry obediently opened the front door. Unfortunately that was just as Tilly, Marcie's cat, was walking by. Benson, saw the cat and set off in hot pursuit, barking frantically.
"Oops!" Henry grimaced apologetically. I scowled at him.
"Wait there!" I ordered bluntly and, without time to change my footwear, set off after my errant hound.

Caught up in the heat of the chase, Benson disappeared at full speed out of sight around the corner.
"Bloomin' dog!" I muttered as I followed on behind. My

slipper caught on the neighbour's holly bush, so I stopped for a second to rescue it from the prickles, only to find the prickles winning the battle with both the fabric and my fingers. "Ouch!" I yelped, but I was not the only one. There was a screeching of brakes and a mighty crash, followed instantly by a stomach-churning yelp. The barking stopped and silence echoed through the air. "No!" I whimpered as dread filled my heart. A chill cascaded down my body, and fear-filled tears rose up in my eyes. I discarded my entangled slipper and ran barefoot to the scene.

Nothing could have prepared me for the dreadful spectacle that lay around the corner... The mangled wreck of an expensive, black car with a geyser of steam pouring out from its bonnet was embedded in Petra's front wall. Its shocked and distressed owner stood red-faced surveying the damage with steam pouring out of his ears (or at least that's how it appeared, until he moved away from the bonnet). A disapproving Marcie stood in the judgement seat of her front garden with her arms crossed, her head shaking and her mouth pursed whilst the guilty perpetrator of the crime, Benson, (thankfully still alive) cowered in a corner with a nasty scratch on his nose. It seemed that he had escaped the collision but not the castigation and was currently being held hostage against Marcie's garden fence by a furious Tilly. I exhaled with relief at Benson's lucky escape and smiled at the sight of him with his tail between his legs, whimpering and cowering at the threat of this scrap of a cat. He looked at me pitifully and whined, seeking deliverance from his predicament, but I chose to let him suffer a little longer in the hope of a lesson learned.

Instead I turned my attention to the owner of the car. He lifted his head and glowered at me, his hefty, black eyebrows indicating very clearly his disgust at my lack of dog-handling skills. My relief evaporated, my smile disappeared and my stomach churned again as I realised his identity - Mr Pinkerton, the twins' new Headmaster. Swallowing hard, I mustered all my courage and approached him apologetically.

"I am really, really sorry, Mr Pinkerton!" I said, grovelling for all I was worth. "I really don't know what got into my dog this morning. Are you okay?"

Mr Pinkerton, standing beside his ruined Mercedes, looked at me then looked at his steaming car bonnet.

"What do you think?" he hissed ungraciously.

Suddenly Benson let out another enormous yelp. We turned around just in time to see Tilly swipe at him once more. Then, using his back as a springboard, she made her escape over the fence.

"I'd better get him and make sure that he doesn't cause any more problems," I mumbled meekly.

"I think you better had," came the terse reply.

Grabbing Benson by the collar, I looked up in dismay to see the twins standing at the corner of the road gleefully observing their Headmaster's misfortune. I attempted some covert arm gesticulations in the hopes of getting them to go back inside, out of sight. Too late! Mr Pinkerton spotted them.

"Yours?" he asked sourly.

"Yes!" I beamed.

"Hmmm. I might have known.... They're as troublesome as your dog!"

This was only the twins' second term at school and they had already managed to make quite an impression. Their multi-coloured attire (courtesy of my mother), unsolicited artwork (mainly on the school toilet walls) and constant giggling, snickering and squabbling had given them notoriety in the staffroom. Much to my dismay, they had been dubbed *The Kray Twinettes*.

"You'd better take them to school before you're late," Mr Pinkerton barked.

"Absolutely!" I agreed, grateful for the opportunity to escape.

Holding Benson tightly by the collar, I stepped forward to cross the road. As I did, I felt a warm, soft, squidgy mass ooze between my bare toes. Sheepishly, I looked down, as did Mr Pinkerton. He smirked. I wretched. Benson looked innocent. I chose not to comment but instead squelched bravely towards my house with the smell of dog poo lingering in my nose.

Chapter 17

The Turning Point

"The trouble with you is that you've forgotten how to have fun!" observed my mother shortly after her arrival. "Ever since Ben left you've been as miserable as sin. For the boys' sake, you need to dig deep and remember what it's like to laugh and to play. They're only little and you're altogether too serious with them. I don't think you see the disappointment on their faces when you quash their fun. Sometimes they get crushed in the process." I baulked with guilt at that thought. She surveyed my face and, recognising that her point had been made, she continued on to lighter more practical matters.

"Now let's think about what we can do with them when they get home from school… and before you suggest it…" she continued, clearly reading my thoughts, "tidying their bedrooms is NOT one of the options!"

I wrinkled my nose in disapproval. Sometimes the truth is a difficult thing to hear. I wanted to justify myself; to rattle off a list of all the creative things that I had engaged in with my boys, but I could not think of even one. For the last few months the television had been Henry and Alfie's entertainer and the housework my refuge. I had tried to regain control of my life by controlling my surroundings. It had provided me with a false but nonetheless reassuring sense of security and stability, but it had also ignored that which was most important – my sons' needs.

The truth may have hurt, but it is the knowledge of the truth that sets you free, and if there was one thing I did not feel, it was free! I resolved to reprioritise my life for the twins' sake and to inject laughter back into my household. Racking my brain for fun ideas, I found its store cupboard empty. I looked helplessly up at my mother for inspiration. She groaned.
"Really? You can't think of anything?" She asked gently. I shook my head and shuffled my feet; childlike behaviour returning to me as I contemplated the emptiness inside. I rested in her strength and waited patiently for her to concoct a plan.

Whilst the children were out at school, I set about tackling the dust warrens that had established themselves in the lesser used rooms. Pulling open the door to the study, armed with the hoover, I marched in with intent. No crevice was safe from this mighty weapon of mass suction. Annihilation was its purpose and I was its handler. Swiftly, and skilfully we descended on the unsuspecting room. Our surprise attack was effective and lethal - the accumulated community of dust bunnies disappeared within seconds. I marvelled as the skirting boards turned from dirty grey to gleaming white and admired the richness of the floor as it regained its original colour.
"Now for the cobwebs!" I thought to myself and lifted the nozzle high, flailing it around playfully like an elephant's

The Turning Point

trunk. In my enthusiasm, I knocked one of the pictures off the wall and it fell to the floor with a crash. Shards of glass sprayed on my newly hoovered floor.
"Drat!" I muttered glibly, picking up the damaged frame. A chess pieces fell out onto the floor – The king. I stood there silently, cradling the fallen piece in my hand and staring at my prized possession shattered before me. "I guess that's game over!" I mused sadly.

Staring at our broken promise, tears trickled down my cheeks. At last I understood the fatal mistake that we had made: we had mistaken these chess pieces for a sign of the guaranteed success of our marriage when in reality they were only that, a signpost - an indicator of the direction that we should take. That signpost was never designed to take us to our destination. Only we could do that. Neither was it a guarantee that we would not meet obstacles along the way; after all, most roads have potholes. We had not considered any of this but had blindly followed our signpost to that place called *marriage*. Our mistake? We abdicated responsibility for our journey of life to a signpost, by assuming that fate would carry us all the way. As soon as we set off on the track of marriage and reached the mid-point of contentment we took our hands off the wheel!

With a flounce of orange chiffon, Davina burst into the room.
"There you are! I've been calling you! What are you...?" She stopped dead in her tracks as she saw my tear-streaked face. Spotting the broken frame in my lap, she understood immediately the source of my grief. Quietly she started picking up the pieces of glass from the floor, then she reached gently into my lap to remove the king. "It's time you let him go!" she whispered.

"We're home!" Davina called, as she delivered the boys safely back from school. She removed their coats, dramatically wafting them onto the bannisters. "Now go and get yourselves a drink and a snack," she ordered, patting the boys on their backs and ushering them forward. She watched as they disappeared off into the kitchen and then waited for their reaction.
"Oh Wow!" they exclaimed together.
"Jelly and ice cream for a snack! Cool!" shouted Alfie approvingly.
"This is SO much better than those boring apples, Mummy!" remarked Henry, with green jelly dribbling down his chin.
"It was Nanny's idea," I said, pointing to Davina. She grinned impishly and then produced four giant glasses of lemonade with multi-coloured, curly straws.
"Right!" She announced authoritatively. "Let the burping contest begin!"

The boys looked up in disbelief, first at me then at my mum.
"But burping's rude! Mummy always tells us off when we burp."
"Quite so! It is rude… except of course… when it's a competition! Isn't that right darling?" she said looking at me for consent. I nodded my head and attempted a smile. I was struggling to engage in the frivolity of the occasion, so I entered into a forced compliance. Undeterred, she continued with her plan. "So here are the rules: burping is the only thing allowed. No extending the rules any lower, Henry, if you know what I mean." Davina pointed playfully at Henry's bottom. Henry giggled. "You can use as much lemonade as you like to help you. We'll each take it in turns and it's the first one to burp their way to ten points that wins. There's one point for a small burp, two

The Turning Point

for a good one and three for a whopper. I'm the judge and my decision is final. Oh and one more rule..." The boys both looked up, wide-eyed and eager. She had their full attention. "Mummy has to play too!"
"What!" I protested, horrified.
"Yay!" came the approving cheers of the twins. Davina gave me a you-know-you-have-no-choice-now look and ushered me to the table. I took my place grudgingly.

"Henry first!" she announced. "On your marks... Get set... Go!" Henry took a huge gulp of lemonade and we all waited, watching him avidly. Nothing. He gulped again and then giggled.
"Stop looking! I can't do it if you're looking!" Just then a small pop left his mouth.
"Is that it?" asked Alfie.
"Well you do better!" challenged Henry.
"I will!" Alfie took a large slug of lemonade and let rip.
"Not bad!" applauded Davina. "One point for you, Henry, and two for you, Alfie. Now, Laurie, it's your turn."
"Oh I really don't think so. Let's just leave it to the boys. This is their competition."
"Pleeeeeease have a go Mummy!" begged Alfie. I made the mistake of looking into his big, blue, puppy-dog eyes and melted.
"Oh alright!" I agreed with just a little irritation. I ingested a mouthful of bubbles and let out a token burp.
"Half a point!" announced Davina disapprovingly. "Your turn, Henry."

Henry looked mischievous and pointed to his empty glass. "Oh my, Henry!" I giggled. "We're definitely expecting a good one this time!" Henry sank back confidently in his chair and opened his mouth. A loud roaring sound jettisoned out.

"Wow!" admired Alfie, high fiving him.
"A definite three!" winked Davina.

"My turn!" squealed Alfie in excitement. We all sat forward, riveted with expectation. Even I was now fully engaged in the proceedings. Smiling, he surveyed his audience, milking the moment for all it was worth. "Ready?" he asked and then sucked as hard as he could, his shoulders rising as he drank. Leaning forward with a cheeky grin, he opened his mouth and emitted a long, staccato-like belch. He sat back with pride.
"Awesome!" cheered Henry.
"Two points!" announced Davina.
"What?" protested Alfie. "That's not fair!" Now fully immersed in the competition, I came to his defence.
"That definitely should've been a three, Mum. It may not have been as powerful as Henry's burp, but it was just as impressive." The two boys nodded in agreement, crossed their arms defensively and looked up at my mother. Davina gave a wry smile.
"I thought you didn't want to play?" she teased. "Alright! I declare it a three!"
"Yay!" came the jubilant cheers of the twins, who promptly got up and did a silly jig. I roared with laughter so they extended their dance for a little longer.

"Your turn again, Laurie. Now I don't want any of your pompous airs and graces this time. I remember when you could burp the alphabet in one burp, all for a bar of chocolate!"
"Seriously, Mum! Could you really burp the WHOLE alphabet?" asked Alfie, open-mouthed with astonishment.
"Well… sort of…" I replied, slightly embarrassed. Henry and Alfie were staring at me goggle-eyed in disbelief. "It wasn't really the WHOLE alphabet though… I normally

only got to P."
"Wow! That's amazing!" exclaimed Henry. "Can you do it now?"
"Pleeeeease!" chipped in Alfie. I giggled at their faces.
"Oh alright! Just for you two, but you're not to tell anyone. I'll do my best, but I really am very rusty." I leant over my lemonade and sucked hard. A little too hard. I choked and the lemonade shot up the back of my mouth and out of my nostrils, covering the twins. Davina and the boys fell about laughing. So did I.
"Let me try again!" I requested, taking another slug of lemonade. "Here goes: A-B-C-...."

With a combination of burps and letters I shattered my defensive outer shell and reclaimed my personality and sense of fun. I rediscovered belly laughs - the sort that ripple through every muscle in your body, quickening your senses and lightening your mood – and remembered what it was like to relax and spend time with those you love.

I won the competition hands down, along with the admiration of my sons. Davina produced a winners' trophy made out of tin foil, and I stood on the kitchen chair to receive it. Henry and Alfie applauded loudly and danced another jig.

The laughter continued all afternoon and re-established itself permanently within our home. Occasionally, as time went on, we would sacrifice ourselves to the banality of life, but those moments were only cursory because that day I reconnected with the twins and myself, and we all saw the benefits.

The twins started to flourish again and their behaviour began to quickly improve. Their wall art stopped instantly as they refocused their artistic talents onto more constructive activities with me. Their aggression lightened as did the atmosphere of our home. Their reputation at school gradually dissolved too and it began to reflect in their reports. As praised increased, I no longer feared parents' evenings or encounters with teachers. I even caught Mr Pinkerton smiling at the twins once. At least I think I did.... Of course, it could always have been wind!

Chapter 18

The Magician

Slowly, I started to extend my social boundaries again, with a little help from my mother.
"Why don't you give Darcy a call? She's been begging to come over for months."
"Soon, Mum. Soon."
"Why? What will change if you wait? You need to start letting people back into your life again. You can't hide away for ever." The scolding of her voice and the kindness of her eyes momentarily pierced my barricades. I squirmed a little and then hurriedly resumed my defensive position.
"I'm not hiding! I'm just… recovering."
"Well you've recovered for long enough. She's arriving at 4pm." With a waft of organza, Davina waltzed out of the room, leaving me in a haze of shock and a cloud of panic.
"But I'm not ready!" I wailed but there was no-one in the room to hear.

Facing others in the midst of failure is one of life's hardest mountains to climb. The easier option is to stay in the valley and hide, but that is actually deception because the bottom of the valley is a lonely, cold, comfortless place. The safest place is at the top of the mountain where there are no shadows to engulf you.

Just before 4pm, the doorbell chimed and the twins scampered to the door, flinging it wide open.
"Auntie Darcy!" they squealed and wrapped their arms around her hips, squeezing her as hard as they could. She responded with raucous laughter, her trademark infectious laugh; an echo from our childhood days. It stirred my soul and I realised how stupid I had been to shut her out. True friendships are not just about the good times, they are there to carry us through our trials.

Darcy lumbered forward with her arms wide open, a child still attached to each leg. She hugged me as only a true friend can, transferring strength and love with one embrace. She looked at me and smiled.
"Thanks for letting me come. I've wanted so much to be here for you." I nodded, too overwhelmed to speak. Davina took control over the situation.
"Right you two," she said, peeling the boys off Darcy's legs. "Let Darcy go. You can play with her again later. She needs to speak to Mummy first."
"But Daddy will be here soon!" objected Henry. Alfie jumped on the bandwagon:
"And then we won't get to see her!" he wailed dramatically, then cheekily opening one eye to see if he had hit the mark.
"Hmmmm… Give them both five minutes and then you may go in."
"Okay!" agreed the boys grudgingly and stomped off glumly with their shoulders stooped forwards and their heads hung low.

I had felt my hackles rise at the mention of Ben's forthcoming arrival, the rucksack still weighing heavily on my heart. Darcy sensed my mood change.

"Are you okay?" she asked, placing an arm around my shoulders.
"Yeah! I'm fine. I'm used to this situation now," I lied.

We settled down on the sofa with coffees in hand and biscuits poised. I nibbled nervously, not knowing where to start. Darcy sensed my unease, so she stretched out her hand and gently touched my arm.
"It's okay you know. You don't need to say anything. I just wanted to come. To be here for you. That's all." I felt the familiar wetness on my cheek as the warmth of her words stirred my heart, unveiling the trauma within. I stifled a sob and began to mumble.
"Sorry Darcy. I'm normally okay. Really I am."
"Sure!"
"I'm just tired. That's all."
"Of course!" she said, nodding, yet scrutinising my face for the real truth. "You've got a lot to cope with. The boys are still young. They must be hard work."
"Actually, that's not it. I mean, they do need quite a lot of looking after (as does the house) but that's not the problem. The thing that drains me is… Ben."
"Why? Is he still giving you grief?" I saw the protective anger appear on Darcy's face as she considered Ben's likely crimes and passed instant judgement in defence of her friend. I shook my head.
"No! No! It's not like that at all. In fact, he doesn't have anything to do with me anymore and he's always polite and kind when I see him. The trouble is that I don't know him anymore and I don't know how to treat him. When I see him, he just makes me feel useless and…. and…" I hesitated, afraid to utter the word.
"And?" Darcy craned her neck forward, awaiting my revelation. I braced myself and confronted the truth.
"… and jealous." I hung my head in shame.

"Jealous? What of?"
"Everything! Jealous of Kelly; jealous that he's the boys' hero; jealous of his lifestyle. He just waltzes in here, takes all the fun and then leaves me to do all the hard work. I get jealous that he's having fun and…." The door flung open.
"Is five minutes up yet?" enquired the boys optimistically as they bundled into the room. Their toothy grins flashed like gleaming, white swords, slicing the heaviness of the atmosphere into smithereens.

They looked at Darcy and then looked at me.
"Mummy, have you been crying?" asked Alfie, stepping forward to wipe my cheek. The tenderness of his touch rescued me from my bog of misery.
"Crying? Crying? You know that Mummy's don't cry… They…." I got up from my seat. "They…" I took a purposeful step towards him, my eyes glinting with mischief.
"Yes?" asked Alfie, backing away from me in exhilarated expectation. I took another step and raised my hands menacingly.
"…They eat little boys instead!" I roared. With a squeal of delight Henry and Alfie fled the room, retreating to the garden for safety.

Darcy and I chased them both around for a while. When we finally caught them, we tickled and hugged them into submission and then all collapsed in an exhausted heap on the lawn. Benson, who never liked to miss out on fun, joined us and snuggled into my side, resting his wet nose on my stomach. There we remained, an interwoven heap of bodies, enjoying the comfort of friendship and family.

Darcy was the first to stir.
"Did you know that I'm a magician?" she announced.

"Really?" gasped the boys in awe.
"Yes. I'll show you if you like."
"Yes please!" they enthused in unison.
"Okay then. Run and fetch me a couple of tennis balls." They shot off immediately and when they were out of earshot, Darcy revealed her plan.

The boys soon returned with expectant eyes and handed over three, rather scruffy tennis balls. Benson immediately poised himself for pursuit.
"Not this time boy, you're coming with me into the kitchen. We'll leave Henry and Alfie to Darcy the Magnificent."
Darcy led the boys by the hand through the garden gate to the front of the garage. Quietly, I shut Benson in the kitchen and assumed my secret post.

"Right boys. Is there anything special about these tennis balls?" Darcy enquired, handing the balls to Henry and Alfie for inspection.
"There's a little hole in this one," declared Alfie honestly.
"And a bit of chewing gum on this one!" added Henry.
"And..." Alfie started, but was promptly interrupted by Darcy.
"I realise that they're not perfect, but what I meant was... Is there anything magic about these balls?"
"No." They said, shaking their heads. "They're just ours."
"Hmmm. Well let's see what I can do about that! Hold the balls out in front of me. Right! Jiggery, pokery, loads of hokery, balls you must do all that's spoke by me." The boys looked up at her, watching her every move. Darcy took the first ball. "Are you watching carefully boys? Here goes!" She threw the first ball over the garage roof. The boys watched as it disappeared from view then looked up in confusion. Darcy smiled cheekily. "Ball, I command you to come back!" Seconds later, to the astonishment of the

boys, the ball came flying back over the roof.
"Wow!" they marvelled.
"Try mine!" squealed Henry, thrusting a dog-eaten ball into Darcy's hand. Darcy obliged and threw the ball over the roof.
"Henry's ball, I command you to come back." Again the ball came hurtling back. Darcy winked knowingly and repeated it seamlessly a few times. The boys stood in amazement.
"I think that's enough now, don't you?" Darcy declared.
"Just one more time, pleeeeease?" pleaded Alfie. Darcy stared into his little face and then conceded.
"Okay then!"

Suddenly Ben appeared around the corner.
"Hi boys!" he beamed, but then he spotted Darcy. He averted his eyes in shame before quickly regaining his composure and an exaggerated smile.
"Darcy! It's great to see you!" he lied, struggling inwardly.
"Daddy!" the boys chirped automatically, but they were so entranced by Darcy that they failed to pay him any further attention.
"Look Dad, Darcy's a magician. She can make the balls come back," explained Henry and, with no warning, both boys simultaneously hurled all three tennis balls over the garage roof. They fixed their eyes expectantly, awaiting their return, but nothing came. Instead there was a large clatter and a muffled scream from the other side.

Realising what had happened as a result of the unexpected launch of the green missiles, Darcy flung the gate open and ran into the garden, closely followed by the others. Sadly, I had no such freedom of movement. Still clutching a tennis ball firmly in one hand, I found myself pinned like a Catherine Wheel to the holly bush at the back of the garage,

my hair and legs splayed out amidst an array of bright, red berries. A sea of rubbish lay strewn across the grass where the dustbin had upturned as I fell. They all stopped dead as they reached me. I saw the disappointment and pity on Ben's face and wished for the ability to disappear, but it was not to be. I looked at Ben. He looked at me. Then I did the only thing that I could do in the situation… Still, pinned to the bush, I smiled and waggled my fingers at him.
"Hi Ben!" I said as nonchalantly as I could manage. "The kids' things are in the kitchen. Just help yourself."
"Sure. Erm… Would you like me to help you first?"
"No thanks! I'm fine," I lied.

I watched Ben stroll over to the kitchen and felt a tsunami of disappointment approach me. I had intended to be so glamorous and capable when he arrived, but instead I had managed the appearance of some deranged creature pinned onto a specimen board. I was just starting to submerge under the wave when its power was broken by the feel of four loving arms and the familiar snorts of Darcy's laugh.
"It's okay Mummy, we'll get you out of here!" assured Alfie as he and Henry pulled me forward with only a few accompanying ripping sounds.
"Look! Benson's here to help too," added Henry. Benson ran towards me at full pelt, his tail wagging. He jumped up unsympathetically and, snatching the ball from my hand, left a trail of slobber down my arm."
"Great!" I mumbled, sarcastically. "Can it get any worse?"

Limping back to the house with scratched arms, Einstein hair, shattered pride and ripped trousers, I hastily bundled the boys into their coats and ushered them into Ben's arms. Mustering my courage and, gathering my emotions, I followed them outside and stood by the roadside waving them off. I stood there smiling, a big toothy smile, yet all

A Rampage of Grace

the time I was painfully aware of my dishevelled appearance and of the wind caressing my newly-naked, scratched butt cheeks.

A perfectly coiffured Marcie appeared in her garden and waved. Automatically, I returned the gesture and smiled.
"Everything alright?" she enquired with her usual air of nosiness.
"Absolutely!" I affirmed. "Never better!"
"Good, good!" she replied vacuously, plunging her trowel into her flowerbed. With Marcie engrossed in her gardening, I started my retreat and, wishing to hide my nakedness, walked backwards towards my garden gate. She looked up again and bemused, tilted her head to one side. For the second time that day, I tried to appear nonchalant and normal. Smiling and waving at her constantly, I continued my reverse down the drive.

I appreciate that walking backwards down a path was not the normal protocol in the neighbourhood, but on that occasion it was a necessity... After all, even when our life is in tatters, we still put on a good front for our neighbours to see.

Chapter 19

Aim High!

"What's the matter, darling?" I asked Henry as he sat glumly in the armchair, his head resting dolefully in his hands.
"Nothing!" came the untruthful reply.
"Really?" I screwed up my nose and wrinkled my mouth in my best I-don't-think-you're-being-completely-honest look. He turned his head away and, like lava down the side of a volcano, hot tears flowed steadily down his ruddy cheeks.
"What is it, sweetheart?" I implored, cupping his chin in my hand and gazing into his sorrowful eyes.
"I-I… I miss Daddy!" he blurted and then turned his head away again, ashamed of the betrayal. It was clear that he did not want to hurt my feelings, so I scooped him up into my arms and hugged him. I would like to say that I scooped him up effortlessly, but at six years-old, he was now too heavy for that. Instead, like a championship weightlifter, I attempted to lift him three times before successfully raising him into the air and then collapsing in a united heap upon the armchair.
"It's okay to miss him… I do too." Henry looked surprised at that statement.
"Really?"

"Yes, really!" I nodded. "It's okay to miss someone you love…" We sat and cuddled for a while.
"It's hard, Mummy. Now that he lives in America, we hardly ever get to see him."
"You see him every night on Skype," I encouraged, although even I recognized that this was a second-rate substitute. He looked at me with disbelief, incredulous at my shallow reply. I conceded. "Yeah, I know, it's not the same, is it?" He shook his head.
"I miss the fun stuff he always did with us."
"Are you saying I'm not fun?" I joked, trying to cajole him out of depression.
"You are…" he acknowledged reluctantly, "but Daddy is a different sort of fun."
"How?"
"Well, he wrestles with us and takes us on bike rides and does active sort of stuff. You do more… Mmmm… Crazy stuff."
"Crazy stuff?"
"Yup!"
"Like what?"
"Like magic tricks…"
"Fair enough! Point made!" I interrupted, not wishing to go further down this line. I smiled gently at him and wiped his cheeks. "Let me see what I can do. Okay? I can't replace Daddy, but I'll do my best."

"Come on boys! I've got a surprise for you. We're going out so hurry up!" I bellowed up the stairs.
"Where are we going?" Alfie asked.
"I'm not telling, otherwise it wouldn't be a surprise. Just trust me!"

The two of them charged down the stairs and presented themselves like troops ready for inspection. I straightened their jumpers and tucked in their T-shirts.
"Ready?"
"Ready!" they chorused.

We did not have far to go - the woods were only a few miles away - but I went by a circuitous route in order to confuse the twins and add to the mystery of our expedition.

We stopped for an ice cream along the way and I gave them their first clue to our destination.
"Where we are going is ever so high. It's ever so high, right up in the sky." I smiled enigmatically, proud of my poetic creation.
"How does that help?" moaned Alfie.
"Any idea, Henry?" I enquired optimistically, ignoring Alfie's belligerence.
"Nope!"
"Alright, we'll drive a bit further and I'll give you another clue."

I turned back on myself and drove towards the woods, stopping halfway to deliver my next teaser.
"If you go down to the woods today, you're sure of a big surprise. If you go down to the woods today, you're going up in the skies," I sang. They both looked at each other as if I had gone completely mad.
"That's not a clue, that's just weird!" proclaimed Henry with disgust.
"Come on guys; join in with the fun of it. Can you think where we might be going?"
"Heaven!" suggested Alfie unhelpfully. The two boys disintegrated into peals of laughter. I started to feel mildly annoyed, but I continued on optimistically and stopped 400

yards before the destination.
"Final clue guys. There's a bar of chocolate in it for the one who guesses this." Suddenly I had their attention.
"Here it is: walking on wire doesn't get much higher."
They looked at each other blankly and then suddenly Alfie beamed; the penny had clearly dropped.
"The high ropes course! You're taking us on the high ropes course! Oh Mummy, say that you are! Please say that you are!" Suddenly, the car filled with excitement, enthusiasm and expectation. I grinned and said nothing, enjoying the gentle buzz of my boys on the back seat.

I pulled into the car park triumphantly. At last I had hit the boys' hot buttons. They were excited and clearly engaged.
"Okay. One more surprise. Shut your eyes." They obeyed instantly and I rummaged in the carrier bag beside me.
"Ta da!" I chirped, proudly holding out their new camouflage jackets. "We can hardly go on an adventure like this without dressing up for the occasion."
"Yay!" Henry was the first to grab his jacket and put it on admiringly. We all followed suit. Then I produced the shoe polish….

A few minutes later with three blackened faces and camouflage jackets zipped up into position, we marched proudly into the reception area for the *Jungle Challenge*. A man poked his head out from behind some giant leaves and grinned.
"Welcome troops!" he said. His voice seemed familiar, evoking in me a distant but elusive memory. I studied his bronzen face, half-hidden under a mop of unruly, blonde hair. Memories of aeroplanes and parachutes flashed through my mind, locating him on my life map. Unperturbed by my scrutiny, he smiled. It was an unmistakeably dazzling smile. Now, there was no doubt as

to his identity.
"Mike?" I asked. He looked blank. "It's me... Laurie." Still nothing. I bumbled on, tripping over my words with embarrassment. "We met up near Newcastle... I did a parachute jump... Several years ago... For my hen night... It didn't go too well..."
"Oh my! I do remember you! You landed in a cow field and got chased by a bull and..." I cut him off in mid-flow.
"Yes! That's the one."
"Sorry! I didn't recognise you. You look so different." I took it as a compliment because last time I had seen him I had been a lot heavier.
"Really? How?" I asked flirtatiously, fishing for a compliment.
"Well, last time I saw you, it was you that was blacked out, not your face!" He threw his head back in laughter. My ego crashed to the floor along with my tin of shoe polish.

Sensing my dismay, Mike moved swiftly on.
"So who have we got here then?" he enquired, squatting down to face the twins.
"I'm Alfie and this is Henry and we're here to do the high ropes."
"The high ropes, eh? Feeling brave are we?" Alfie and Henry both nodded eagerly. "And is Mummy doing it too? Or is she just going to watch?" he asked provocatively, shooting me a cheeky look.
"Of course I am!" I protested, raising my blackened nose indignantly in the air. He laughed.
"Excellent! Well come with me and we'll get you kitted out."

With my harness firmly (a little too firmly) in place, I lurched forward towards the first obstacle. Mike pointed towards the course.

"Okay guys, listen up. There are only two rules on this course. The first is: when you're up you're up; there is no turning back! The second is: there is only to be one person on an obstacle at a time and no more than two on each platform. Is that clear?" He spoke with clarity and authority and my boys stood in awe. "Right! Who's first?"
"Alfie, you go first because you're nearest." I suggested decisively. "I'll go in the middle; that way I can help you both."

Alfie stepped forward and waited for his safety harness to be attached to the wire.
"Right young man, off you go!" Mike instructed. Alfie jumped confidently onto the cargo net and scrambled up effortlessly. By the time I had my safety harness attached, he was already onto the third obstacle.
"So much for a bonding experience!" I muttered. "Looks like it's you and me, Henry." Henry beamed and then gave me an appreciative cuddle.
"Off you go Mum!"
"See you on the platform!" I declared optimistically and jumped onto the net. The rope sank under my weight and my ascent was somewhat slower than I anticipated. Henry waited patiently and watched as I hauled myself up onto the platform. Instantly, he was onto the net and reached me in seconds, hardly giving me time to recover. My heart sank, but I encouraged him nonetheless. "Well done Henry! You were quick! I'll meet you over the other side."

I looked at the next obstacle – a log suspended 30 feet above the ground with a single rope to pull yourself along and balance. It had seemed so innocuous from down below, but now that I surveyed the ground far beneath and felt the slippery moss underfoot on the beam, the daunting reality of this 'adventure' played on my mind. I tentatively

Aim High!

placed my foot on the log and inched my way across, breathing deeply as I went. The rope swayed, my feet slipped and my heartbeat quickened as a surge of adrenalin started to overwhelm my body. I turned to Henry and fixed a fraudulent smile on my face.
"I won't be a minute! It's good fun isn't it?" Terror coursed through my veins.

I turned my attention again to the platform. It was only a couple of steps away. I was going to do it! With a final flurry of footwork, I made it across and collapsed onto the platform, hugging the central, wooden pole tight. Really tight. Relief flooded my already swamped system and tears welled up in my eyes.
"Are you okay, Mum?" It was Henry. He, like his brother, had crossed the beam effortlessly in seconds.
"I'm fine," I lied. "Where's Alfie?"
"He's over there. He's just finishing the course!" I looked over to where Henry was pointing just in time to see Alfie running across the final wooden bridge. I suddenly became woefully aware of my physical deficiencies. I had encroached on Ben's territory and was paying the price. Nausea and light-headedness overcame me leaving me unable to control my body or my senses. I stood frozen to the spot.
"Go on then, Mum!" Henry encouraged. But I could not. The world was spinning around me and the wooden mast was all that enabled me to stay upright. I lashed myself tightly to it with my arms, my knuckles turning white as I held on with all my might.
"I'll be okay in a minute, Henry." My speech slurred as a cacophony of sensations scrambled my brain. "Really I will."

I heard the disgruntled murmurs from the people

backlogged behind me.
"What's going on?"
"What's the hold up?"
"What's she waiting for?"
"Oh, for goodness sake!"

"Are you alright up there?" It was Mike. He squinted up at me from below, his hand shielding his eyes from the sun and his ever-present, dazzling smile radiating comfort to my soul. I tried to answer, but only a squeak came out. He recognised the signs of terror. "I'm coming up!" he reassured. Tears of relief and shame streaked down my blackened face.

Within a few seconds, Mike traversed the obstacles and was standing by my side, beaming with reassurance and positivity. He took one look at my face and realised that I had hit the point of no return. He did not even try to persuade me to carry on.
"Do you need me to get you down?" he offered sympathetically. I nodded meekly. "In that case, wait there… Oh! Silly me! You can't go anywhere can you?" he quipped, gently nudging me back into reality. "Give me two minutes and I'll be back. You'll look after her, won't you, young man?"
"Definitely!" Henry replied, hugging me around my waist. Henry peered up at my face, his concerned, blue eyes contrasting sharply with his shoe-polished cheeks. "Don't worry Mummy! I've got you!"

We stood for a while in a silence that was broken only by the gentle rustle of the trees and the grumble of the queue. A blackbird flew past then turned and rested on a branch opposite. It tilted its head quizzically as it surveyed the scene. Even the woodland had become aware of my unfortunate predicament! I heard a faint buzzing and shuddered at the thought of an audience of wasps and bees. However, the buzzing became a whirring and the whirring grew closer and louder. Despite my curiosity, I could not bring myself to ease my clutch on the pole enough to look down. When you are on the rough sea of vertigo, the side of the ship is a perilous place to be. I preferred the safety of being lashed to the mast!

I stared outwards, dreaming of the comfort of my feet upon dry, firm land; imagining myself running freely and fearlessly through rich grassy fields. My thought stream was interrupted as Mike's face suddenly appeared above the platform closely followed by the rest of him and the cage of a yellow crane.
"Lift Madam?" he grinned.

Terror left as help arrived, but the numbness of my body did not depart. I was still frozen to the spot. Mike chuckled silently and stood beside me again. Finger by finger he prised my rigor mortis hands away from the pole and then helped me inch my way across the platform to the safety of the crane, where I collapsed into a crumpled heap. I raised my head up just in time to catch a glimpse of Henry effortlessly traversing the course.

Mike turned to me and smiled impishly.
"Which floor Madam?"
"Ground! Definitely ground!"

Chapter 20

Davina's Trails

"For goodness sake! Can't you get anything right?" Marcie's scathing words resounded around the smoothie-splattered kitchen; her fiery, verbal arrow scoring a direct hit on my pride. I winced and reassured myself that it was an easy mistake to make. Anyone can forget to put the lid on the liquidiser!

Armed with a cloth and some kitchen roll, I repentantly started to mop up the strawberry and banana slop that had oozed its way into every crevice of Marcie's kitchen.
"..... You really need to think before you do things. It's just not okay to go to people's houses and..." I let Marcie's tirade wash over me. I was drenched in smoothie and was not about to receive a soaking of failure and disgrace as well. I continued mopping and waited until she had finished and her perfectly made-up face had settled back into her well-rehearsed façade.
 "There now! We're all spic and span again," she trilled triumphantly.
"Would you like me to try again?" I offered. Her body recoiled, her smile slipped and horror seeped into her piercing, grey eyes.

"No! Just go and sit down and let me do it. Honestly!" I heard the mistrust in her voice and obediently complied.

Carefully, Marcie replenished and restarted the liquidiser. Within seconds she had blended a perfect, pink liquid and poured it into five matching tumblers without spilling a drop.
"There you go. Easy! All done!" she announced patronisingly in her sweetest tones. "Now, where's my bell?" She located it in one of her perfectly-ordered kitchen cupboards and with a delicate hand movement and tuneful, tinkling sound, summoned the boys.

"Honestly Mum, I struggle with Marcie. I never seem to measure up to her standards, and then I go making it worse by messing up big time like I did today! Sometimes the way she looks down at me makes me want to throttle her."
"Red or white dear?" asked Davina, ignoring my moans and concentrating instead on my ever-depleting wine rack.
"Red, please... I don't know how she does it. Everything in her life seems so perfect: her house; her kitchen cupboards; her clothes; her hair; her son, Josh. Even her front garden hasn't got a dandelion in sight!" I paused and surveyed my tangled bushes and weed-filled beds. An empty plastic bag blew across the pavement and settled on my roseless thorns like an unwelcome flag of failure.
"I doubt everything with Marcie is as perfect as it seems, darling," Davina reassured wisely. "I suspect that the difference between you and Marcie is that you wear your mess on the outside!" On that note, Davina swept out of the room, leaving a trail of contemplation behind her.

Davina's Trails

"That's really naughty! Bottom step both of you, now!" I bellowed in my less-than-perfect parenting style. I ushered the twins to the hallway and, after plonking Henry on the bottom stair, grabbed Alfie by the hand and led him up to the top.

"But this is the top step, not the bottom step, Mummy, and you said that you wanted us both to sit on the bottom step!" Alfie challenged contrarily. I shot him one of my glares and he retreated back into submission.

"This is rubbish!" scowled Henry.

"Yeah!" supported Alfie, feeling a little braver again. "Josh's mum would never treat him like this. She doesn't shout."

"Really? Well, when you've finished doing your time here, we can go across and find out exactly how Josh would've been treated, shall we? Then Marcie will get to find out exactly what you boys have been up to!" I was irritated by Alfie's comment but recognised his valiant attempt at deflecting my attention away from their crime. "Seven minutes! Starting now... and no talking or I'll start your time again!" They both bowed their heads and picked their toes while I returned to the lounge and surveyed the giant, green moustache that they had chalked onto the television screen in a moment of experimentation!

For the second time that day, I armed myself with weapons of mass cleanliness and set about restoring a home. I was clearly not entirely successful because from that day onwards all the television actors had a greenish hue to their skin tone.

Seven minutes and two contrite apologies later, the twins set off in search of more mischief.

"So why don't you struggle with Henry and Alfie?" mused Davina unexpectedly over her glass of red wine that evening.

"What?"

"You said earlier that you struggle with how Marcie treats you and yet you never struggle with your feelings towards the boys, even when they cover your television screen in green chalk and are rude to you!"

"But that's different!"

"How is it different?"

"Well the boys don't mean anything by it. Marcie does."

"But what if Marcie doesn't mean it? What if she just doesn't know how to cope with disorder?"

"But that's ridiculous! I'm not always clumsy and yet Marcie's always bitchy and rude to me."

"Well… That's your interpretation of events. If you were to ask her, she may see it differently." Frustration rose up within me as my mum challenged my feelings towards Marcie. I clutched determinedly onto the offence of earlier, refusing to let it go. Like a cat stalking its prey, Davina refused to drop the subject too, choosing instead to change her approach. "But can't you see that the twins and Marcie all challenge you and yet your reaction to each of them is different. Why?"

"Well… Errrrm… I'm supposed to teach Henry and Alfie right from wrong and train them to be respectful. They're still little, so it's okay when they mess up. Marcie, on the other hand… Well, she should know better!" The words exploded from my mouth as I clutched at flimsy straws of justification. I removed their bitter aftertaste with a glug of wine and defensively pulled a sofa cushion onto my lap.

Davina ran her finger around the top of her glass, causing a high pitched squeal. She mused mystically over the red sea and then peered at me through her pointed, purple glasses.

Davina's Trails

"I'm not convinced that's the difference. I still think there's more to it..."

"Go on then! What do you think the difference is?" I asked mockingly. After a lifetime of Davina's chaotic and airy musings, I braced myself to receive her latest obscure theory but was pleasantly surprised at the solidity of her reply.

"I think it's all about love. The fact is that you love Henry and Alfie no matter what happens. There are no conditions. They can be as naughty as they like or as rude as they dare and you still love them. However, with Marcie it's different. Your love for her is conditional. It's dependent on her reaction and behaviour towards you."

"I guess so... But I think it's natural to change my feelings towards someone when they're being unkind," I protested. Davina tilted her head to one side in disapproval.

"Really? If it's natural then why don't you do that with the twins?"

"That's an absurd comparison! They're my sons and Marcie's just my neighbour!"

"But aren't we all called to love our neighbours?" Davina chided. She changed tack. "Well, what about Darcy then? You've never been frustrated with your feelings towards her and yet the two of you have had many fallings out over the years."

"Yes, but that's Darcy! I've known her for years, and anyway, Darcy's lovely. No-one in their right mind could get frustrated with her. Marcie's different."

"Darcy wasn't so lovely when she dropped your friendship for her new boyfriend!"

"Hmmmm. I'd forgotten that." The pain of the memory stung my heart momentarily. I chose to disarm it with flashbacks of our more joyous times together. "I'm sure Darcy would never do that again. She's a true friend."

"But what if she did?"

"Well she wouldn't!" I protested.
"But what if you're wrong? What if Darcy did hurt you again? What would you do then?" I considered this distasteful concept carefully before replying.
"Then I would forgive her and love her anyway."
"Why?"
"Because she's Darcy!" I replied fondly. Davina smiled.
"And this is Marcie. So why won't you extend her the same arm of grace that you do to Darcy?"
"Because Marcie is not Darcy!" I exclaimed crossly, indignant at the comparison. "And anyway, Marcie is always having a dig at me. I don't see why I should overlook all her snide comments. There are limits!"
"And that is exactly my point!" Davina declared triumphantly, placing her empty glass on the side. "You have placed a limit on your love for Marcie and that limit is dictated by her behaviour towards you. When you learn to remove that limit you will change your relationship with Marcie forever!"

Without another word, Davina stood up and shimmied flamboyantly out of the room in a waft of orange chiffon. Her trail of wisdom remained and challenged me for the rest of the evening.

Chapter 21

Snakes Alive!

As I got into bed that evening, I was still grumbling over the day's events and my challenging conversation with my mother. I knew it was essential to drop the offence that I carried towards Marcie, but I refused to release it; instead, I clung on to my pride. The lack of peace in my heart reflected in the torrent of thoughts that swept through my mind, churning up uncomfortable feelings and causing me to toss and turn. I lay there for what seemed like hours, until eventually I overcame the restlessness and fell into a fretful sleep...

"For goodness sake! Can't you get anything right?" Marcie's scathing words resounded in my head as I watched the day's catastrophe replay in my dream. I surveyed the scene of devastation and was ashamed at the disaster I had unleashed in her perfect home. Familiar oppressive feelings overwhelmed me and I wanted to retreat.
"Not yet!" came the voice. "Just keep watching."
"For what?"

"You'll see..."

I watched myself set about the cleaning of the kitchen with dismay. Discouragement was written all over my face. I witnessed the accusatory scowls that Marcie threw in my direction and listened to every condemning word that she spoke over me.

"….. You really need to think before you do things. It's just not okay to go to people's houses and wreck them. I've worked long and hard to make this house nice and I'm so disappointed that you treat it so carelessly. Why can't you be like other normal people? I can't even trust you with the simplest of tasks! All you need to do is to think first, but oh no! You are Laurie Driver who doesn't think! Instead you just go charging in like an overweight bull in a china shop. I don't know of anyone else that has as many disasters as you do. Pass me the mop. No! Not like that! Wring it out first! Honestly! It's like having another child in the house! …"

I could not bear to listen to anymore. It was too painful. I turned my head away.
"So what was I supposed to learn from that exactly?" I asked the voice.
"Nothing! I am just showing you your interpretation of events. You will only start to learn when you see it with my eyes."

With that the scene replayed itself. I saw myself fill the liquidiser with fruit and milk and willed myself to pick up the lid but to no avail. The sequence of events remained unchanged. I winced as I watched myself go towards the lid and then get distracted by a squirrel in the garden scavenging for nuts. Then I watched with dread as I saw myself return empty-handed to the blender. Marcie was ferreting around in the larder for some straws and wittering away about her latest holiday. I saw my finger press the switch and the explosion of pink milk that ensued. It covered every cupboard, tin and surface within five feet. The flood of disappointment reached me even in my dream.

Yet again I focused on the fullness and strength of Marcie's reaction: the horror that swept across her face as she surveyed the scene; her scowl of anger and her… Oh my! I jumped backwards in disgust. A giant python was coiling itself around her ankles and quickly moving up her body. Within seconds, it engulfed her until only her eyes were visible.

"Do something! Can't you do something?" I pleaded.
"There's no need. Just watch and learn," the voice responded calmly.
The python's head appeared from around Marcie's shoulders. It opened its mouth and started to speak.
"For goodness sake! Can't you get anything right?" came its words. The snake continued spouting every venomous syllable that had left Marcie's mouth that day. As it spoke, I saw arrows of *dismay*, *discouragement*, *judgement* and *shame* fly out of its scarlet gullet. They headed directly for me and embedded in my back. I watched as I saw myself wince and then recognised the transformation when I steeled myself to block out the torrent of abuse. As I did so, the new arrows failed to make their target; instead they glanced off my back and vanished instantly. The others started to fall off me onto the floor until just one arrow remained – it was labelled *Shame*.
"Why is that arrow still there?" I asked.
"It is hooked on your clothing," the voice replied. I had been so intent on watching the situation unfold that I had

not noticed the waistcoat I was wearing in this dream – a green, woollen waistcoat labelled *Pride*.

"Without pride there can be no shame," the voice explained.

"Look again at Marcie," the voice instructed. Reluctantly, I turned my head towards her. I stared, mesmerised at the movement of the python around her. Its body seemed to move in two directions at once. Suddenly a second head appeared from behind her back. I recoiled in horror.
"There are two?"
"Yes."
"But what are they?"
"Look closely at their trails and markings and you will identify them. Each one has its own distinctive pattern." I stepped forward to view them closer and noticed the letters hidden in their triangular patterns. I read their words aloud.
"*Inferiority* and *Criticism*?"
"Yes! Those are what came against you today. Not Marcie." The voice paused briefly to allow me to absorb this truth. "It was the snake that spoke." I looked again at Marcie, fully engulfed by the two pythons, unable to move freely. My heart filled with pity for her plight.
"Can she be set free?"
"Yes." The voice was softer towards me now as revelation dawned in my heart.
"How?"
"By love. Unconditional love."
"But how do I do that when I struggle so much with my feelings towards her?"
"All you have to do is to hate the sin and love the sinner. These snakes are not visible in your realm, but their characteristics are still easy to spot – they always leave a trail of devastation behind them. Their mandate is to

destroy that which is good. When you learn to differentiate between snakes and people then you will learn to love my people as I do."

Chapter 22

An Unlikely Duet

"Morning, Mum."
"Morning, darling!"
"I had the most amazing dream last ni... Oh my goodness! Whatever are you wearing?"
"What do you mean?" said Davina with a knowing smirk.
"You... Well... You look so... sensible!"
"I have no idea what you're referring to!" she teased.

Davina was dressed in a dark blue pencil skirt, tailored, white shirt and pink cardigan. Even her hair was tamed into a stylish chignon with invisible fastenings. The only clues to her normal attire were her bohemian, dangly earrings, bright lipstick and footwear – her trademark, rainbow platforms were still very firmly attached to her feet. These sedate clothes suited her figure, showing off her striking looks to perfection, but they masked the personality within and presented an altogether misleading persona. I viewed her outfit with suspicion.

"What are you up to?"
"Nothing! I just thought that I'd go out for the day. That's all."

"And where exactly did you say you were going?"
"I didn't!" she replied elusively. The lack of information was starting to niggle at me. It was uncharacteristic for Davina to withhold vital facts. Something was amiss
"Hmmmm. You've been disappearing off a lot recently, so I'm guessing there's a man involved." Davina smiled at this suggestion and tapped the side of her nose with her finger, making it clear that she was not about to impart the details.
"See you later!" she declared and then started towards the door, briefly stopping to pose one last question. "Are you still planning on going to the church fete this afternoon?"
"Erm. Yes. I think so."
"In that case, I might see you there." With one final, exaggerated air-kiss she was gone.

"Come along, Henry. It's not much further."
"But I don't want to go to some stupid church crate!"
"It's not a crate. It's a fete and it's not stupid. It'll be fun!" I declared optimistically, looking at the dark clouds looming overhead, secretly hoping that there would be some cover available when we arrived.
"What is a fete, Mummy?" enquired Alfie cheerily.
"It's a mish mash of things, Alfie. There'll be lots of stalls where you can have fun and win prizes and other stalls where you can buy cakes and drinks. They'll probably have a bouncy castle too; they did last year." Even Henry's ears pricked up at this final suggestion and miraculously his objections evaporated and his pace quickened.

A couple of minutes later, we arrived at the church hall and headed around the back. With £2 each in their pockets to spend, the boys immediately made a beeline for the

An Unlikely Duet

inflatable pirate ship that was anchored in the middle of the field. I chose a more leisurely option and sauntered slowly around the stalls. With many familiar faces from school and plenty of school friends for the twins to play with, I soon relaxed into the event.

I made my way to the independent jewellery stall and surveyed their pieces. An unusual green necklace caught my eye. I picked it up carefully and inspected the intricate, Aztec design on each bead.
"I thought that was pretty too!" whispered Marcie unexpectedly in my ear. Startled, I jumped back in surprise, knocking over one of their displays. Marcie frowned in disapproval. "Oh dear! Are you sure you should be touching that. After all you wouldn't want to break it? You know what you're like." Her accusation activated my hot button and my blood started to boil. Spiteful thoughts flooded through my mind, heading for my tongue. I felt them building and forming with every second that I stood under the influence of her critical expression. Just as I was on the brink of opening my mouth to release a tidal wave of toxic words, something amazing happened. Flashes of the previous night's dream played through my mind and for the first time I saw the reality of the situation before me. I recognised the voice of the snake, and realised that this was not Marcie speaking but that which tormented her. As the truth set me free, a cooling flow washed through me, neutralising the heat and dispatching the acrid feelings that had polluted my heart and so nearly damaged our friendship. I visualised the image of poor, helpless Marcie smothered by the pythons; overcome by her own personal battle with criticism and inferiority. None of this was really aimed at me; it was merely the overflow of the broken areas of her life spilling into mine. Compassion rose within me, forming a tear in my eye. I stepped

forward with open arms and hugged her more lovingly than ever before.

"Hello, Marcie! I didn't know you were going to be here today."
"Well you wouldn't! It was a last minute decision. Josh was bored and I thought it might be fun. When we arrived, he took one look at the pirate ship and proved me right." We both looked wistfully over at the pirate ship. Unfortunately we were just in time to see Alfie forcing Josh to walk the plank. Thankfully, the smile on Josh's face suggested that he was a willing participant in his own demise. Marcie was less convinced and looked on with overprotective disapproval.
"Boys will be boys!" I suggested optimistically.
"And bullies will be bullies!" she corrected, before rushing off to save her precious Josh.

Deflated by my encounter with Marcie, I quickly lost interest in the stalls, seeking instead a remedial cup of tea. Spotting a marquee labelled *refreshments,* I headed across the field. Two red-faced women, chuckling away to themselves, passed me as I went. They had just left the refreshments tent and kept looking back over their shoulders.
"She's a scream! Who'd have thought…"
"I know… I always thought Frederick… " I failed to hear the rest of their conversation because I was distracted by the sight of another large lady choking on a rather vibrant fairy cake as she left the tent. She was turning blue, but still could not stop laughing. A portly man in a straw hat came to her rescue by walloping her hard on her back. The cake dislodged and, jettisoning out of her mouth, landed

An Unlikely Duet

unannounced in a nearby drink, whilst the lady landed on an unsuspecting passer-by. Regaining her composure and her pinkish hue, she then turned and thanked the man profusely for his heavier-than-expected, helping hand. Undeterred by her choking experience, she then tackled the remainder of her cake with gusto.

It seemed that everyone who left the refreshments marquee did so with a smile on their face. I was intrigued and in desperate need of refreshment, so I called the boys over.
"Henry! Alfie! Come on! Let's have something to drink."
Henry and Alfie looked disappointed.
"Oh!" they chorused, rounding their shoulders and dropping their heads low to accentuate their disapproval. I resorted to enticement.
"There's probably chocolate cake." The improvement in their demeanour was nothing short of miraculous. Their heads perked up, their shoulders levelled and they happily ran ahead of me into the tent. I smiled quietly to myself, marvelling at the power of chocolate and its impact on modern parenting.

Two steps later, I heard a most unexpected yet familiar voice emerge from the tent:
"Boys!"
"Nanny!" was their joyful response. I peered through the door to the marquee and saw my mother standing behind a red and white, gingham tablecloth, serving cakes alongside the vicar.

"Mum?"
"Laurie!" Davina called delightedly, waving her arms in a flamboyant gesture that sent the vicar's hat flying. "Come and meet Freddie. He's the vicar of St Mungo's." I stepped forward suspiciously. "Freddie, this is my

daughter, Laurie, the one that I've told you all about."
"Nice to meet you," I said politely as I tried to decipher the unspoken sentiments between them. "So you're Freddie, the one that Mum's told me nothing about!" I quipped mischievously. Davina smiled enigmatically. The vicar blushed and extended his hand towards me.
"Frederick. Most people call me Frederick."
"Oh! Don't be so stuffy, Freddie!" Davina protested. I shook his hand, then he wandered off hastily to hide behind a large slice of Victoria Sponge, which he thrust upon a rather unsuspecting, nervous, old lady, who was actually waiting for a dainty fondant fancy.

"So I guess this explains your change of attire and mysterious disappearances, does it?"
"Not exactly. You see, the reason I keep vanishing every Thursday is because I've been attending The *Alpha Course* that Freddie's been running at St Mungo's. It's really rather good. I've learnt ever such a lot. It's quite changed my thinking about Christianity and hot cross buns?"
"Hot cross buns?"
"Yes! It turns out that the cross on the top of the buns is to symbolise the cross that Jesus died on."
"Ah! Just a little different to the explanation that you gave me when I was growing up!"
"Oh!" Davina grimaced. "Sorry about that! I really did think that it was their way of covering up the cracks in the top. Maybe I should've asked someone."
"Maybe... Anyway, you still haven't explained why the sudden change of clothes."
"It's simple really. I knew that I'd be serving lots of cream-laden cakes today, and I realised that all of my outfits were too dangly, flouncy and downright impractical. People may like chiffon cakes, but no-one wants chiffon in their cake!" I chuckled at her explanation and felt reassured that nothing

about her had really changed. "But if it makes you feel any better, Laurie, I shan't be wearing this again. I've found it far too restrictive. I haven't been able to tell half of my stories in this outfit. After all, how on earth am I supposed to demonstrate the constipated ballerina that I saw in Budapest when I'm wearing a pencil skirt? It's simply impossible!" With that Davina wandered off to join Frederick and serve the hungry, baying crowds of Lower Tweedle.

Chapter 23
Cutting the Straps

I lay lazily on the sofa, listening to Alfie read out loud. I smiled at his perfect, little fingers clutching tightly onto the coloured pages and beamed with tearful pride as he confidently mastered the text.
"The dwarves loved having Snow White living with them in their cottage and enjoyed the tasty dinners that welcomed them home each night," he read. I smiled at Alfie in encouragement and nodded for him to continue. "... but the thing that the dwarves liked most about Snow White was her kidneys."
"What?" Images of the dwarves as black-market organ traders flashed through my mind. "Let me have a look at that..." I scanned his book and shrieked with laughter. "No silly! Not *kidneys*... *Kindness*! The dwarves liked her kindness!"

Alfie and I were still sniggering at his mistake when the computer started to ring. That dreaded, familiar, daily ringtone.
"It's Daddy!" squealed Alfie loudly, running to the computer.
"No!" I screamed silently and retreated to the kitchen.

I tried not to hear their conversation. I did not want to know how good Ben's life was in America but, no matter how much I busied myself around the kitchen, I heard it all. With every syllable that left Ben's mouth, tension, rejection and hatred coursed through my veins. An unstoppable flow. I gritted my teeth and found an onion to chop. I knew it would soon be over (his calls never lasted long), and then I would be free again to carry on with my life. However, today my escape route was cut off abruptly by the voice in my head – that familiar voice that often challenged me and course corrected me on the rough seas of life with the rudder of wisdom. This time its challenge to me was simple:
"Are you ready yet?" the voice enquired.
"Ready for what?" I asked, but there was no follow-up explanation.

Just then Henry appeared at the door.
"Mummy, Daddy says he'd like to speak to you."
"Oh joy!" I mumbled sarcastically and walked towards the computer as a criminal to the gallows.

"Hi, Laurie!" Ben offered warmly.
"Hello," I replied coldly, hatred chilling my response.
"How are you?"
"Fine." I disliked the tension between us but did not know how to break it without coming down from my high horse of judgment and disapproval.
"Good. That's good."
"Henry said that you wanted to speak to me. What about?" I was keen to get this over and done with.
"Yes, that's right. Erm… I wanted to… Erm… I wanted to… I wondered…" My curiosity was piqued now. I had never seen Ben so sheepish. I stared at his face examining every crease for clues. It all seemed unfamiliar to me now.

His skin, no longer radiant, had taken on a greyish hue and his bluebell eyes seemed to have faded to a pale, stale grey.
"Yes?"
"I want a divorce!" he blurted. An arrow hit my heart. It was a bull's-eye.

I gasped inwardly but smiled outwardly, fighting to retain my composure. Noxious chemicals rallied and positioned themselves ready to flood my system. I breathed in deeply and closed my eyes, desperately searching for the words to speak out loud, but I knew that I could not trust myself to be kind. The voice knew too and came to my rescue.
"Ask him why?" the voice instructed. So I did.
"Why now?"

Ben looked crestfallen at my question and hung his head. He started to sob. His tears warmed my heart and melted the icicles of hatred and revenge. My heart reached out to him as I recognized his humanness and remembered the real Ben - the Ben that had been hidden from me for so long, hidden behind a façade of selfish requests and a determination to appear whole at all costs. The façade crumbled brick by brick with every word of explanation that left his mouth.
"It's Kelly…" The mere mention of her name sent chills through my system. I reached for the floodgates of poison but was halted in my tracks by Ben's next statement.
"She's ill… She's… She's very ill… and I want to… before…"

I never heard the rest of his explanation for he collapsed in a deluge of tears that swept me out onto the sea of emotion. Waves of bitterness and jealousy clashed with waves of pity and love. A terrible storm ensued and I was tossed to and fro as thoughts clashed with thoughts, emotions with emotions, revenge with forgiveness, pride with humility, self-righteousness with compassion. I started to drown, weighted down by stubbornness and judgment, my heart encased in concrete. I felt myself sinking, being dragged down, rucksack first.

The voice spoke again:
"Are you ready? Ready to cut the straps? It is time."

For the first time I understood the real price of unforgiveness. It was a price too high. I longed for freedom, laughter and joy, not oppression, bitterness and pain. I desired a pure heart and kindness, all of which had been lost in the shipwreck of betrayal. I had been so intent on viewing everything from my throne of judgment that I had not noticed the hardening of my own heart. I had not realised that I was adrift, lost on a sea of bitterness.

In that moment of clarity and turmoil, I made the hardest decision of my life - the decision to forgive; to cut the straps of pride and overrule the judgment that I had issued against Ben and Kelly. This was no longer an issue of right or wrong or of self-justification. Ben was no longer the accused and I the innocent victim. I was now guilty too. Guilty of unforgiveness and that unforgiveness was killing *me*, poisoning *my* system.

I looked at the screen. Ben was staring at me, awaiting my decision. He knew the power that I wielded in that moment, and so did I. If I said no, then he would have to wait years, but if I said yes, then he would be free in a matter of months.

What he did not understand was that I also wielded the same power over myself and that, by making the right choice, I too would be free in a matter of seconds.

Trembling, I smiled nervously at him, bracing myself for what I must do.
"There's something I need you to know first, Ben," I started. He looked at me quizzically.
"What is it?"
"You need to know that…" I stopped and inhaled deeply, rallying every ounce of resolve that I possessed. "You need to know that I forgive you and Kelly." The words echoed around my head, ministering to my soul. Caught up in the wave of self-healing, I repeated them again, just using different words. "I don't hold anything against either of you anymore." I felt the tsunami of freedom flooding in, caused by the power of the vibrations of my choice. Joy and kindness started to take their rightful places as the rucksack dropped off my heart. Perspective reordered itself instantly and my vision expanded to encompass positive thoughts towards them. I was no longer viewing things through the murky waters of self-pity. "I am genuinely sorry to hear about Kelly. I hope that she'll be okay. Is there any hope for her?" These were not empty words but compassionate ones. I really did want the best for them because I was finally free, no longer attached to them with cords of jealousy and rejection. Ben hung his head and grimaced.
"There is an outside chance that she'll get through this, but right now it's not looking good."
"Oh! I'm sorry," I said, followed by an awkward silence.

After what seemed like forever, I broke the tension with my decision.
"If you want a divorce, then I won't stand in your way," I whispered, hardly daring to air the words. Pausing for a moment to consider the implications of a divorce, I

A Rampage of Grace

considered the vows that we had both taken on our wedding day, especially the one that had frightened me the most – *until death us do part*. "I just want to make one request, Ben..." I added.
"What?" he asked suspiciously.
"When you declare the reason for the divorce on the papers, I don't want you to use the words *irretrievable breakdown*. Please find some other wording." Ben looked quizzical.
"What?" he seemed confused, so I explained.
"You see, it never was irretrievable. It was always a matter of choice." Ben's expression froze for a moment as he considered my words, then he brushed them lightly away with a pacifying,
"Sure, Laurie. Sure. Whatever you say. Thank you!" A look of relief softened his features and a hint of colour returned to his face; he had got what he had come for. An awkward silence fell again.
"I've got to go now, Laurie," he lied. "Thank you again. I'll be in touch."

The Skype call ended and I stared at the screen. Numbness approached me as I considered the weight of our impending divorce, but then I noticed my lightness of heart. I started to grin as the reality of my true freedom sank in - in a moment of bitterness I had made a choice to forgive and the feelings of freedom and forgiveness had followed. My situation had not changed but my outlook and heart had. More importantly, I was no longer carrying that rucksack.

Chapter 24

Monsters in the Mist

Six months later:

Davina burst into my bedroom with an enigmatic smile and a bubble of energy.
"Morning darling!" she chirped. I yawned sleepily and then studied her face. She was poised, clearly waiting for my attention.
"What? What is it?" I mumbled, lifting up my alarm clock to check the time. It was still only seven o'clock, and on a Saturday too. So much for my lie-in!
"Nothing!" she lied playfully, placing her hand upon her chin.
"Then why have you woken me up?"
"No reason," she teased, waggling her fingers. I wrinkled my nose in annoyance. Guessing games at seven in the morning were definitely not my idea of a pleasant wake up call.

The early morning sunlight streamed through a chink in the curtains and reflected off her face highlighting her radiance. She waggled her fingers again and the light refracted through her diamond ring, causing a rainbow on the ceiling.

Diamond ring? What diamond? What ring? Oh my! I sat up hurriedly and grabbed her hand.

"Let me see that! Wow! That's a whopper!"

"Certainly is!" beamed Davina proudly.

"It's beautiful! But when? How? I mean…"

"Last night. Freddie proposed over dinner."

"Where?"

"In *Le Petit Chat;* that new French restaurant. He popped the question over our starters. Apparently he intended to do it after pudding, but he was so nervous that he realised that he wouldn't have been able to eat at all if he left it that long! He'd prepared everything – the table in the corner, the ring, the music. It was so surreal that I half expected his snails to pop out of their shells and serenade us!"

"Aww! That's fantastic, Mum! I am so pleased for you!"

I sat back dreamily, basking in the rays of light and the warmth of her news. A troubled expression crossed my face. "What's wrong?" she asked.

"It's just that I can't get my head around the thought of you being a vicar's wife… Actually I can't even get my head around the thought of you as a wife at all. You're not exactly renowned for your domestic ways!"

"Me neither, darling! Me neither." Davina tossed her head and floated towards the door, her voluminous nightdress glinting in the sun.

"You must invite him around. I'll cook you both a celebratory dinner," I shouted after her as she left my bedroom. Her face peeked cheekily back around the door.

"He's already coming… Tonight… Six o'clock… He's bringing his brother, David, too. I was going to cook, but now that you've offered, I'll leave it to you." Her face disappeared and the joy of her news filled my room.

"Laurie, it's Marcie. What are you up to this afternoon?"
"Nothing much. Why?" I replied with expectations of a cream tea invitation floating seductively through my head.
"Great! I knew you wouldn't have anything worthwhile to do!" she said honestly. "I need to practice my monster makeup for an exam on Monday and I think your face would be absolutely perfect!"
"Ah! Well… I'm not sure…."
"You are wonderful! See you at one!" she instructed bossily and hung up.

I spent the next five minutes in front of the mirror scrutinising my face for hints of monster. With the exception of the discovery of a rogue hair or two, my search proved inconclusive.

"Would you sit still, for goodness sake! You're such a fidget! Even Josh behaves better than this."
"Yes, but I doubt that Josh has ever sat for three hours in one spot without moving. Can't I at least have a cup of tea?"
"No you can't! How can I possibly finish your mouth if you're sipping tea? Anyway, I've almost finished. Just a bit more protrusion on your bottom lip and a few more black lines under your eyes and we'll be done. Then it just needs to set." Marcie grinned at me through her perfect makeup and continued to dab my face with copious quantities of grey and black goo. My bottom lip started to drag downwards with the weight and I dribbled out of the side of my mouth. Marcie scowled. I attempted a grin but failed miserably.
"What's the time?" I mumbled incoherently whilst dodging her brush.

A Rampage of Grace

"It's four-thirty. It'll be midnight soon if you don't sit still!" she chided. I exhaled a deep, guttural moan and submitted myself to the completion of the process.

At five o'clock exactly, a fair-haired, blue-eyed gorilla dressed in jeans and a pink, cashmere jumper crossed the road from Marcie's to mine. Most of my neighbours were inside at the time, although a couple of passers-by stopped to stare, so I avoided their gazes by fixing my eyes straight ahead until I was safely indoors. I surveyed my face for the second time that day. The gorilla face, whilst clearly amateur in application, was none-the-less an impressive transformation of my radiant, fair skin.

Despite Marcie's four hours of intensive work in creating this mask, I estimated that it would only take ten to fifteen minutes to remove, if I applied myself to the task. With that in mind, I set to work immediately preparing the dinner. Carefully calculating every chore, I made sure that I left sufficient time to return my face to a more acceptable state before the dinner guests arrived. I abandoned my ambitious plans of a gourmet menu, settling instead for a traditional roast – lamb studded with rosemary and garlic, roasted potatoes and a selection of vegetables. It was a safe menu, but the best that I could produce with such limited time.

The meat and potatoes were in the oven in no time at all and I started to gain momentum. Next, I turned my attention to the starter. Realising that I no longer had time to prepare my own, I rummaged in the fridge and grabbed two packets of shop bought pâté. Removing all of the tell-tale packaging (which I buried deep within the bin), I transferred them both into one of my own dishes and roughed up the edges to give it a homemade look. A sprig of slightly sorry-looking parsley later and the deception was complete. Nobody would ever guess (apart from my mum, who had taught me the trick in the first place).

I attempted a similar feat with three shop-bought chocolate mousses, ambitiously trying to create a layered effect by alternating two different types of chocolate. Sadly my layers bled together and I had to settle instead for a more rustic, marbled effect.
"At least I'm guaranteed that they'll think I made that one!" I consoled myself. "Right! I just need to turn the meat over and then it's bye, bye gorilla!" I muttered, opening the oven door, still with my carving fork in hand. I was immediately engulfed by a dense cloud of hot steam, which obliterated my view and my senses as it scorched my skin. I felt my face start to melt.

"Cooeee! It's only us. We're a bit early, but I knew you wouldn't mind. You did get my text, didn't you?" asked Davina blindly as she stepped into the steam-filled kitchen.

I peered up through the steam to see three unidentifiable, blurry figures approaching me. Davina was still chattering away blithely.
"Let me introduce you. Laura this is David. David this is my daughter, Laura, but then I believe you already know each other." The steam subsided and I emerged from the mist with my gorilla-face dripping black pools of melted goo onto the kitchen floor and my sharp carving fork held menacingly in hand. In a bid to override my unusual facial appearance, I tried to welcome them with a smile. The resultant movement in my cheek muscles caused the whole of the left side of my gorilla-face to slide down into a mutant lump. I saw the shock on their faces and felt the disappointment in my heart. Reluctantly I held out my

A Rampage of Grace

hand to welcome Freddie's brother – David... David Pinkerton... the twins' headmaster!

David's thorn-like eyebrows knitted together in an all-too-familiar look of disdain. I withered inwardly but outwardly extended my hand to him in a gesture of friendship and a bid to redeem the situation. Under most circumstances, this olive branch would have succeeded in changing the atmosphere, but on this occasion it only resulted in him changing his jumper... A necessary act since I inadvertently cut a hole in his original one with the carving fork that I had forgotten was in my hand!

In a reconstruction of the aftermath of that fateful car crash, David's face turned puce and he glowered at me. With kaftan billowing, Davina raced to the rescue. Grasping the helm of the situation, she raised both her arms in the air and dramatically attempted to part the red sea of fury before her.
"STOP!" she yelled. Everyone halted and looked at her. Even David's eyebrows stood to attention! "Right! Laurie, you go and clean your face! Freddie, you get David a drink! I'll take over here!" she ordered, arming herself with a peeler.

With the situation diffused, Davina steered the evening back on course, embarking on an elaborate rendition of her adventures in the markets of Marrakech. So it was that I ended up ascending the stairs of my house in the English village of Lower Tweedle to the makeshift droning of a camel and bleating of a goat.

Chapter 25

A Table Full of Opposites

Half an hour later, I reappeared fresh-faced and freshly clothed in the living room. Davina and Freddie were lounging comfortably on the sofa whilst David's portly frame was moulded into the large armchair in the corner. His red wine, balanced precariously on his rather ample stomach, perfectly complimented the hues of his plump, red face. With the passing of time and the enjoyment of my mother's company, he appeared to have relaxed. His eyebrows had transformed from a thorny, knitted barricade into two somewhat softer hedgerows bedecked with occasional beads of sweat. A quirksome expression rippled across his mouth as I entered the room. I guessed it was a smile.

"Laura! Come and sit down; I've poured you a glass of wine. It's about time you got to know David. After all, he's going to be your uncle soon!" Davina teased. David and I looked at each other in horror, clearly neither of us were happy at the prospect of such a close, irreversible link.

"So… Mr Pinkerton…" I began awkwardly in an attempt to initiate conversation. David smiled wryly and leaned forward, adopting a supercilious stance towards me. His pompous display of authority was severed immediately by Davina.

"David! Call him David! He's family now!" David sat grumpily back in his chair, muttering.

"I'm still Mr Pinkerton to you at school."

"Obviously!" I agreed compliantly, amused by his reaction to our newfound equality.

"And I don't think anyone needs to know about our new relationship do you?" he added defensively.

"Relationship?" I teased with mock shock. David blushed at my inference.

"I mean this uncle business!" he clarified. "Assuming that this wedding goes ahead, that is!"

"Don't worry, David. Your secret will be safe with me," I assured him. "At school, I'll just pretend that you're a blustery, old headmaster that I'd prefer to avoid. That way no-one will suspect anything. Will that help?" Mr Pinkerton's eyebrows raised like Tower Bridge and his portly chest expanded in affront. I diffused him with an innocent smile and he settled suspiciously back into his chair. Davina changed the subject.

"No need to worry whether the wedding's going ahead or not," Davina declared. "The date's been set. Hasn't it Freddie?"

"Yes!" beamed Freddie proudly, his warm, soft face radiating pleasure. His face was round like David's but gentle and kind. His eyebrows, whilst dense, merely served to frame the softness of his eyes and to highlight his warm character. They reminded me very much of a faithful, shaggy dog.

"So? When's it to be?" I enquired.

"Four months from now. June the 14th. At St. Mungo's of course."

"Of course!" David and I agreed in unison.

Dinner was an awkward affair with long drawn out pauses. Even my mother and I, despite our best efforts, were unable to rescue the conversation given David's propensity for monosyllabic answers. I became fascinated by the contrast of the two brothers. Freddie was such a smiley, affable man, always enthusiastically there with an elaborate tale to tell, whilst David seemed to be unapproachable, prickly and angry. I determined to understand the contradiction in their two characters.

"So, Freddie, what was David like as a child? I mean, he can't always have been the serious headmaster that we see today?"
"Oh no! He was anything but!" enthused Freddie. "David was just fun to be around, always teaching me new things, like how to fish and climb trees. He even showed me how to track down the badger that lived in the woods behind our house."
"So you're a bit of a nature buff then David?"
"Maybe," he replied unhelpfully. Freddie continued.
"Obviously, as David got older he wanted to do his own stuff and didn't really want a younger brother hanging around. I suppose that's the problem with us being five years apart. He started going out with his friends and I was left at home. I guess we drifted apart a bit after that, didn't we David?" David grunted in response. It was impossible to tell whether the grunt was in agreement or disapproval, so I determined to find out.

"So, David, tell me about Freddie? What was he like when he was little?" I asked.

"He was good," came the flat response. I refused to be palmed off that easily.

"Good? That doesn't tell me much. He can't have been good all of the time. Go on, spill the beans… Was he cheeky or naughty? Was he an annoying younger brother who nicked your toys and whinged, or did you enjoy having him around?" Freddie beamed at my enthusiastic pursuit of his childhood. David, on the other hand, set his cutlery down and snarled in annoyance (at least I am assuming that it was a snarl and not another smile).

"He was good. Always good! In fact, I don't think he ever did anything wrong. Or at least in Mother's eyes he didn't. In her eyes he could do no wrong." With that he picked up his cutlery again and proceeded to sever a piece of lamb in two.

"That's not true, David!" protested Freddie. "I was always in trouble. She was forever telling me off about my muddy trousers and the worms and spiders that I deposited on the living room carpet. She got particularly cross with me when she was entertaining Lady Candling and I did that. Apparently, the shock almost killed the old dowager!" Freddie, Davina and I descended into peals of laughter, but David just scowled. I tried another approach.

"Oh come on David, don't be so serious. Even you must have found that just a little bit funny!"

"Actually, I never knew about it. I was only ever told what Freddie did right and what I did wrong!" he said venomously, spitting cauliflower cheese projectiles from his mouth as he spoke. The pain of his statement resonated uncomfortably around the room, leaving an awkward silence across us all.

It was at that moment that I recognised the divide between the two brothers – bitterness and jealousy. David, who had started off as an inspirational, lively character like Freddie, had nurtured those two feelings towards his brother and mother for years and in doing so had destroyed himself. By his own insistence on unforgiveness, he had morphed into a disagreeable human being, whilst Freddie, who had nurtured no such feelings, had gone on to flourish into his full potential.

I pondered upon the size of David's rucksack and the pressure on his bones. I thanked God that I had laid mine down, along with the poison of bitterness and jealousy that could have tainted the happiness of my life. Finally I understood the metamorphosis that I had escaped.

"Pudding anyone?" offered Davina
.

Chapter 26

Marcie's Mum!

"Laurie, it's Marcie!" came the desperate voice at the other end of the phone. "I need your help. Please come!" The line went dead.

All manner of scenarios flashed through my head. Reacting immediately and abandoning my plans for homemade sausage rolls, I left the half-rolled pastry and rolling pin on the side and a dusting of flour on the worktop, dog and floor.

Ripping off my apron with one hand, I grabbed for my shoes with the other, only to find one missing.
"Benson! Benson! Where's my other shoe?" I squawked at the top of my voice. Benson's scruffy, black face appeared proudly around the kitchen door with my soggy shoe hanging from his mouth. I tutted loudly and removed it from his gentle jaws, then bravely ignored the cold, wet feeling as I slipped my shoe on and squelched my way rapidly out of the house.

"Thank God you're here!" Marcie exclaimed when she opened her front door. Surprisingly, she appeared

impeccably dressed and very composed. Her lime green twin set was neatly buttoned and offset with a pale pink and cream chiffon scarf, which accentuated her milky-white skin tone perfectly. Her make-up was flawless without even a hint of a wrinkle or furrow on her brow and her blonde hair was perfectly coiffured, with every curl in place. Even her exotic perfume filled the hallway without the slightest whiff of distress. I was bemused by the discord between her perfect appearance and her frantic phone call. "Come in! Come in!" she barked urgently. "We need to get a move on."
"But what's the problem?" I enquired. "It sounded so urgent."
"Oh it is! It is!" she whispered breathily. I looked into her steely grey eyes and spotted a fleck of desperation. I realised that whatever the situation was, it was grave indeed, for I had never before seen Marcie exhibit any weakness in her flawless façade.

"It's my mother you see..."
"Is she okay?" I interrupted, immediately imagining hospital bedlam and near-death scenarios. "Do you need me to look after Josh today?" Marcie looked both irritated and perplexed by my offer of assistance.
"No! No I don't! My mother is fine!"
"Really?"
"Yes! She's arriving today at 4pm."
"Oh! Right! So what's the problem then?" Marcie held me squarely at the shoulders and looked at me with total sincerity. I steadied myself, awaiting the explanation of the horror that had so clearly distressed my friend.
"The house isn't ready!" she announced dramatically. My jaw dropped open in disbelief and irritation at the vacuousness of Marcie's trauma. "There's still so much to do! She's bound to find fault with everything; I just know

she will!"

For the first time, I saw Marcie in a new light. Never before had I seen her so defensive and desperate to achieve the accolade of approval from another. Normally she would be the one handing out the awards and the judgements. Yet today she was so stressed that she subconsciously ran her hand through her perfectly coiffured hair, dislodged a curl and did not even notice, let alone try to rectify it. I was amused to see the loose curl cascading down her forehead, a sign of her inherent humanness displayed at last. Somehow, it warmed my heart towards her.

"So what do you need help with?" I asked softly.
"Oh! Where to start?" she wailed. "I guess the kitchen and lounge. If you can help with those then I can crack on with her bedroom and the food. Honestly, those rooms are a real mess!"

I wandered into the kitchen and surveyed the scene – everything positioned perfectly in its allocated place, all work surfaces clear apart from a small, neat pile of washing-up placed precisely beside the sink. I looked around incredulous, remembering the chaotic mess that I had just left behind at my house.
"What exactly do you think needs doing in here?" I enquired tentatively.
"Well dusting of course!" replied Marcie handing me a pair of white gloves. "Look!" and with that she put on a white glove and swiped a finger across the shelf. Triumphantly and with revulsion she exhibited the very feint, grey smear that appeared on the material. "She'll spot it. I know she will! It all needs dusting!"

Arguing was pointless. This crisis, though dubious in substance, was real enough to Marcie. So, as a friend, I humoured her and decided to support her through it. I was quickly dispatched off to the lounge with my orders, a pair of white gloves, a can of polish and some neatly folded dusters. As I set about my pointless task, I wished with all my heart that my house would one day be this clean.

When 3.30pm came, Marcie cast a critical eye and finger over every room and every surface. Nothing escaped her eagle eyes. Finally, when the inspection was over and my rooms had passed muster, she broke into a relieved smile and declared,
"Perfect! Thank you!"

"How long's your mother staying for?" I enquired.
"A whole week!" she replied, despairingly.
"But that's great because it gives me plenty of time to meet her. Maybe you could come over to dinner one night." Marcie's face lit up at the invitation and then dropped seconds later as she remembered the ongoing state of my house.
"Maybe you should come over here instead," she offered.
"It might be a bit…"
"Cleaner?" I offered, laughing. She nodded, ashamed.
"Tuesday? Say 6 o'clock?"
"Perfect!"

By the time Tuesday evening came, I felt nervous. The thought of meeting anyone who was capable of unnerving the unshakable Marcie was a dreadful prospect, and I started to regret ever suggesting the dinner invitation. So, filled with fear and trepidation, at 6 o'clock exactly, I

marched the boys, still wrestling with their shirt collars and ties, across the road.
"It's itchy!" wailed Alfie.
"It's stiff!" moaned Henry.
"Hush now! You both look very smart."

I rang the doorbell. Marcie answered and gasped with admiration and relief at the twins' formal, crisp clothing and smooth blonde hair (courtesy of copious quantities of hair gel).
"Wow! Don't you two boys look gorgeous? And my dear Laurie, I'm so glad you're here!" Marcie exuded, giving me an uncharacteristically warm hug. She was so pleased to see me that she even launched into an involuntary compliment. "You look..." but stopped as soon as she saw my choice of outfit – a simple skirt and shirt combination that I had found in my local supermarket. I could see her wrestling with herself to find something positive to say. The delay was both noticeable and uncomfortable. Finally, she settled on a phrase and delivered it with a well-rehearsed, professional smile. "You look... so you!"
"That's great! I would hate to look like anyone else!" I replied, batting off offence. "Now, why don't you introduce me to your mother?"

Marcie nodded and ushered me into the house and into the lounge. I held my breath in anticipation of my first encounter with the tyrannical matriarch and contemplated the manner of my first greeting (even considering a curtsey). However, I was surprised to find a tiny, wizened, white-haired old lady sitting comfortably on the soft, cream couch. Dressed in a pale, blue twin set, she was as immaculately dressed as her daughter, only softer in appearance. She beamed at us all. I relaxed into a false sense of security.

"So, you must be Laura. I've heard so much about you from Marcella."
"Marcella?" I repeated, confused. Marcie blushed.
"That's me. Mummy's the only one to call me that. Personally, I prefer to be called Marcie."
"But that's not your name! Your name is Marcella," insisted Janice firmly but in a sweet voice. Janice turned to my two boys and looked at them approvingly. "And who do we have here then? Two fine young gentlemen if ever I saw them!" The twins beamed at such praise.
"I'm Henry!" announced Henry, puffing his chest out.
"And I'm Alfie."
"Henry and Alfred, eh? Fine names!"
"No! I'm not Alfred. I'm Alfie," corrected Alfie indignantly.
"Yes, yes, I know the nickname, but I would prefer to call you by your proper name." Alfie looked at me pleadingly, so I came to his assistance.
"His full name is Alfie, not Alfred. Ben and I thought that it was more informal, friendly and befitting of our family personality."
"Hmmmmmm," came the sneer of disapproval. I withered inside. I had not even been there five minutes and yet had already fallen short of Janice's yardstick. I sensed a difficult evening ahead and thought it best to release the boys from the trauma.
"Run along and find Josh. I'm sure he's been looking forward to seeing you."
"Yes!" corrected Janice subtly, "*Joshua* is in his room waiting for you."

Sit up straight for goodness sake Marcella!; *This lamb is nice, although a little pink for most people!*; *From the left*

Marcella! From the left! You should always serve people from the left. The barrage of criticism aimed at Marcie was unrelenting. I watched helplessly as Janice picked and tore at everything Marcie did, publicly exposing the bones and flesh of Marcie's flawless façade. At times I felt like I glimpsed Marcie's heart faltering, but each time she managed to restart it and recover her rhythm. However, I saw that with each blow it beat a little fainter, the destruction beginning to show. I leapt to her rescue.
"Marcie, this is amazing! You really have gone to so much effort. It tastes fabulous!" Marcie smiled meekly at me, appreciative of my rescue attempt. However, my flimsy, inflatable lifeboat was soon punctured by Janice's piercing tongue.
"Oh no! She can do much better than this! Can't you Marcella?"

I tried another tack – distraction – in an attempt to relaunch the lifeboat.
"So, Janice, tell me – what was Marcie like as a child? I bet she was a proper little madam."
"Actually, she wasn't. She was always very beautiful and so well-behaved. In fact, most of the other mothers used to admire Marcella very much and use her as a role model for their own children."
"Really? Wow! A role model, eh?" Marcie nodded and sighed. "But what about the real Marcie? What was she really like behind that perfect façade?"
"Whatever do you mean?"
"I mean, what kind of person was she? What did she enjoy doing? What things made her laugh and cry? What were her naughty little habits, the ones that make a mother smile?" Marcie looked at me quizzically, as did Janice. A silence followed whilst Janice considered the question; a question that delved uncomfortably deeper than the safety

net of appearances.

"That's hard to say. She didn't really do much laughing, crying or playing. She was too busy helping me with the W.I. She was great at selling jam you know. Nobody could resist Marcella and her beautiful, blonde curls."

"There was one thing, Mum," offered Marcie. "I did used to like playing in the river with the other kids. Do you remember?" Marcie's face shone as she replayed fond memories in her mind. "I even caught a fish once with my bare hands and rowed down the river on a car door!"

"Oh yes!" sneered Janice. "How could I forget? I soon put a stop to all that nonsense! You kept ruining your pretty dresses. It was about then that I introduced you to sewing and baking... and you never looked back!" Janice sat back with a self-satisfied, triumphant smile. Marcie nodded sadly, a distant, delightful memory quashed with a single blow.

In that instant, I finally understood Marcie. Her critical tongue was neither malicious nor vindictive but one that had been trained over many years by a critical mother, who believed that perfection was the definition of success. That recipe for success had omitted two essential ingredients – love and fun. I made it my mission there and then to reintroduce those elements back into Marcie's life.

Chapter 27

Back to School

"Do I have to?" I whined, in a throwback to my childhood days.
"Yes you do! Now hold still!" snapped Davina as she picked up the eyeliner and drew more freckles on my nose.
"But I can't imagine that he would even want to see me there... I mean, it's not as if we get along."
"Which is exactly why you need to go!" she insisted. "Look, you're going to be family soon so, if nothing else, do this for me." Davina looked at me with wide, brown, beseeching eyes followed quickly by a cheeky grin. Resistance was futile!
"Anyway, why does it have to be a school-themed party?" I moaned miserably. "Surely, that's like a busman's holiday for David?"
"Well, David's not one for parties; this way at least he can pretend he's still at work. After all, that is where he spends his life."
"If he doesn't like parties, then why throw one for him?"
"It was my idea. I want to remind David of his fun side and to tease out of him the sociable person that he used to be."
"I think it will take a bit more than teasing out! More like winching out! Anyway, even if you do succeed, I imagine

that David will feel a bit isolated being the only person not in fancy dress. I know I wouldn't like it." Davina mused for a minute and then replied.
"But he will already be in costume!"
"Huh?"
"He's coming straight from work... He'll be dressed as a headmaster!"

Davina placed the final touches on my face and then we posed together, as school mistress and pupil, in front of the mirror. She was dressed in a starched, white shirt, a green, triangular, tweed skirt, support tights and brown, lace-up, flat shoes. The only hint to her true personality was the bright orange and purple flower adorning her hair.
"There! A proper matron, even if I do say so myself. And look at you in your red school dress and tie. You look adorable!"

I surveyed my reflection and begged to differ. I felt ridiculous! Not only had my mum dressed me up as a freckly five year-old, but she had also blacked out my two front teeth in an attempt at recreating those precious toothless days. Sadly, her concept had not merged successfully with reality - I now looked like a demented old hag! By contrast, Henry and Alfie looked smart and normal in their school uniform and seemed blissfully unaware of the ridicularity of their mother.

Just as I was contemplating a change of costume, Davina looked at her watch and gasped.
"Quick everybody! We need to go! We've got to get there before David, or we'll spoil the surprise." Grudgingly, I moved to the front door and out to the car. This was never going to be my finest hour, but my one consolation was that nobody I knew would be there.

"It's Laurie isn't it?" came a familiar voice, as I bit into yet another profiterole from the buffet table. The cream oozed out, cascading down my chin like an avalanche. My stomach dropped with disappointment as I gazed upon the handsome face of Mike, the instructor. I smiled, forgetting my teeth. His eyebrows raised in shock and he stifled a laugh.

"Primary schoolgirl?" he guessed, playfully.
"Yup," I admitted shamefully. "It was my mum's brainchild. It seemed like a good idea at the time. And you...?"
"Came as a sixth-former. I thought it would be less embarrassing than turning up in shorts and a flat cap. Although, maybe I should've advised Uncle Freddie on his costume!" he laughed, pointing at Freddie's chunky legs protruding from a pair of oversized, grey shorts. Freddie turned and waved.
"Uncle?" I questioned.
"Yes! Freddie's my uncle. He's the vicar at St Mungo's. Do you know him?" Thrown by this revelation, I hesitated a bit before replying.
"Yes. Yes I do... He's marrying my mother... Next month."
"Wow!" he beamed. "What a small world!"
"Yes. Yes it is." I agreed, trying to assemble the pieces together in my mind but finding one piece missing. "So tell me, Mike... If Freddie's your uncle, then who's your father?"
"Why David of course! I'm a Pinkerton. Can't you tell?" he teased.

I glanced over at David. His portly frame was hunched heavily over the bar whilst, in an attempt at avoiding all conversation with the guests who had come there to honour

him, his grumpy, red face and piggy eyes focused on his pint of beer. Occasionally, his hefty black eyebrows would twitch into life and enter into their own private party, but for the most part, all was still. Mike beamed at me animatedly with his dazzling smile, washing me with a wave of warmth. His blonde tousled hair fell easily about his face as his charm radiated out.
"I'm told that I look more like my mother!" he whispered, winking cheekily.

The rest of the evening passed all-too-quickly in the company of Mike. Our banter was free-flowing, as was the wine, and for a while I forgot the heartache of the past. He reflected fondly on my high ropes disaster and politely omitted any mention of my parachute jump. Instead, he lavished his attentions on my two boys and on replenishing my wine glass.

Freddie called the evening to a close.
"Thank you everyone for coming. I'm sure you'll all agree that it's been a fabulous evening with not a detention in sight! Now, all that remains, before we leave, is for me to ask you all to join me as we give three cheers for my brother, David - the birthday boy. Hip, hip…" Everyone in the room chorused in unison with three emphatic and heartfelt hoorays, but the sentiment eluded David, deflected by his force-field of bitterness. He responded out of politeness instead of out of his heart – dipping his head in acknowledgement and feigning a smile of thanks. In doing so, he resembled a nodding British bulldog that you find in the back of cars, only with slightly less appeal.

I went in search of our coats, but Mike pulled me back gently. Smiling, he reached forward slowly, skilfully entering a space reserved only for those I trusted, and

rubbed some rogue eyeliner off my chin.
"That's better!" he declared softly. With an impish grin, he added, "You know… If we're going to be cousins, then I should at least have your phone number…"

Chapter 28

A Date with the Past

"... Thank you so much Mike! I'll see you there at eleven." I put down the receiver and laughed. This was a date that I was really looking forward to.

"I don't understand why you won't tell me where we're going," complained Marcie. "And why can't I wear my blue suit? You're wearing what you want." I ignored her snide reference to my casual attire and sought to chivvy her out of the house.
"Hush! All will be revealed in good time. For now, all you need to know is that you'll like it. Won't she boys?" I asked, appealing to Henry and Alfie, my partners in crime.
"Definitely!" they chorused.

Marcie conceded and walked reluctantly over to my car, ushering Josh ahead of her. Josh clumsily clambered in between the twins whilst Marcie elegantly entered the passenger side and sat down. She positioned her legs perfectly together at a slight angle, as all well-bred women are trained to do. Then, she carefully unwound the seatbelt in a way that showed off her immaculate nails.

"First stop *Jethro's!*" I declared proudly as soon as the car was underway. Marcie looked horrified. *Jethro's* was the cheapest café bar in town, notorious for its dated décor, basic seating, good cake and superb toilets. It was a family-run cafe that welcomed everyone no matter what their situation. Young, old, rich and poor (well actually, not too many of the rich) gathered together to enjoy the unique hospitality extended by this gregarious family. Jethro was a plump, northern ball of mischief, who loved children and specialised in annoying mothers by handing out messy craft to the kids - craft containing permanent felt tips and even worse… glitter! His wife, Helga, was an Austrian lady who clearly revelled in the notoriety extended to her home country by the film *The Sound of Music* - every now and then she would burst out enthusiastic renditions of *Edelweiss*, attempt to yodel or round up the children and march around the café to some strange new song that she had invented. I knew that Marcie would never dream of going there voluntarily; it just was not refined enough for her. Whereas we loved it and frequented it often!

"*Jethro's*? Why on earth do we have to go there? Surely if we need to go to a café bar, then we could go to *The Venetian* instead," Marcie moaned haughtily. "The cappuccino's exquisite there and it's beautifully clean and tranquil."
"And boring!" muttered Josh (a little too loudly). Marcie shot him a stare and his eyes fell to the floor.
"Just trust me, Marcie. Trust me," I whispered as reassuringly as possible. Marcie looked uncomfortable and very suspicious, but she acquiesced and sat back silently in her seat.

A Date with the Past

Minutes later, I pulled into the car park behind *Jethro's*. Marcie looked at me imploringly, but I ignored her and smiled.
"Right boys! Have you got the bag?" Henry and Alfie nodded. "In that case... ALL CHANGE!" I opened the car doors and everyone piled out. I led the way into the back of the café.
"Morning Jethro!" I called as we headed towards the toilets.
"Ah! Morning, Laurie. This must be Marcie!" he said with a disturbing wink (or at least it disturbed Marcie).
"Is it still alright to use your toilets?" I asked.
"Definitely!" he said, grinning.

"How does that man know my name?" asked Marcie, horrified. I smirked. I was really enjoying this. Marcie led a neatly packaged life and never liked to go anywhere that pushed her out of her comfort zone. She was clearly already in uncharted waters and paddling frantically.
"Stop worrying about everything, Marcie. Just go in here and put this on." I handed her some pink tracksuit bottoms, a white T-shirt and a pair of scruffy trainers. She grimaced.
"Seriously?"
"Seriously! You need to trust me on this one because you'll regret it if you don't." Marcie braced herself and took the clothes. She entered into the ladies' toilets, reappearing five minutes later in her new attire. Josh was already changed and stood beaming in the corridor. The twins had lent him some of their play clothes, which he had eagerly embraced. He was never allowed to wear anything that was not considered smart, so he was enjoying this opportunity to dress scruffily.

"We are going out the back way, aren't we?" Marcie enquired. "I wouldn't want anyone to see me like …. Like THIS." Her sneer made me giggle. When I had recovered my composure and we were on the way out to the car, I reassured her.

"Don't worry, Marcie. I promise you that no-one will see you where we're going!" I waited until she was strapped in before adding, "Except for Mike that is."

Mike was waiting for us by the river with a beaming smile and three canoes.

"I thought you'd changed your minds," he teased, tapping his watch.

"No way! Right! Marcie! Mike has planned a fun day for us all on the river (hence the scruffy clothes)." Marcie looked bemused and immediately started protesting.

"I don't think so! I'm far too old to mess about on the water. I can't believe that you thought that I would enjoy that, Laurie. Surely you know me better than that?"

"Ah, but Marcie... Remember the fun that you used to have as a child? Wouldn't you like to recreate that for Josh and show him all the things you learnt?" Marcie looked at Josh's face, which glowed with excitement and anticipation. She thought for a moment and then tried to sidestep her role.

"Why don't I just watch and you two can take Josh out on the water?" Mike and I had anticipated this reaction and had agreed in advance that we would not give Marcie a way out, so he launched our pre-planned counterattack.

"I'm sorry Marcie, but that won't work. The ratio for today needs to be one adult to one child. If you don't do it, then Josh will just have to miss out... I've already promised Laurie that I'll look after Henry." Josh's face fell. He looked desperate.

"Pleeeease Mum. Can't we do it? Just this once?" Marcie looked at his face and relented but clung onto her

irritation. She looked furious.
"Well, I shall have a go, but I'm not happy, Laurie! I'm not happy at all!"

Marcie edged grumpily down to the water's edge. Mike winked at me triumphantly and Marcie's date with the past began.

Mike started us off gently with some basic canoeing skills, teaching us how to use the paddles correctly and change direction. Then, he led us on a short expedition up the river. Alfie and I giggled as we struggled in vain to go in a straight line, veering off instead at obscure angles. Mike and Henry forged ahead confidently, stopping at times to allow us all to catch up. Marcie took a while to get started. It was difficult for her to hold the paddle without ruining her perfectly manicured nails. I watched as she frustratedly attempted several different grips on the paddle, all of which were completely ineffective.
"Come on Marcie, you slowcoach!" I yelled, trying to bait her into action. It seemed to do the trick. She threw aside her self-consciousness, grasped the paddle firmly and gritted her teeth.
"Come on Josh! Let's show them!" Josh sat up excitedly as Marcie leant forward determinedly and rowed them competently down the river, (overtaking our canoe in just a few strokes). "Now who's the slowcoach?" she yelled.

Exhilarated after an hour on the river, we returned to the original river bank.
"Excellent!" declared Mike. "Once we've had some lunch, you'll all be ready for round two!"
"Round two?"

"Yep! ... Raft building."
"Woo hoo!" yelled the boys. Marcie smiled approvingly.

With a flurry of packaging and a murmur of munches, we all gobbled down our lunch. In the centre of the picnic rug, I dumped some sorry looking sausage rolls along with a pre-packed tub of hummus and some rather rustic carrot sticks. In her usual fashion, Marcie had spent hours preparing exquisite morsels to delight both our taste buds and our eyes. She carefully arranged them on patterned plates and then delicately positioned them on the rug. I rolled my eyes in disapproval.

Marcie, it seems was caught between two worlds – the world of perfection and the world of fun – but even so, she was keen to get started on the raft building.
"Finished?" she encouraged us eagerly as she removed our plates before we were ready.
"Apparently so!" I murmured, dryly.
"Come on then!" she enthused as she led the way to where Mike was standing.

"I've got a variety of things here for you to use to make a raft," he said. "You'll need to use the barrels underneath for flotation, but what you use for the platform is up to you. When you've built your rafts, you can have a race down the river. It's going to be Laurie and the twins against you and Josh. I'm going to be neutral. I'll help you all while you're building and I'll referee from my canoe. Is everyone clear?" We all nodded. "In that case, off you go!"

We set about our rafts eagerly - bracing together logs and barrels and balancing planks and old fence panels for platforms. The boys learnt about knots and teamwork, and Marcie and I learnt to be children again. With giggling and guffawing, we chomped our way through the task, oblivious to the hours passing. Marcie was so focused on building the very best raft that she never noticed her broken nails, grimy clothes and fallen hair. Glimpses of the real Marcie had appeared at last.

Josh and she worked carefully and systematically together, whilst the twins and I took a more chaotic approach. Eventually, despite all our deficiencies, our water-worthy vessels were ready, so we proudly dragged them down the bank and placed them expectantly on the water. I waded into the river, as did Marcie, to hold them still whilst the boys clambered on. Mike handed us each an oar and set out the course.
"The first raft to make it to the weeping willow is the winner."
"But what if the rafts break up?" I asked, concerned.
"They won't; you've all made them really well, but even if they did, it wouldn't matter… This part of the river is very shallow. On the count of three then… One… Two… THREE!"

The twins and I pushed off from the bank and started to row. Unfortunately, with three of us rowing in different directions, we started to spin. Marcie and Josh slowly sailed by, waving mockingly.
"Losers!" they chanted as they took the lead.
"Right! That's it! Come on boys, let's get them!"
"Yeah!" Henry and Alfie shouted. With renewed determination, we all stuck our oars into the water and pulled with all our might. My oar unexpectedly caught in the river weeds causing me to unbalance. The raft tipped precariously as I tried to right myself, depositing me unceremoniously into the water.
"Mum!" yelled Alfie.

"Don't worry about me!" I spluttered. "Keep rowing!"

The boys obediently did as they were told and started to make much better progress without me. They started to overtake Marcie and Josh and the race in earnest began. First one raft then the other inched ahead, the weeping willow looming fast. Marcie and Josh started to break away, so I resorted to dirty tactics.
"Splash them!" I yelled to Henry and Alfie. Henry continued to row whilst Alfie immediately set about bombarding Marcie and Josh with handfuls of water. Josh instantly forgot the race and entered the fight, moving to the side of his raft in order to get a better shot.
"No!" yelled Marcie as the sudden shift in weight caused the raft to tilt dramatically, plummeting Josh off the side. In a flailing attempt at retaliation, Josh grabbed at the twins' raft as he went in. Their raft upended and they tipped into the water too. The boys descended into fits of giggles as they furiously flung water at each other. Marcie, who had managed to remain on board, smiled as she watched the fun. Then, to my amazement, she jumped in too and joined in!

The rafts did not survive the chaos. They started to break apart, but such was the intensity of the water fight that none of the participants noticed the barrels starting to float away. They escaped as far as the fallen tree trunk downriver where they congregated in the stiller waters awaiting the rescue party to begin.

As we dragged the final barrels and planks to the shore, we all collapsed into dishevelled, exhausted piles of happiness. I looked over at Marcie, just in time to see Josh give her a huge, soggy hug.

"Thank you so much for today, Mum! It's been... It's been..."

"I know, Josh. It's been wonderful. I'm only sorry that we haven't done it before."

Marcie, with a beaming smile and a tear of happiness, turned to Mike and I.

"Thank you!" she mouthed. "Thank you for making me remember." Then she got up and headed towards the car, leaving the empty shell of her false façade behind. The real Marcie had emerged at last.

"Where shall we go now?" I asked. Everyone considered the question. Suddenly Marcie's face lit up.

"I know!" she exclaimed, excitedly. "Let's go to *Jethro's*!"

Chapter 29

The House of Cards

"I'm coming home!" garbled Ben.
"What do you mean *home*?" I asked protectively. Ben was no longer part of our home and I did not want him back.
"Back to the UK. Back to England."
"But I thought you and Kelly liked America. I thought you were both happy there." Ben coughed and the sound on Skype broke up for a minute. "Ben! I can't hear you. You're breaking up."
"No! We've broken up!" he replied, tears streaking down his face. "Everything was a lie... The illness... The marriage... Everything!" I reeled backwards with the force of the barrage of his revelation and carefully dodged the shards of his shattered situation. I did not want them piercing my life.

"What do you mean the illness was a lie? Surely you can't fake a terminal illness? I mean... Kelly wouldn't be that heartless...? Would she?" My thoughts tumbled out as my brain struggled to comprehend the situation. Ben grimaced. "She had me convinced for sure!"
"Well, did she seem ill?" I asked insensitively.
"No, not really. It was supposedly a degenerative illness -

one of those latent illnesses which, conveniently, has no symptoms in the early stages other than fatigue. At least that's what she told me."

"But what did the doctors say? Surely they wouldn't have been fooled?"

"She never let me go with her to the hospital," he admitted remorsefully. "She said that it would upset her too much to have me there. It was all a pack of lies and I believed every word she said."

"Oh!" I exclaimed dumbfounded. "So what did she go to hospital for?"

"Don't you understand? She never went! There never were any hospital visits. It was all lies! All made up!"

Shell-shocked, I sat silently for a moment, confused and astounded. I had only answered this Skype call because I was nearest to the computer. I was expecting to say hello, exchange a few pleasantries and then get the boys. I was not supposed to receive an outpouring, especially not from Ben. After all, we no longer really spoke any more. Of course we were civil and friendly, but there was no sharing of information, no exchange of life-stories, just a distance that I had come to rely on. A void - separated by both the ocean and an emotional emptiness towards each other. I struggled to reposition myself. To steady my feelings so that I could cope with this lifequake. To display compassion whilst satiating my curiosity. To dispatch triumphant thoughts and replace them with empathy. To dispel anger towards Kelly and redirect it towards the snake.

"I don't understand," I continued after a few moments. Why would she do this?" Ben looked up at the screen.

"For money," he stated coldly, but I still looked blank. He spelt it out for me. "So that I'd marry her."

"But that's crazy!"
"Yup!"
"Couldn't she have encouraged you to marry her some other way?"
"I guess. But the fact is that she knew that I didn't want to marry her. Not deep down. Not after... after... what happened with us." Ben hung his head in shame. I saw his remorse but ignored it. We were beyond that stage. I ploughed on with my questioning.

"Kelly must've realised that you'd find out one day. Like... when she didn't die?"
"Oh, she'd planned it very well... Thought of everything. She said that there was a slim chance that she would pull through, but that she needed to go away to a specialist clinic. Like a mug, I gave her the money each time. Each time she went away, she came back exhausted, telling me harrowing tales of the treatments she'd been through. She was very convincing."
"So where did she go?" I was fascinated and, forgetting all sensitivity towards Ben's feelings, delved further.
"She went to a friends in *The Hamptons*."
"To do what?"
"Find herself someone richer. She spent her time partying. All-night parties from what I can gather. That's why she was so exhausted." I giggled at this point. Ben looked hurt and then chuckled grudgingly too. "I know... It sounds ridiculous."
"But didn't you suspect *anything*?"
"Not a thing!" he said shaking his head. "I trusted her fully."
"I know that feeling!" I blurted out. Ben looked shocked. "Sorry!" I apologised. He nodded.
"That's okay, I deserve it."

A Rampage of Grace

"So, how did you find out?"
"It was simple really. I was supposed to be away on a business trip, but it got cancelled at the last minute. I thought I'd surprise her, so I came home unannounced. She was in the other room and did not hear me come in. She was on the phone to her friend, Sheryl, confirming the arrangements for their next weekend away and extolling the virtues of their last trip. Apparently someone called Gregory was really looking forward to her next visit." This time compassion did kick in. I knew only too well the blow of betrayal and the sinking feeling that comes with watching your life-dreams ebb away. I looked at Ben's face. He looked lost. He had built his life on mythical foundations and his house of cards had tumbled down.

Suddenly a thought came to me.
"Ben?"
"Yes?"
"Did you ever find out why Kelly left her last employer? The one before she came to us." Ben closed his eyes and nodded.
"I made some enquiries the other day. Turns out that she was having an affair with her employer. His wife found out and threw her out instantly."
"Hence the black eye?"
"Yes," Ben confirmed, nodding. I pondered for a moment and then aired my thoughts
"Tell me... Was he wealthy too?"
"Very!" Ben hung his head in despair.

"So what now?"
"I'm coming back to the UK to start again."
"And Kelly?"
"She's hit me with a massive bill for alimony and moved in with Gregory." Ben sighed, the sigh of a man who has

learned his lesson through the school of hard knocks. The sigh of a man who has resigned himself to fate. The sigh of a man looking at a pile of fallen cards. The sigh of a man who has lost sight of his hope and his future.

Chapter 30

Rivalry

Mike and I watched with glee over the next few months as Marcie unfolded before our eyes. At first, we thought her river fun experience was a one-off; that she was too entrenched in her controlling, critical ways to release herself into the fun and chaos of the future. We were wrong! Slowly but surely she unfurled to reveal her soft, inner petals, her beautiful, warm smile and her wonderful sense of adventure.

"...Come on you two. It'll be fun!" Marcie pleaded.
"Really? How can any form of art be fun? We'll all be bored, especially the children!" I moaned. "Can't we just wait until they're older to do art galleries?" Marcie looked surprised and started to protest.
"But this isn't a gallery! It's..." I interrupted her before she had a chance to defend her proposition.
"Let's go to the cinema instead! There's bound to be something good on that we'll all like." It was a feeble attempt at sidestepping Marcie's suggestion, but the thought of traipsing over to Croydon to attend something

called *Human Art* just did not appeal. Mike saw the disappointment on Marcie's face and intervened.
"Come on, Laurie. Let's do it for Marcie. You never know, you might just like it. I'm sure there's an art lover in there somewhere." He smiled at me, winked and then nudged me gently under the ribs. I screwed up my nose and groaned playfully. He could be so persuasive!
"Alright then!" I conceded. "But I'm going in jeans. I'm not dressing up! I refuse to pretend to be something I'm not!" I declared petulantly. Marcie giggled.
"That's fine. Neither am I."
"You're not?"
"No!" With a cheeky grin, Marcie headed to the door. "I'll pick you all up in an hour then."

I watched as Marcie left, gently opening the door and shooting us a final smile before she disappeared out of view. Not the false, practised smile of years gone by (the one that appeared no matter how grumpy she was feeling), but a kind, warm, natural smile that lit up the room. There was an ease about her now. A softening of her mannerisms. A softening of her clothing. A softening of her heart.

"I spy with my little eye…" The game went on for ages! I marvelled at Mike's patience. Boredom had set in with me after only the second round and we were now half an hour into it.
"Are we nearly there yet?" enquired Josh. My thoughts exactly!
"Just five minutes to go," Marcie replied, wryly.

Five minutes later, she pulled up outside a giant warehouse. It was nothing like the snobby kind of fine art building that

Rivalry

I had expected. Actually, when I thought about it, I realised that I did not know what to expect. My prejudice against art and all things fine had meant that I had never even ventured near a gallery, let alone stepped foot inside one, so my perceptions were both fictional and flawed. In fact, I had rejected Marcie's suggestion outright, without even giving her a chance to explain what we were going to see. I cast my eyes suspiciously over the building and was annoyed to see the giant paint splodges that adorned the sides of the warehouse and the childlike banner across the doorway.

"That's just the sort of modern art that I can't bear!" I snarled, my worst prejudices confirmed. "No doubt, it's supposed to symbolise the inner child and all that rubbish!" Marcie sniggered but stayed graciously silent.

"Come on everyone. This is my treat!" she declared.

Marcie led the way to the door and, after waiting for us all to catch up with her, swished the door open flamboyantly... to reveal the paint-splattered revolution that was *Human Art*.

"Ta da!" she trilled.

"Oh my!" I gasped.

"Told you we'd have fun!" she winked.

The punky, red-haired lady in the kiosk looked bored as she chewed her gum and rummaged under her desk. She handed us each a pair of goggles and a white, plastic boiler suit complete with hood. Then, after directing us to the changing rooms, she issued us with our instructions:

"Once you're in your gear, you can either head into the general area or into any of the themed rooms." This was clearly a well-rehearsed speech that she had delivered many times, for she gave it without any glimmer of joy and in a disinterested, monotone voice. "It's up to you whether you want to make some art to take home with you, or just mess about. Either way, you've got one hour, so have fun and remember the rule... Boiler suits and goggles must be worn at all times when you're in the paint area. Other than that... anything goes!"

When Willy Wonka designed his chocolate factory, I can only believe that he used this place as inspiration. With its rivers of paint and imaginative rooms, all that it lacked was the Oompa Loompas. However, in this paint-filled emporium of fun, orange-coloured men would not have looked out of place!

"Stop! Stop!" I pleaded, clutching my sides. The stitch from laughing was excruciating.
"Too late!" Marcie declared, firing her paint-filled water pistol at me again. I raised my white umbrella and the green jetstream ricocheted off, leaving an artistic trail.
"Got you, Mum!" yelled Henry as he drenched me with a yellow supersoaker and somersaulted behind a padded pillar. My umbrella was little defence against his superior weapon, so I headed for the paint cannon in the corner.
"This is war!" I shouted. Mike anticipated my plan and cut me off, reaching the cannon seconds before me. I retreated behind a pillar just in time – a torrent of red paint whooshed past my head.

I knew that it would take about 30 seconds for the cannon to recharge, so I grabbed the blue supersoaker beside me and motioned to Josh and Alfie to follow me. I ran like a crazed woman at Mike and Marcie, drenching them both in blue paint. Josh and Alfie followed closely, covering my back against Henry whilst simultaneously launching paint-

Rivalry

filled water bombs at Henry, Marcie and Mike. A siren sounded to indicate that our ten minutes in that room was over. We ditched our weapons and headed for the door.

Mike's normally-brilliant, white smile appeared slightly yellow because of his blue, paint-covered face. As he went past he pulled me close, and swiped some red paint off my face, brandishing it victoriously.
"Thought you could get the better of me did ya? Gotcha!"
"Judging by your blue face, I think you'll find that I got you!"
"Really? Is that so?" he drawled, pulling me closer.
"Hmmm. Let's see." He kissed me gently. Our painted faces slid softly against each other, turning our lips purple.
"Hu-hum," Marcie coughed. I blushed with embarrassment, but thankfully no-one could see it under my red and purple paint.

When we left the room, I pressed the button on the outside and watched as jets of water appeared from the ceiling washing our rampage of paint away. Swirls of brilliant colour cascaded down the plastic walls, before mixing together to form a murky, brown whirlpool in the centre of the room. All traces of our explosion of colour and wild warfare were soon sucked down a small drain in the centre. I watched as the last trickle of brown ebbed away. The white room was now ready for the next team of people who were eagerly queuing outside.

The remaining hour was a wonderful, fun-filled time. Everything was padded, slippery and safe. Each of us left an impression on the place – a painted bodily impression on the walls and floors. We competed to see who could do the highest splat on the wall. Surprisingly it was Marcie that won. She proved that she was an accomplished trampolinist as she bounced her way to the heights and launched herself against the padded walls. Whereas Mike excelled on the paint slide, picking up tremendous speed and showing great control to produce perfect leg splats on the padded bumper at the end. However, the boys preferred to expend their energy on the belly slides – long plastic runs doused in paint. By the time they had finished several bouts of sliding along on their stomachs at full speed, their boiler suits were a sludgy, brown mess.

The siren sounded one last time to indicate that our session was up, so we obediently entered the *Cool Down Room*. Here we had the opportunity to create a human art canvas to take home as a memento. A time to create our own. The walls were bedecked with an assortment of paper for us to use. We finally settled on a large sheet of beige paper and created a ring of handprints on it; a reminder of this wonderful day of fun and unity.

"Coming kids?" I asked cheerily.
"Yes!" they chorused happily.
"Final room then!" They looked at me excitedly. "The shower room!" I explained. Their faces fell.

By the time the evening came, the twins, exhausted from the fun of the day, were curled up comfortably on the sofa watching their favourite action movie. As usual, I was busy in the kitchen. The doorbell went.

Quickly, I tried to wipe the pastry mix off my hands before leaping towards the front door. Mike got there first. I came around the corner just in time to see the hackles rise on

Ben's neck as he spied Mike for the very first time.

Chapter 31

Seconds?

Over the next few weeks, Ben appeared a lot. The frequency of his visits began to annoy me because I did not like his intrusion into my privacy. I preferred instead to lead completely separate lives, although I recognised that was not a realistic expectation given that we shared the twins. Alfie and Henry loved having their Dad nearby again, relishing every moment they spent with him. Ben led them on expeditions across muddy terrains (often delivering back two, unidentifiable, slimy, brown packages) and regularly played football with them. He sat and read with them under the big oak tree in the park and chatted endlessly with them on the benches. I suppose that they discussed boys' stuff, but whatever the content the twins were riveted. I watched as they blossomed (all three of them) and then felt guilty for begrudging Ben the time with them. He was revealing to his sons the footsteps that lead to manhood and they were eager to follow him on that path.

One day I stood watching wistfully out of the kitchen window as Ben played with the twins in the park opposite.

Mike approached me from behind and gently held me.

"What're you thinking?" he asked softly as he nuzzled his chin into my neck.

"Nothing much. I'm just looking really. They all look so happy together."

"Yeah. They do," he sighed.

"It's odd really."

"What is?"

"Seeing Ben out there with the boys. It's as if we were never apart… and yet we are." Mike instinctively released his grip on me.

"Do you wish you were still with him?" he asked tentatively. I thought for a moment, searching my heart for the truth.

"No… Definitely not! Of course, I'm sad that our marriage broke up and God knows that I wish it hadn't, but to consider restoring it now is unrealistic. To ignore all the pain that has passed between us and pretend that it hasn't happened? I don't think I could do that. Actually, I know that I couldn't. And even more important… I wouldn't want to. For me, I'm just sad that the children will never experience a family unit as it's intended to be. They'll always be part of something broken. I feel like I've given them second best; like they've missed out on something pure." Mike seemed relieved and nuzzled into me again, kissing me gently.

"So, no regrets about us then?" he asked. I spun around to face him and smiled.

"None at all! You know that I love you, Mike. My thoughts were for the children not me. You needn't worry. Ben's come back into their lives, not mine."

Mike beamed with his boyish, familiar grin and a lock of hair fell cheekily over his forehead. He blew it back, winked and lightened the mood.

Seconds?

"In that case missus, are you up for an adventure this afternoon? If Ben's got the boys then we can go off together. I know this wicked little picnic spot down by the river and, if we're really lucky, we'll be able to search out the otter that lives down there."
"Sounds great to me!" I replied happily.

We spent that afternoon cycling and walking; frolicking and searching; laughing and smiling; eating and drinking. A heady cocktail of excitement and exercise mixed with a dash of romance and a sprinkling of good food. I smiled as we cycled slowly back, enjoying every moment of our time together. Autumn was in full force and I marvelled at the golden hues of the leaves as we cycled through the tree-lined avenues. As we pulled up outside my house, I noticed that the cherry tree had already started to shed some leaves. Winter was close by and I had not even felt its approach.

"I'm going away!" Mike announced excitedly out of the blue. "For a month."
"What!" I exclaimed, shocked by the revelation. "But where? How? Why?" I almost wailed that last word. Why now? Why him? Why so long? So many *whys* rushed through my head. Mike seemed oblivious to my panic and simply smiled.
"Don't worry!" he reassured. "It's the four week expedition to South America. Remember? I told you about it months ago. I just wasn't sure if it would come off because I didn't make the original team. That's why I never mentioned it again. Well it has come off! Someone has dropped out; he had to – he got attacked by a tribe of angry natives on the last expedition. Apparently he's still in hospital. Luckily for me!" He grinned proudly as if that

explanation would reassure me. As if the time apart would be tolerable because it had the word *expedition* attached to the time span.

"Oh! That's great!" I uttered half-heartedly, thinly veiling my disappointment. "When do you go?"
"Friday."
"What?"
"It doesn't give us much time, I know, but I'll soon be back again. You wait and see."

At first things seemed normal without Mike around. I spent much of my time distracted by the final arrangements of Davina and Freddie's imminent wedding. Finishing touches were still required for Henry and Alfie's pageboy outfits and the final decisions regarding the buffet were still in progress. Davina kept turning up at the house all of a fluster. Organisation was not her strong point, at least not when it came to weddings!
"Darling, I just don't know what to do! Freddie's family are so conservative and yet I so want to honour them and make them feel welcome, but they do make it so very hard for me."
"Why? What's happened?"
"Well, it's David... I conceded to going with the traditional suits and cravats rather than the chinos and open-necked, satin shirts that I'd originally planned. However, even now David is refusing to wear the waistcoat and cravat that I've chosen! I tell you... I despair of that man!"
"But, I don't understand. Why won't he wear them?"
"He says they're too gaudy. Honestly! Just because he's a boring, old buffoon who only wears grey or black, he thinks he can dictate the dress code at our wedding." I listened

Seconds?

attentively to my mother's protestations and considered her claims. David was most definitely not one of my favourite people, nor was he renowned for his fashion prowess, but if my suspicions were right then it was possible that he had a point.

"So, what colour scheme have you chosen?" I asked cagily. Davina's face lit up at the opportunity to reveal her artistic expression.

"Everything is going to be so sunny, Laurie! People will go away smiling and filled with warmth and rays of delight." My eyes widened with enlightenment at her enigmatic explanation. I recognised her terminology and my stomach sank.

"You've chosen rainbows haven't you?" I asked dryly.

"Of course I have!" she beamed.

"But what about Freddie? Didn't he have a say in it? What colours did he want?"

"Freddie doesn't care… He's colour blind. Anyway, as far as he's concerned he'll just go with the flow, so long as it's in a church. That was his only stipulation. And as he quite rightly pointed out to me when I first suggested the colour scheme… God loves rainbows… He invented them!" She nodded triumphantly and beamed again. I grimaced.

"So if rainbow colours are your theme, what exactly have you asked David to wear?"

"Nothing too extreme, just a blue suit with orange waistcoat and purple cravat. Only three colours. Not seven."

For the next 30 minutes I sat with my mum and reasoned with her, finally reaching a compromise that we both felt would be acceptable to all concerned. Davina refused to relinquish her three colour dress code for the supporting groomsmen, even threatening to raise it to five at one point (just to spite David). However, after much toing and froing, she left victorious with her colour scheme intact but

David's reputation in mind.

Over the weeks that Mike was away, Ben was brilliant with both Davina and myself. When the wedding proved overwhelming, he calmed Davina down and offered sound, sensible advice. When frustration barricaded my thoughts, he stepped in and gently restored peace. When heaviness hit me, he lightened the atmosphere and rallied the twins. When my workload proved too much, he stopped to help me prepare their tea.

"Why don't you join us?" I asked one evening. He looked surprised.
"Seriously?"
"Sure. Why not? The kids'll love it. It's only pizza. It's our film evening. Normally you have to wear pyjamas to take part, but we'll let you off. Just this once."
"Okay. Sounds fab! Thanks. What're we watching?"
"I haven't decided yet. Any preference?" I asked. Ben grinned.
"*Chitty Chitty Bang Bang*?" he suggested. I giggled and nodded.

That night we all sat together on the sofa - Ben at one end, me at the other with the two boys sandwiched in between. Unashamedly, we bumjogged our way through the theme song, hid behind cushions from the Childcatcher, sang at every opportunity and munched our way through several packets of popcorn. This rare moment of unity delighted the boys and brought a new dimension to the atmosphere.

"Do you mind if I put the boys to bed?" Ben asked when the film had finished. "It's been so long since I last did

Seconds?

that." I hesitated at this request because it felt like he was pushing a boundary, but I could find no logical reason to refuse, so I capitulated.

"Of course. That's fine. I'll come up and kiss them good night when you're finished."

"Thanks. I really appreciate it," he beamed and led the twins upstairs.

After a few minutes, I crept up the stairs and peeked into the twins' bedroom. Ben was bent over Henry, tucking him in. Alfie was already curled up tight. Henry reached up his arms and pulled Ben down towards him. He held his Dad tightly.

"I love you, Dad."

"I love you too, son," he whispered.

They lingered there for a moment, enjoying the embrace. Ben pulled back gently and wiped away a tear. I retreated to the top of the stairs before he spotted me and pretended to have just arrived. Ben came out of their room and smiled.

"They're ready for you," he said softly. I wandered into their room. Alfie grinned.

"Night, Mum!" he whispered.

"Na night, Alfie" I replied, kissing him tenderly on his cheek. "Sleep well." He closed his eyes tight and smiled. I crept towards Henry who was staring up at the ceiling. I knew that look; it was the one that he used when he was thinking deep, sad thoughts.

"Are you okay?" I asked.

"I guess so!" he replied noncommittally. I waited, knowing that if I stayed quiet long enough, then he would reveal his deep thoughts to me. He did. "Mum, can I ask you something?"

"Of course."

"Are you and Dad going to get back together?" I saw the optimism in Henry's eyes and felt the sting in my heart as I delivered his disappointment.
"No, Henry, we're not!"
"But why not?" he asked in a tormented tone.
"Because we've hurt each other too deeply and because we both have new lives now. You can never go back, Henry; only forward. We're not going to get back together. It's impossible."
"But Freddie says that nothing's impossible with God."
"Does he now? Well I'm only human Henry."

I wandered thoughtfully down the stairs and into the kitchen. I flicked the kettle on and automatically set out a single coffee mug.
"That smells good!" said Ben.
"Oh! Sorry! I didn't think to make you one."
"That's okay. I'll make mine myself."

The atmosphere between us felt strained. The room fell into an awkward silence. Ben was the first to speak.
"Laurie?" he said. I looked up and nodded. "I've been thinking..."
"Really? That's a first!" I teased, trying to lighten the mood. He smiled briefly at my humour and then continued. "I realise that what I did was terrible... Truly terrible... To you and the boys... but I was wondering..."
"Please don't!"
"Don't what?"
"Don't continue. I know what you're going to say." I looked into his bluebell eyes and recognised the flame of hope. I opened my mouth and extinguished it in one breath. "I don't want to try again." The blue turned to grey as the light snuffed out. He hung his head low.
"But it would be different this time, I know it would."

Seconds?

"Why would it? What's changed?"
"I have!" he declared firmly. "I never realised what I had until it was gone and by then it was too late. I would never betray you again, Laurie. I would always cherish you and the boys, if only you'd give me a second chance."

I heard his words but they were exactly that – words. Empty words. Their hollowness echoed around my heart, failing to generate any resonance; I felt nothing. My heart was now closed to Ben. I had made my choice and my choice was Mike.
"You're just lonely, Ben. Just lonely. You want me because you're lonely and missing the boys, but that isn't a good reason to get back together. We're divorced now and I've moved on. You need to do the same. I remember reading once on the ceiling of a church that God has plans to give you hope and a future. Maybe you need to learn to fly alone for a while, to pilot your own plane so that you can find that future."

Ben stood motionless, rejected and embarrassed. His breathing slowed and he escaped into deep thought. The tension was unbearable. I fiddled with my coffee cup and the clink of the china roused him.
"I think I'd better go!" he said.
"I think that would be wise." I watched as he placed his undrunk coffee upon the counter and headed out of the kitchen. I stood still while he made his own way out and waited until I heard the front door bang shut, then I breathed a sigh of relief.

Bronzen and very grubby Mike returned three days later.
"Hello gorgeous!" he said, grabbing me by the waist. "You

are such a sight for sore eyes! I have really missed you!" He held me tight and I felt warmth and security flow back through my veins. "I love you, Laurie."

"I love you too, Mike." He held me firmly in his arms for several minutes more before pulling back and gazing into my face.

"So, what's happened while I've been away?"

"Nothing much!" I lied.

Chapter 32

Repetition

With my eyes tight shut, I stood up and faced the altar of St Mungo's church. The gasps of the congregation rippled towards me as each row turned to face the bride. Normally they are gasps of astonishment as people take in the radiance and beauty of the woman proceeding up the aisle, but in this case I was not convinced. The gasps were deep, long and seemed to me to have a shocked edge to them. I feared the worst.

Davina advanced slowly but surely up the aisle until she was level with me. Tentatively, I opened my eyes, held my breath and turned to face her. I was relieved to find her in a diaphanous, ivory, chiffon dress with an indigo, silk, three quarter-sleeved jacket. I am not quite sure what I had expected; maybe some outlandish creation or a dress that was a homage to all things rainbow, but I was wrong. Fundamentally, she had chosen well and looked stunning - every inch the beautiful, capable woman that I knew her to be.

Of course, she had accessorised in line with her rainbow colour scheme, but these were touches that merely personalised an otherwise beautiful ensemble. In her hands she held a bouquet of red, orange, yellow, blue, indigo and violet flowers interspersed with green foliage, but with a softening of white gipsofila. Never had so many colours coexisted in one bouquet, and yet the differing heights and colours had masterfully blended to produce a glorious display of international unity and clever colour combinations. Delicate, French cornflowers rested easily against fragrant, Indonesian lilies. Traditional, British roses offset modern, African orchids. Bright red anemones contrasted perfectly with orange and yellow amaryllis to form a harmony of colour. The entire bouquet was a living canvas perfectly blended by the paintbrush of heaven.

Davina's trademark features were still present even on this most memorable day: A (new) pair of rainbow wedges adorned her feet, complimenting her bouquet beautifully. Her lips were painted with her usual, bright, red lipstick, although it seemed more vibrant today, a vibrancy which merely served to highlight the joyous smile that illuminated her face. She had waited a lifetime for this occasion and she was clearly enjoying every moment.

Freddie and David stood nervously at the front awaiting Davina's arrival. David stood stiffly with military-style precision - a stance that would have been the same whether he had been awaiting an executioner or his brother's bride. Freddie, on the other hand, was smiling and fidgety, clearly full of nervous excitement. He peeked over his shoulder and set eyes on Davina for the first time. I shall never forget the warmth and radiance that filled his face, instantly portraying the deep love that he held for her and the joy that she brought him.

Henry and Alfie followed on behind in their velvet, indigo page boy outfits. They grumped along avoiding all eye contact with the congregation, and ignoring the cacophony of *oohs* and *aahs* as they passed the pews. Clearly humiliated by their unusual attire, they were even more unimpressed by their rainbow boots and ring cushion.

At one point Henry stopped to adjust his dungarees, which had snagged on his orange shirt. As he bent over, his tasselled, velvet hat fell to the floor. Josh sniggered from one of the pews. Henry shot a daggers look back and then folded his arms in protest throughout the rest of the service. Alfie continued on angelically out of sheer loyalty to his beloved grandmother.

The service was conducted by the bishop, a longstanding friend of Freddie's. I recognised him instantly from the summer fete as the portly man in the straw hat, although I hoped that his back-slapping skills would not be required today! The church was packed, not just with friends and family, but with Mungonians, as I liked to call them (people who attended Freddie's church). Even Ben had turned out to wish Davina and Freddie well, although primarily he came to see his sons' performance as page boys. Judging by the mixed expressions on his face he was feeling a combination of fatherly pride to see his sons honoured and of compassion for their embarrassing attire.

The service was flawless and very moving. I watched tearfully as my mum and Freddie exchanged vows and rings. Promises of forever. Life-long commitments. David's face resounded disapproval (although that may have still been a remnant of frustration at his outfit) but neither Davina nor Freddie seemed to notice because they were caught up in the sincerity and joy of their moment.

We all sat down for the sermon. Bishop Parkinson (or *Parky* as Freddie called him) stood at the front and smiled.
"Ladies and gentlemen. Firstly, I want to thank you all for coming to support Freddie and Davina on this, their special day. As a close friend of Freddie's over the years, I find it a particular privilege and honour to marry him today because, after watching his relationship with Davina unfurl, I have no doubt that this is a match made in heaven." Davina and Freddie giggled and blushed at this endorsement. I felt Ben's eyes boring into the back of my head, but I determined not to look at him, turning instead to smile at Mike beside me. He smiled back. I hugged his arm tight and rested my head on his shoulder. I loved that peaceful feeling. The Bishop continued. "It requires effort, love, forbearance and humility to keep a marriage healthy and alive. There's no room for egos, nor selfish desires, for on this day two become one."

An elderly lady, Mrs Dawson in the third row, rummaged noisily in her bag for a mint and then proceeded to fill the knave with crinkling wrapper sounds. Mike squeezed my hand, Alfie yawned and Henry snuggled in close. The elderly lady choked on her mint. Liz ran to her aid and patted her on the back. The mint jettisoned into the aisle along with her false teeth. The Bishop pressed on ignoring the commotion.

"The bible says that there is *a hope and a future for everyone, a plan to prosper and not to harm.*" My heart quickened as I heard him refer to the very essence of my conversation with Ben. I snapped my head around and saw Ben sitting there wide-eyed and attentive. Clearly the significance had hit him too. "Many people erroneously believe that when they marry, their partner becomes their hope and their future. That is not only a mistake, but it is also a huge responsibility to place on anyone's shoulders! Too huge! When that is the case, if one falters so does the other. Where is the strength in that? No! Marriage is intended to be a relationship where the emphasis is on giving not receiving." Alfie nodded off to sleep and started to snore gently. I removed his tasselled hat and ran my hand slowly through his blonde curls.

"We are all capable of fulfilling our hope and future - our destiny here on this earth. No-one can steal that hope from you. No matter how bad you feel or how horrendously you've been treated, to believe that someone can ruin your destiny is to believe a lie! It is yours and yours alone. No-one can steal it BUT..." The bishop paused for dramatic effect. There was silence in the church as we waited with expectation. Mrs Dawson rummaged again. "You can be tricked into giving it away."

I heard a muffled sob from the back of the church and instinctively knew it was Ben. My heart went out to him as these words echoed through his soul, but equally I knew that it was no longer my place to comfort him. Anyway, Mike was looking at me so I could not turn around. He did not understand the significance of this sermon to Ben. How could he? I had never told him about my conversation with Ben. I felt guilty. The weight of the lie of omission rested heavily on my shoulders. Suddenly, the peace between us disappeared and I did not feel so comfortable after all.

The Bishop continued,
"First, we must each learn to fly solo. Only then do we become a trustworthy co-pilot." My jaw dropped open. It was as if the bishop had been eavesdropping on our conversation.

"I have watched as Davina has lavished herself, in all her fullness, on everyone here and in doing so brought strength and encouragement to Freddie and joy to all our lives. It has also been my pleasure to watch a previously lonely Freddie embrace and incorporate Davina into his life. In doing so, the buoyancy and life have returned to his ministry (and thankfully to his sermons)." The congregation all chuckled at that comment. Freddie simply blushed. "These two beautiful individuals have come together today with their unique flavours and have united to form a wondrous melting pot of potential. I can't wait to see what comes of this mighty union!" At this point, the Bishop stepped down from the lectern and walked up to Davina and Freddie.

"Congratulations Mr and Mrs Pinkerton on your covenant promise here today! May you love each other unconditionally, support each other wholeheartedly and enable each other to reach the fullness of your potentials here on this earth."

The Bishop finished his address with a huge grin which contagiously spread to the whole of the church, finally erupting in a spontaneous round of applause. Joy resonated through the congregation, closely followed by a hymn.

We all stood as the organist stumbled her way through an unrecognisable and painful version of *Lord of the Dance*. The congregation tried their best to hold fast to the original tune and keep up with the organists' variable timing. I zoned out and began to consider what the fullness of my potential might look like. How could I find it? How would I know that I was on the right path? I looked at Henry and Alfie, who were bumshuffling impatiently beside me, and felt a glow in my heart. Without a doubt, they were part of my destiny, part of my role here on earth. I had a responsibility to nurture and bring them into the fullness of their promise, but I knew that I could not settle there. They were not my lot. Not my sole purpose. One day they would be gone from my home and I would remain. No, there was definitely more, much more. How could I unlock that potential?

I glanced around the ceiling of the church because last time that I had mused on a deep question the answer had been written on a ceiling. I looked up, but this time there were only chubby little cherubs and floating clouds. I groaned. Why, oh why had the designer of this church gone for pictures not words? Why could not all churches be the same? I was disappointed not to find the answer, yet inside I had a conviction – a conviction that told me the answer was nearby.

I scrutinised every wall and scanned every banner. Nothing! I flicked through the hymn book. Nothing! Feeling like a ship adrift on the ocean, I sat back in the pew, disappointed and disheartened. Something caught my attention… a small red book, wedged between two kneeling cushions. Reverently, I picked it up with its worn leather cover and ragged pages. I opened it up carefully, like a child with a treasure. This book had clearly been well loved by someone for there were scrawlings, notes and highlighted passages throughout… an outpouring of someone's personal thoughts and revelations. It felt intrusive to continue, like reading someone's personal diary… but I carried on anyway.

Flicking furiously, I huddled furtively over the book, seeking something but with no treasure map to find it. There was no *X* to mark the spot, so I searched until I came upon a page that was so highlighted and underlined that there was little or no white paper left showing. A page so filled with treasure that the owner could not bear to part with a single word. Hungrily, I started to read this page of the little bible. It was labelled *John 10*.

I devoured the meaty chunks of text, digesting every morsel, all the time searching for one specific chunk to savour – the one that would satisfy my question. I did not have to scavenge for long, for I found a verse that leapt off the page and satisfied my hunger. Over and over I read verse 27, chewing on its truth:

My sheep listen to my voice; I know them, and they follow me.

"I know that voice!" I uttered audibly. In my excitement I had forgotten the service and my surroundings. The hymn was over and all had fallen silent in the church for the final prayer. Disapproving heads turned towards me. I blushed with embarrassment.

"What?" asked Mike, looking bemused.

"Nothing!" I lied again.

But it was not nothing. It was the answer that I had been searching for. It was my way forward. Ironically, it was also what had already guided me this far. My heart settled peacefully as I considered my future and knew that to realise that potential, all I had to do was listen and follow.

When the final hymn started, I was all but spent emotionally – I had experienced tears of joy, pangs of guilt, voracious emptiness and total peace all in the space of an hour. I ushered the twins down the aisle, heading towards the light. Many people nodded and smiled fondly at me as I passed them. All except one – Ben. He sat with tear-streaked cheeks oblivious to everyone, lost in a sea of failure. For one moment, I considered rescuing him - throwing him a lifeline of comfort - but I wisely decided against it. Our paths were no longer connected and I wished to leave it that way.

Bishop Parkinson had spotted Ben too, so he quickly dispensed with the formalities of handshaking and headed towards him - scooping up Ben's emotions and replacing them with wise counsel.

I left them to it and continued towards the door. David,

dressed smartly in his dark blue suit, pale mauve waistcoat and purple cravat, brushed haughtily past me as he tried to catch up with Freddie. A protruding nail on the end of a pew caught his trouser leg, which ripped to reveal the flash of his bright orange socks beneath. So public! So out of character! The clothing compromise that he had hoped to hide was now on show for all to see. I smiled contentedly and headed out for the photographs.

Chapter 33

Rainbow Rooms

The marquee was beautiful, bedecked with flamboyant flowers from around the world. Each flower was a masterpiece in its own right, but when deliberately combined together and placed in substantial Greek urns, the effect was quite simply stunning (and surprisingly tasteful). Soft, cream voile draped from the top and sides of the marquee, providing a sumptuous feel to this makeshift room. The chairs around the tables were enrobed with ivory covers and finished with large ribbon bows. Seven different colours of ribbon had been used to create an endless sea of rainbows that brought a vibrance and freshness to the room.

I sat down at a large, round table, choosing a purple-bowed chair. Unfortunately that left Henry and Alfie arguing over the available red and orange chairs on the other side.
"I'm not sitting on an orange chair!" stamped a rather cross Henry.
"Nor am I!" wailed Alfie.
"Why ever not?" I enquired.
"I've had enough of orange!" complained Henry,

pointing to his pageboy shirt.
"So have I!" agreed Alfie grumpily.

Mr and Mrs Fortescue (the Vergers of St Mungo's), who were seated on the other side of Mike, took pity on the twins and offered to allow them to swap to their green and blue chairs.
"Thank you ever so much, Mrs Fortescue!" I said gratefully.
"Oh it's no problem dear. Call me Violet... after all you are the vicar's daughter now!" She winked. I winced. The thought of such a respectable and responsible position did not sit well with me. It felt stifling. I preferred something less formal – *the baker's daughter* – or freer – *the artist's daughter* – or radical – *the rock star's daughter*. As I thought about it a bit more, I decided to scrap that last position... too much fame, notoriety and strangeness. Earthy and normal were more my style.

My contemplation was rudely interrupted by more frenzied squabbling.
"... But I want green!" argued Alfie.
"But I got here first!" protested Henry.
"But it's my favourite colour!"
"So what!" Henry stuck out his tongue, crossed his arms and sat smugly on the green-ribboned chair. Alfie saw red and resorted to violence, trying as hard as he could to forcibly evict his brother. I looked over at the Fortescues. Violet was staring at me with raised eyebrows of disapproval and a tightly pursed mouth. Oh dear! We had been in our new found social position for less than an hour and had already let the side down!

The wedding buffet was delicious with something to

suit everyone. My mother had specifically arranged for all of the food to be placed in colour order so that it provided a dramatic visual impact that was empathetic to her theme. Unfortunately it did make for some odd display combinations. The salmon terrine found itself next to the strawberry panna cotta (which sadly left old Mrs Dawson, who had forgotten her glasses and was unable to read the labels, with an unusual taste sensation when she mixed them both together with her salad). The beetroot and red cabbage were placed next to the blackcurrant cheesecake, but thankfully that was an obvious mismatch which the guests managed to avoid. However, the one area of the buffet that proved to be the undoing of most people was the brown section, where sweet and savoury sauces were placed side by side. Mysteriously, many of the guests, despite diligently scrutinising the labels, still found themselves with hog roast and chocolate sauce or profiteroles and gravy!

Bemused, I stared at my own plate of chocolate covered roast potatoes and attempted a decontamination process whilst pondering on my own mistake. Out of the corner of my eye, I caught the red faces of Henry, Alfie and Josh surveying the room and sniggering at the misfortunes of the other guests. They were laughing so much that they struggled to eat their own unsullied dinners and I realised that something was afoot. It was then, with horror, that I remembered spotting the boys earlier loitering guiltily around the buffet table. I suspected that a bit of label swapping had taken place, courtesy of their mischievous hands. Just then Henry caught my eye as I scraped yet another of my potatoes clean and he immediately averted his eyes and grimaced. Guilty as charged!

The wedding meal was wonderfully relaxed with no table plans and no top table. Everyone (except David of course) mingled easily and chatted for hours. Jugs of Pimms circulated freely as did the pink lemonade. There was no dire disco, instead they had opted for a ceilidh to suit all ages. Even the boys joined in the dancing; laughing when they got it wrong and whooping with delight when they got it right. Marcie stayed true to her conversion and laughed her way through it all, even resorting to going barefoot for much of the night. Mike's best friend, Dominic, accompanied her through most of the dances, where they laughed, smiled and exchanged glints and glances.

"Have you seen?" Mike asked me, pointing towards Dominic and Marcie.

"Of course! How could I miss them? It's good to see Marcie so relaxed. I honestly never thought I'd see that day."

"I know. She's not quite the starchy pants you first brought down to the river!"

"No, she isn't. In fact, she's quite lovely nowadays."

"She's got you to thank for that," said Mike, smiling proudly. "You were the one who took the time to reconnect her with the real Marcie."

"Actually, it was us. I couldn't have done it without you!" Mike smiled. I am sure that I caught sight of a blush, but it was only there for a second before his bronzen hues covered it over.

"Come on you... Let's dance!" he ordered, dragging me by my arm onto the dance floor, which is where we stayed for the rest of the evening.

The celebrations continued into the night (well actually it was until ten o'clock, but according to old Mrs Dawson that was far too late). It was heart-warming to hear the peals of laughter and the drumming of dancing feet on the wooden floor. Davina adopted her usual position – centre of attention – whilst Freddie clapped and laughed his way from the sidings. She was like a whirlwind, racing from dance to dance and person to person, and he was like a refreshing breeze following calmly in her wake, smiling, adoring and blissfully happy.

The ceilidh caller yelled:
"Would everyone please join us for the final dance, *The Conga*, which will be led by the bride and groom!" Guests rushed eagerly back onto the dance floor and shoved their way into position. Henry and Alfie led the way for us. Mike and I dutifully followed. I looked at my mother's face. She was in a boisterous mood; I had seen that look before.
"This could be interesting!" I whispered to Mike, pointing at Davina. He glanced over briefly and grimaced as she performed a mock can-can from the front of the line.
"Oh! I see what you mean. Still, Dad's in no danger," he said, pointing at David who was still firmly planted in his seat.

The music started up and we were off. The procession snaked its way around the tables, gently at first. Then Davina picked up the pace and made a break for the door, leading the line out into the mud-ridden garden. She had no mercy. Rainbow wedges or not, Davina would and could tackle any terrain, unlike many of the guests in their stiletto heels. Round the trees we went, through thorny bushes and over cobbled paths. One by one the guests dropped out, with cries of:
"Ah! My shoe!"

"Ouch! That hurt!"
"Where are we going?" and,
"What was that?"

Eventually the stalwart, mud-caked guests who had survived the ordeal snaked their way back in. Davina led us onto the stage, much to the surprise of the band. Unfortunately it was also to her own surprise since her muddy wedges slipped on the shiny platform. She fell backwards causing a domino effect on all of us in the remaining line. Henry managed to dodge out of the way of Bishop Parky, and Alfie landed safely on me. Once again, Mike proved a safe, sturdy pair of arms, catching me as I fell and cushioning my landing with his muscular chest. Sadly for David, he was walking past the line just at the point that Uncle George toppled off the stage. David did not see him coming and as a result ended up as an involuntary human crash mat. Uncle George laughed playfully. David harrumphed grumpily.

Mike gently pulled me up with a beaming smile.
"You know," he said. "I'm definitely coming around to the idea."
"What idea?" I asked puzzled.
"The idea of Mrs Pinkerton."
"Yes, it's funny isn't it? I never imagined my mum married, let alone as a vicar's wife and a Pinkerton!" I chuckled, but Mike smiled wryly and drew me closer. He stroked my hair tenderly and then smiled.
"No!" he whispered softly. "I meant you. The idea of you being Mrs Pinkerton. My Mrs Pinkerton." My heart skipped a beat and I gasped. "So what do you think?" he asked.

Think! He wanted me to think! He had just dropped an amazing bombshell, a dream that I had never dared to dream, and now he expected me to think and even worse to give a coherent response. Even if I could think, my heart was beating so loudly that it drowned out all my thoughts. I wanted to respond, but in the muddle of that moment I could not, so I did the only thing that I could do in the circumstances... I sidestepped the issue.

"I think somebody has had too much Pimms!" I quipped, tapping him playfully on the nose. "Let's see how you feel about it all tomorrow. You've just had a nasty knock on your chest; it might have affected your heart! Maybe it'll be back to normal in the morning." He laughed and pulled me in closer.
"Or maybe it won't! Let's just see what tomorrow brings."

Mike and I summoned the boys and headed off towards the car. Externally I was silent, but internally a maelstrom was raging. Thoughts swirled unchecked through my mind – thoughts of future, present and past; thoughts of dreams unfulfilled and unspoken. I stilled my heart and clamped it tight. Was I really ready for this step again? Half of me shouted yes and the other half screamed no. What was my dream? Was my desire to marry or to marry Mike? I had never thought about it before, but now I was standing in the spotlight and tomorrow was looming fast.

Chapter 34

Black

Some tomorrows never come and others bring surprises and redirection. This one came... and did all those things.

The day started when I was rudely awoken by a poke in the ribs. It was Alfie turning over in my bed. His little face ended up inches from mine and I could smell the remnants of yesterday's garlic on his warm breath. Sleepily, he opened one eye and grinned.
"Morning, Mum." He whispered.
"Morning gorgeous!" I replied. Henry groaned.
"Shhh!" he mumbled grumpily.

We had ended up sleeping together the previous night out of sheer exhaustion. Mike had dropped us off after the wedding, leaving us to go straight upstairs to bed. The twins never made it to their own room. Instead, they collapsed in an exhausted heap of happiness on my bed. I did not have the heart to disturb them, so I just clambered in between them and pulled the duvet snugly up. It was a decision that I now regretted because my ribs were hurting, my nose was reeling from the assault of Alfie's breath and it was only six o'clock in the morning. I had forgotten that the twins were such early risers.

"Let's go and have breakfast!" suggested Alfie enthusiastically.
"In a bit, Alfie. In a bit. Just let me lie here a bit longer," I pleaded sleepily. By now Henry had woken up too.
"Why don't we make some biscuits?" he suggested.
"Yeah! Great idea! We can take them on our bike ride!" chirped Alfie in agreement.
"Biscuits? Bike ride? What are you talking about?" I mumbled, abandoning the idea of sleep.
"Mike said he'll take us all out on our bikes today. Don't you remember? He said so in the car last night." I did not remember. In fact I had not heard anything that was said in the car last night. Nothing at all. I had been too distracted!

The twins swamped me with enthusiastic pleas, until eventually I capitulated and trudged dopily downstairs. Still half asleep, I soon found myself stood in a billow of flour, with cocoa powder stains up my dressing gown sleeve, rolling out chocolate chip biscuits at half past six in the morning. As I rolled mechanically back and forth, my mind and heart wrestled to and fro. I had entered into one failed marriage and I was determined not to repeat my mistake. My heart said marry, but my head said no. Over and over again. The same debate. To and fro…
"Mummy? Are you sure you're supposed to roll them that thin?" asked Henry, pointing at the now almost transparent cookie dough.
"Whoops! No! Sorry, I wasn't concentrating. I was thinking."
"What about?"
"Nothing that concerns you," I lied.

Marcie called, just before Mike arrived.
"Hi Laurie. I was planning on taking Josh on a trip to the safari park today. I wondered whether Henry and Alfie would like to come too. I thought they'd enjoy it."
"Well, Mike and I were planning on taking them cycling today, but I'll ask them. They haven't been there for over a year, so they may prefer it." The decision was unanimous... two little voices shouting *safari park* at the top of their lungs and dancing around the lounge with delight. "I guess that's settled then! I'll deliver my two intrepid explorers over to you in an hour."

Armed with backpacks, binoculars, homemade biscuits and bottles of squash, I escorted the twins across the road. Instantly Josh flung open the door and Henry and Alfie charged in without so much as a kiss goodbye. I waited for Marcie.
"You look tired!" she grimaced.
"I am. Late night, early start and..." I was going to mention my dilemma to her, but then thought better of it. Mike's proposition was spur of the moment last night and was probably only a fleeting thought. There was no point in involving Marcie at this stage.
"And?" she probed.
"And the prospect of a bike ride on this chilly day," I said, nicely diverting the topic away from anything important.
"So tell me, how's Dominic? You and he seemed pretty connected yesterday." Just as I said that a red, racy car pulled up and out stepped Dominic. Marcie blushed. I looked at her and raised an eyebrow.
"He's fine thanks. He's coming with us."
"Oh! So that's why you wanted the twins to come - to keep Josh occupied."
"Maybe," she admitted coyly.
"Right! Well I'll leave you to it. What's that saying?

Two's company and three's a crowd."

I was just about to cross the road back to my house when Mike pulled up outside. I braced myself, wondering what his thoughts on marriage would be today. With the twins gone, I had nowhere to hide. It was just going to be Mike and me. I felt a mixture of joy and apprehension, that same feeling that you get before a first date. He got out of his car with a huge bouquet of red roses and an even bigger smile. My heart leapt. I knew what this tomorrow was going to bring and was secretly glad inside. I smiled back at him and stepped out into the road, ready to cross over to his side.

I never saw the car... because I never looked. My eyes were fixed on Mike. I just heard the roaring of the engine and the squealing of the brakes. Mike's face disappeared. My world went black.

Chapter 35

Forever Changed

Tubes, drips and machines invaded my body, taking over the responsibility for my very existence. They carried the burden whilst I could not and kept hope alive. The only sounds in that sterile hospital room were the repetitive bleeping of the monitors and the steadfast gasping of the ventilator. The air was filled with stagnant anaesthetic, unspoken fears and the occasional, evasive waft of faith.

Freddie arrived that fateful day, shortly after I was moved to intensive care. Shocked into silence at my appearance, he simply held Davina tight and prayed quietly by my side.

The overworked, locum registrar entered the room and spoke factually, without emotion or sensitivity.
"You need to prepare yourself for the worst." Even I heard those words from my darkness, from the haze in which I was trapped. I heard the muffled sobs that followed and then… nothing.

I lay there motionless for five long days, stuck in a sea of black nothingness with only the occasional voice to stir my senses and awaken my mind. There were no thoughts, no anxieties, no fears, no boredom, just blackness. It was as if I was outside of time for I had no sense of time. Even if I had wanted to, I could not move my body or open my eyes; there was no longer a connection between myself and reality. Days and days of nothingness for me. Days and days of anguish for those left to sit in that soulless room.

My mother sat constantly by my bed every day, trying to exude positivity and optimism with her words, but the desperation in her eyes drowned it out. Mike came when he could and sat awkwardly in silence, but to his relief, his work drew him away often. Ben stayed at home to look after the twins, but as soon as they were at school or at Marcie's, he came to the hospital and sat faithfully beside me.

Henry and Alfie showed the cheerful resilience that is unique to children - they just accepted Mummy's impromptu hospital stay, without accepting the gravity or the weight of the situation. They peacefully carried on with their lives, seamlessly adapting to the change in their arrangements. No-one told them the full truth about the life that hung in the balance. They were only told the snippets that they needed to hear.

"I'm sorry! I'm so, so sorry! Please don't go! The boys need you... We all need you... I need you!" His sobs penetrated the darkness and I heard his cry. My mind started to make connections and very slowly a memory formed. A memory of my time before, of a life that was mine. Pictures started to appear before my eyes, visions of

the past. Something was starting to switch on inside me, like a cold engine on a snowy winter's morning. I relived the crash and felt the pain, then I heard the voice - the guiding, comforting voice.
"Laura, it's time to fight! You're needed." The voice was firm but reassuring and as it spoke waves of reviving energy coursed through my body. I felt the urge and the power to open my eyes.

"Oh, thank God!" exclaimed Davina. "Nurse! Nurse! She's waking!" Optimism and hospital staff flocked to my bedside like bees to honey. Monitors were read and orders exchanged, but I retained none of it as I started to regain consciousness.

I began to choke as the function rushed back into my body. The nurse quickly extracted a tube from my throat to enable me to breathe on my own. She smiled warmly at me and my eyes learnt to work again as they slowly focused on her soft, kind face. I felt a reassuring squeeze on my left hand and Davina leant over and whispered in my ear.
"Welcome back! You've had us all worried." She kissed my cheek tenderly and I felt the gentle warmth of her lips on my icy cold skin. I tried to speak but all that came out was a grotesque, grating noise.
"Shhh! Don't try to talk yet. Just rest," advised the nurse. Gratefully, I relaxed again.
"Hello, Laurie!" whispered Ben gently as he wiped his tear-streaked cheek. I smiled weakly and attempted a nod.

Doctors and nurses invaded my room on many occasions that day to examine and assess me. They each came with serious faces and furrowed brows but left relaxed and smiling. If this was the fight that I had been assigned to then I had clearly won already. Minute by minute I felt strength returning to my body as the heartbeat of life beat once more within me. At first I responded only with smiles and gentle squeezes, but by the evening I was able to stiffly move my head and speak in softened croaks.

Mike came that evening and flamboyantly lavished a single red rose, a huge card and a kiss on me. He had obviously not remembered how much I disliked single red roses!
"I sneaked this past the nurses' station," he whispered naughtily. "Apparently you're not allowed any flowers on this ward, but I'm sure this one won't hurt." He winked. I smiled, then he leant over me and whispered, "You didn't have to go to all this trouble to avoid my proposal, you know!" I smiled, lapping up the warmth of his eyes and the squeeze of his hand. Reassured by his presence and strength, I relaxed back into my pillow.

Over the coming days, sleep was my constant companion and family and friends my stability. Davina tended to my every need and chatted away about nothing in particular. Mike was demonstrative with his love and gifts but sparing with his time and conversation. Ben sat quietly in the background, occasionally updating me on the latest escapades of Henry and Alfie, but otherwise diligently serving the needs of me and the others in the room.

One of the evenings a doctor appeared, coughing really loudly so as to herald his own entrance.
"I'm afraid I'm going to have to ask you all to wait outside while I run a few tests on Laura. It won't take long. I'll send the nurse for you when I'm finished." Dutifully they all left.

"Now, young lady," he said sternly, turning to me and leaning over the bed. "I hope you'll cross the road more

Forever Changed

carefully in future." He dropped the serious face and chuckled. I nodded.
"Yes. I think I've learnt my lesson."
"Good! Now let's take a look at this left leg of yours. By all accounts it took the brunt of the impact. It was shattered completely, as was your hip but I've done my best to piece them back together again for you. Luckily for you, I'm good at jigsaw puzzles! Now I need to check how successful we were. Tell me... what can you feel in your leg?" I concentrated hard and tried to locate the sensations in my left leg, but I could not find them. My internal GPS system had obviously been corrupted by the accident and needed a reset.
"Nothing," I replied honestly.
"Nothing, eh? Hmmm. Can you wiggle your toes for me?" Again I tried, but again there was no connection. I stared at my toes, but, no matter how much I focused on them, I couldn't get them to move. Panic started to set in. I stared at him with open eyes. He recognised my plight. "Don't worry," he said gently. "It's still early days." He bent over my foot so that I could no longer see either my foot or what he was doing. "What if I do this? What can you feel?"
"Do what?" I asked helplessly, not feeling anything. He ignored my question and kept repeating his.
"Can you feel this?" I just shook my head. Each time he asked I felt nothing. A drop of sorrow trickled down my cheek, quickly followed by a drop of fear. Helplessness bubbled up inside until I could contain it no more and an avalanche of tears cascaded down my face.

The doctor smiled kindly. Then he spoke.
"Would you like anyone back in here with you while we continue our chat?" he asked. I nodded pitifully.
"My mum!" I spluttered, unashamedly feeling like a five year-old again, longing for that maternal reassurance and

calm. Two minutes later, Davina came back into the room, her face pale. As soon as she sat down beside me, the doctor began his summary.

"Of course, we're still at the very beginning of your recovery and by all accounts most of your statistics indicate that you will make a full recovery. There appears to be no internal organ damage and your brain scans appear normal."

"Well that's a surprise!" quipped Davina. She started to relax and smile at the good news. She gently squeezed my hand. I sat with bated breath, knowing that this was merely the flattery before the assault. The doctor continued. "What is difficult to assess at this stage is what recovery you will have in your left leg. There is clearly some nerve damage caused by the impact to the spine and at the moment it's hard to identify just how significant that damage actually is. I would have expected some movement or feeling by now, but currently there are no signs of it. The bones will knit back together again for sure, and the blood flow is good, but without the feeling in your leg you need to face the possibility that…" he paused to fiddle with his glasses, then lowered his eyes. "You may not walk again." I gasped sharply, as did Davina. I squeezed her hand so tightly that her knuckles turned white, almost as white as her face. Silence screamed around the room.

Finally Davina spoke, a glint of hope in her eyes.
"But you can't be sure, can you? I mean, you don't actually know that she won't walk again, do you?" The doctor shook his head.
"No, I don't know for sure. All I can say with any certainty is that I've seen people in Laura's situation many times before, people with similar levels of injuries and responses, and only one in a hundred ever walks again and even less are able to walk unassisted." Davina, clearly encouraged

by these improved odds, turned to me with fire in her eyes. "You can be that one, Laura! It has to be someone. That one can be you! You just have to fight for it!" I felt a surge through my body again, a spiritual confirmation of the voice that I had heard. So this was the fight that lay ahead of me – the fight for my mobility. The battle seemed daunting and big, but I knew that the victory was already mine.

Chapter 36

The Dirty Fight

This fight was dirty and long. With every skittle of hope came a bowling ball of failure or pain to knock it down. Unrelenting. Unforgiving. Strike one! Strike two! Game over!

Time and again I experienced defeat, but time and again I braced myself for another game. Failure and pain came thick and fast at me, but I learnt to disarm them quickly and bowl them into the runners, leaving my skittles of hope intact. Sometimes, the vibrations of the battle caused my hope to wobble but my mum's supportive arm was always there to firmly position it back in place. Occasionally, negative thoughts overwhelmed me to such a degree that they spilt over into other people's lanes but they held firm and graciously ignored my misfires, not allowing them to spoil their game. Together we fought. Day and Night. Always hope-filled. Always determined. Game on!

"It's my turn!" shouted Henry.
"No it's not!" bellowed Alfie.

"Yes it is! It's been five minutes."
"No it hasn't!"
"Yes it..." Alfie did not wait to hear the rest of Henry's protestations, instead he wheeled himself down the corridor and out into the garden.

I sat on the sofa and watched them out of the window as they squabbled over my wheelchair and hurtled about on it. It had become the centrepiece of their playtimes and the focus of much fun. The previous day, they had even attempted stunts off the patio steps, but I had quickly stopped their exploits since this wheelchair was my lifeline to independence and I could not risk damaging it.

Sadly for me, this wheelchair was bitter sweet. It was a constant reminder of the useless state of my leg, my dependence on gadgets to function normally and my inability to move freely. However, it also released me into a level of independence that would otherwise be impossible. I could now make short, unassisted trips to the corner store and nearby park. These independent excursions helped to lift my mood, but their impact was always short-lived because the all-consuming desire to walk never left my mind.

Mike found it hard too. Frustration was written over his face every time he came around. He would gaze upon the wheelchair with disappointment as a myriad of able-bodied, fun dates evaporated from his grasp. His life was based outdoors, his natural habitat the mud banks, deep forests and high cliffs - a life without limits. Mine was now extremely limited - to ramps and smooth surfaces. One ill-placed patch of cloying mud could potentially render me stranded like a beached whale. Like a Dalek, stairs were my nemesis. An out-of-service lift in an inopportune place would relegate me to publicly ascending stairs on my bottom (which to be fair, was never actually an option for a Dalek). White trousers were no longer a possibility; my fashion decisions were now based around practicality.

My physiotherapy was hard and tortuous with daily repetitive practice required. Mike would encourage me fleetingly, but his impatience cried out of every muscle in his body – his leg tapped constantly and his smiles of encouragement were forced, betrayed by the deadness in his eyes. We tried to readjust to our circumstances, but as time progressed and movement in my leg did not, we drifted slowly in opposite directions. Davina tried valiantly to rally our spirits and keep our outlook positive but even I saw the candle of hope diminishing in her eyes. I knew that things needed to change, but I could not see the way forward, so I stuck my head in the sand and carried on as best I could. However, Mike was incapable of remaining stuck for he was slowly going stir-crazy.

One drizzly Friday night, I sat looking out of my lounge window at the rainbow overhead. The brilliance and optimism of its colours mesmerised me, so I did not hear Mike arrive.
"Hello gorgeous!" he said routinely, kissing me on my cheek. I jumped as I was ejected from my dream-like state.
"Hi there handsome!" I replied automatically. I looked him up and down. There was something different about him. He was both tense and relaxed all at the same time – his eyes were smiling and full of release yet his manner was tense and awkward. The contradiction unsettled me.

"Are you okay?" I asked.

"Erm, yeah!" He lowered his eyes and then hesitated.
"What is it? What's wrong?"
"Nothing... Or at least... nothing's wrong. In fact, something's very right." He shuffled his feet on the ground and then looked me in the eye. "You know that South American job that I took a few months ago?"
"Yes," I said slowly, wondering where this was leading.
"Well, they contacted me again yesterday. They've offered me a permanent position." His face brightened considerably at this concept.
"Wow!" I said half-heartedly. "When do you start? I mean... I'm assuming that you're taking it?"
"Definitely! This is a once-in-a-lifetime opportunity. I'll be working and living in the Amazon rainforest. How cool is that? I can't imagine anything more exciting!" I watched his face illuminate with the excitement of this opportunity and knew that it was time to let go. Time to let him experience his adventure and free him into the lifestyle that he craved. A lifestyle that I knew I was unable to share.
"Obviously, I won't be able to come too," I stated calmly, bringing the awkward issue out into the open. "I have the boys... and I have this," I said, patting my wheelchair. "It's hardly suited to forest life!"
"I know! I've thought of that. It will only be for a couple of years and I can come back and visit often. We'll just have to put the idea of a wedding on hold for now and..."

As soon as he said the word *wedding,* something inside me shuddered and I realised how mismatched we now were. There was no basis for a lifelong commitment to Mike; no foundation. His relationship with me was no longer based on a rope of love but on strings of pity and misguided loyalty. I needed to cut those strings and set him free. Gently, I placed a finger upon his lips to sever his flow.

"That's wonderful news. You deserve this opportunity! But let's not try to resurrect something that's dead. You and I both know that it's time for you to go." I smiled warmly and watched as his tension dissolved. He nodded. I had only spoken what we both knew to be true but had denied for so long. I felt peace inside and that peace engulfed him. We rested in silence for a moment or two, but then a wave of guilt hit him and he started to flounder again.
"I don't mean to let you down, Laurie. I just…"
"Shhh! You haven't let me down at all. The boys and I will be just fine. Anyway, I'm on the mend now and we're set in our ways. We wouldn't thank you for a big move right now." We exchanged smiles and peace resumed its rightful place, soon to be usurped by the onset of awkwardness and justification.
"Thanks for being so understanding. You do know that I really value you, don't you? This is nothing to do with you. It's all to do with me… You're very lovely. You need to know that. It's just that this is my dream and I have to follow it."
"I totally understand. You're fine. I want you to achieve your dreams."
"Of course, I want us to stay friends," he said.
"Of course!" I agreed, although we both knew that was never going to be the case.

He stayed for a while longer and then went through the front door for the final time. I watched as he left in body, but knew that he had actually left long before - He had left along with perfection when the accident corrupted our world.

Chapter 37

Defrost

Although Mike and his promises had left my life unexpectedly, my tears for him were short-lived. Instead of sorrow I felt peace and was able to relax more in my daily life. With the burden of my obligations and his expectations lifted, I found faith again in my small accomplishments. Previously my tiny teeters of progress had felt like failures because they fell so short of Mike's hopes for me.

Predictably, the frequency of Ben's visits increased and his attentiveness to me expanded, but I was determined not to let him back into a position of trust, so I held him at arm's length and turned down many of his kind offers.

"You shouldn't be so hard on Ben you know. He's only trying to help," commented Davina one sunny day when, on the basis of independence invasion, I had rudely refused Ben's offer of making a meal. Consequently, he had rapidly retreated into the lounge and I had hopped off into the kitchen to try and single-handedly rustle up some food.
"Hmmm. Trying to wheedle his way back in you mean!" I replied cynically. "Well I don't need his help! I'm doing

just fine without him!" I added crossly.

"I think you're misreading him," she offered gently. Despite her dulcet tones, she hit a nerve with me and I spun around irate.

"I don't think I'm misreading him at all! He left me for Kelly and that didn't work out, so now he's back here hoping for a second chance. Well excuse me, but I am nobody's back-up plan!"

In my crossness I cut my finger and hopped over to the sink to wash away the blood. The red water flowed freely as the red mist continued to surge through my system.

"You wouldn't say that if you'd seen him at the hospital." Davina threw out the bait and waited silently for me to bite. I refused. Intrigued though I was, I remained stuck in a stew of stubbornness. With a soft swish of orange chiffon she left the room and I remained in an uncomfortable pool of unasked questions.

I turned the music up loud in a valiant attempt to drown out my thoughts and emotions. My attempt failed and confusion swept over me. With the silver colander in hand, I turned angrily towards the kitchen table and lost my balance, falling to the floor in a sea of peeled carrots. Frustrated and hurt, I lay there helplessly listening to the thunderous thudding of footsteps as Ben and Davina came running.

"Are you okay?" Ben asked, concern etched across every crevice of his face. I swallowed my pride before replying and reluctantly took his hand.

"I'm fine! I guess I'm still not used to… to… this!" I said disappointedly pointing at my useless leg. He smiled kindly and pulled me onto a chair.

"Please let me help you," he implored. "You don't have to do this on your own."

Defrost

There was something about the kindness and sincerity in his voice that touched my heart. I felt the icy shard inside me start to melt, so I frantically pressed my internal fast freeze button to keep its protective wall alive. I looked into his deep blue eyes but there was no pity there. Pity was an emotion that I was all-too-familiar with now and could spot from ten paces. It was an emotion in people that I had come to despise for it bypassed my sense of self and reduced me to an inadequate object. I searched hard, but there was no pity there. Manipulation and insincerity were absent too. Instead there was just warmth and...

"I'm sorry Laurie, but you're going to have to swallow your pride for once. I'm all for you living an independent life, but you need to take it one step at a time. You still need our help. It's only been a few months since the accident and you're still not used to... to... your situation," Davina said tactfully. I laughed mockingly.

"Go on! Say it! I'm not used to being a cripple! That's what you wanted to say, wasn't it? Don't beat about the bush. Just say it how it is. My leg is useless and now so am I!" I started to cry - tears of frustration and pain flowing freely down my reddened cheeks. Davina hung her head despairingly and just shook it.

"No, Laurie!" she uttered softly after a few moments. "That isn't what I was thinking. I just wanted to pick my words carefully so that I didn't speak anything bad over you. Freddie always says that the power of life and death is in the tongue, so I was just trying to be positive with my words. That was all. I didn't want to extinguish your hope."

"Hope?" I shouted angrily. "Hope? What hope do I have? *Everything* they've tried so far has failed. I still can't feel my leg or my foot. All they're doing is prolonging my agony... Doing exercise after exercise to keep my dead leg alive and to prevent it from withering. They're not really helping. I still can't play ball with my boys or take them cycling. I can't help them up when they fall over. I can't rescue them from muddy fields. For goodness sake, I can't even walk anymore!" Davina and I sat head to head, locked in a frozen stare of frustration. The argument was futile and it changed nothing.

"You're alive aren't you?" she challenged. I averted my eyes in shame and nodded. *"You* are not useless. Your leg is not you. It's your heart that defines you." I examined my heart and felt the weight of the icy hardness within; a defensive wall built from bricks of hurt, anger and injustice. "You need to learn to love again…" she continued. "To love others… To love life… To love yourself." My fast freeze button broke under the pressure and the thawing process began. I felt the icy wall begin to crack as the warmth of my tears cascaded down my porcelain cheeks. My mum held me tight as the ice melted.

Davina and I stayed motionless, locked in an embrace. Finally, the tap, tap, tap of Ben chopping the carrots aroused me. I lifted my head from her tear-sodden shoulder.

"What are you doing?" I asked.

"Helping!" he said in one of those and-your-problem-is tones. I was just about to protest and defend my independence when Davina looked at me sternly with a raised eyebrow. I took her unspoken advice and rejected stubbornness and pride.

"Thank you!" I said. He smiled. "Can I help?" I asked.

"You can if you want to. Why not peel the rest of these?" he suggested handing me the potatoes. Davina left the room to change her top and Ben and I worked together to produce the dinner. He put on some fun music and, after an initial silence, our conversation flowed easily.

Defrost

"Ben?" I said suddenly, prompted by the awareness of an icy shard that still remained within me.
"Yes?" he replied whilst continuing to stir the sauce in the wok.
"I'm sorry." I said bluntly.
"What for?"
"For the way I've been treating you. You've shown me nothing but kindness and I've been horrid and I realise that now." He smiled wryly.
"Yes. Yes, you have!" he said and then turned and shot me one of his big, dimpled grins. I laughed. My apology had clearly been accepted!

I hopped into the lounge where Davina was playing with Henry and Alfie.
"Mum?"
"Yes?"
"I'm sorry!" Davina just smiled reassuringly and beckoned me onto the sofa.
"I know, darling. I know. You're going through a tough time and I understand that."
"Yes, but that's no excuse. You've been there for me all the way and I don't mean to be so ungrateful."
"It's not just me. Ben, Freddie, Marcie. They've all been there too, you know."
"Yeah! I do know. They've all been fantastic and I would never have got this far without any of you." Davina smiled again, encouraged by my change of heart.

"Mum?"
"Yes."
"When we were in the kitchen, you said something about Ben… About when he was in the hospital room…" she nodded. "What did you mean?" Davina shrugged her shoulders and sighed deeply.

"Well, it was funny really... We all reacted very differently to what happened to you. When the news came through, Ben came to the hospital immediately. He was all ashen-faced and concerned. In fact, for the first 24 hours he never left your side, not until he knew that you were out of immediate danger. Even then, he only left to go and look after the boys and as soon as Freddie or Marcie took over he returned. It was difficult for him to be there too because of Mike. He tried to be respectful of Mike's status in your life, so he always stayed at the back of the room when Mike was around. But the truth was that Mike didn't come that often. He didn't seem to be able to cope. All Mike kept asking was whether you would walk again and what kind of life you would be able to lead. It was quite clear to all of us that they were selfish concerns and none of them had you in mind. Ben, on the other hand, cared about no such things. All he was concerned about was you.

"Anyway, I watched as Ben spent every available moment at your bedside, even taking the week off work so that he could be there whilst Mike carried on working, even taking on overtime." I felt the disappointment and betrayal at this disclosure. Mike had professed love and suggested marriage but the reality was that neither had been based on firm foundations and both were conditional offers. Davina paused for a moment before continuing.

"When you were in the coma, Ben often just sat beside you and held your hand. Occasionally, I would see tears streaking down his face as he looked at your broken body and helpless state. Sometimes, he would just pray quietly at the back of the room with Freddie. Freddie never told me exactly what they prayed, but I know that he remarked to me about the depth of compassion and love that Ben showed for you. The thing was, Laurie, you didn't even

Defrost

know that he was there and he had nothing to prove to us because we were just focused on you. He had nothing to gain from his actions. He didn't do it for the boys or for us. He did it all for you and then when you awoke he asked nothing of you and didn't even tell you that he'd been there all the time. If he had been trying to wheedle his way back into your affections, then he could have done that a long time ago by exposing Mike's insincerity. But he didn't.

"Laurie. I know that what he did with Kelly was wrong and I will never say anything different, but the person that I saw in the hospital room was a very different man."
"I see," I mumbled, processing everything that my mum had revealed.
"Do you?"
"Yes, I do." Davina looked at me quizzically, so I explained. "I realise that I've been holding the past against Ben for all this time. I need to release him from that. Everyone deserves the right to change." Davina nodded and smiled.
"Laurie?"
"Yes?"
"Just one more thing… About your leg."
"Yes?"
"There's still hope; I just know it. Don't give up just yet. We're going to see the consultant tomorrow, so let's just see what he has to say."

Chapter 38

Hope

Hope comes in many forms. Though its identity is often veiled by its different packages, it is always unmistakable in its character. True hope is recognisable by its purity and strength. When you think that all is lost and there is nowhere to turn, suddenly in comes hope riding on a white horse with his name engraved on his leg for all to see. Unlike false hope, which offers only a blip of joy and is soon extinguished, there is no mistaking when true hope enters the room. Wherever he enters, faith comes too.

"I realise that this is a hard decision for you," said Mr. Turner, the consultant, gravely, "So I am prepared to give you some time to think about it."
"There's no need," I blurted out desperately. "I want to try." Mr. Turner peered at me over the top of his glasses and surveyed my face. He raised one eyebrow and then nodded.
"You're quite sure?" This time is was my turn to nod. "I cannot stress enough that this is still an experimental procedure and as such it comes with no guarantees."

"I understand that," I replied. "But the only guarantee that I have at this moment is that, without this procedure, I definitely won't walk again."

"I'm afraid so," he conceded. "Very well, I shall prepare all of the paperwork and get it sent to you along with a date. You're looking at a wait of four to six months, unless there's a cancellation."

"That's fine." I felt a flicker of hope ignite inside me. Just when I thought that all doors had been tried and closed, Mr. Turner had opened up a new, hidden door – an experimental door involving a combined stem cell and nerve transplant.

"Do either of you have any more questions?" he asked. I shook my head and looked at my mum. I could tell from the expression on her face that she was still processing all that had been proposed and was suppressing all hope within her for fear of yet another disappointment.

"Mum?" I prompted. She nodded, gathered her thoughts and then spoke.

"So... If (and I realise that it's a big if) this procedure is successful, how long before we'll start to see a result?" Mr. Turner sat back, wrinkled his mouth and twiddled his glasses.

"Honestly? I have no real idea! We should know very quickly if the nerve part of the transplant has taken because Laura will start to feel her foot again. Of course, how much feeling she'll get back I can't say. It may be enough to enable her to walk again... or it may not. That's where the stem cells come in, but they take time and I'm afraid that time varies from person to person. Some babies walk at eight months, others take two years and some... well, they never get there at all. It's the same with this. It's not possible to monitor what the stem cells are doing once they're in Laura's system. At that point, Laura's body will take over and interact with them. Hopefully, they will encourage the reconnection and regrowth of the tissues, nerves and systems that were damaged in the accident but as for time..."

"I see!" said Davina, looking crestfallen. I placed a reassuring hand on her leg.

"It's okay, Mum. I want to do this. I have to give it a try. After all, I have nothing to lose?"

Davina wheeled me out of Mr. Turner's office and down the yellow, antiseptic, hospital corridor. Neither of us spoke – both holding our breath for fear of bursting the fragile bubble of hope that we had just been offered. A shell-shocked silence lingered with us until we reached the car, and even then, neither of us discussed the prospect of the operation ahead until we were at least halfway home.

Normality reigned when we returned to the house, but now it was tinged with frustration. I resented the ramps and grab handles and growled at my wheelchair and stair lift. The burning desire to walk freely had raged to the surface again and I longed to be released into my opportunity for freedom. Two weeks passed before the consultant's letter finally arrived. Up until then, I was like a bear with a sore head and the whole household was consigned to tip-toeing around me on eggshells. However, when I ripped it open and read its contents, my mood did not improve because I found my hope deferred for five months – a hope that was inextricably linked with the date of this operation.

Ben remained unperturbed by my growling grumpiness, consistently meeting me with a beaming smile and bright, bluebell eyes. Occasionally, he disarmed my foulness with kindness, often encouraging the boys in comical activities that dissipated the tension in the air. He was the tonic and I was the gin – his bubbly constituency lightened the situation, whereas my toxicity left people around me incapacitated and stumbling for words.

"You really are a frightful grump you know!" he chided playfully one day. Outraged and completely void of humour, I defended myself.
"So would you be if you were in my situation! I think you'll find I do pretty well under the circumstances! I can't imagine you coping this well!" He pursed his mouth and cocked his head to one side like a budgerigar.
"Maybe!" he replied airily. "Or maybe I would choose to look at what I *have* got in my life and not concern myself with a small mobility issue."
"SMALL MOBILITY ISSUE!" I shouted angrily. "HOW DARE YOU! Get out! Get out now!" I pointed furiously to the front door.
"No!" he responded calmly.
"NO?" I screamed, shocked at his defiance.
"No!" he reiterated firmly. "I refuse to leave this house until you've got things in perspective again. We've all tip-toed around you for the last month but actually that was wrong of us and it's been completely unfair on the boys." Davina, who had heard all the shouting, poked her head around the door, but she hastily retreated when she saw the contretemps.

"Laura, I can't stand by and let this operation become your everything. It needs to be the blessing, the extra. Don't you see?" I wrinkled my brow and shook my head in confusion. I did not see at all, but at least my anger had started to subside. "You've become fixated with walking, as if that defines you. It's almost as if you've forgotten

Hope

how to enjoy life and yet so little of your life has actually changed." I went to interrupt him, to protest about my many afflictions, but he prevented me by showing me the palm of his hand. Kneeling down beside me, he looked earnestly into my eyes and continued gently. "I'm not saying that it isn't hard for you because I know it is. Over these last few months, I've watched you battle tirelessly to function normally again. Remember… I saw you lying there in the hospital bed, helplessly teetering between life and death. But you chose life! Life isn't dependent on mobility; it's dependent on how you interact with it." I started to understand and sat back in remorse, aware of my victim mentality. Ben continued.

"The boys need you back. They've been faithfully waiting for *you* to return. They don't need a mum who can walk perfectly. They just need *you*, their mum. They need you to start engaging with them again, taking an interest in their lives. Henry did a picture of the solar system yesterday, which he put his heart and soul into. He spent ages on it and came to show you, but you just grunted and didn't even take time to notice the details that he had so lovingly put in. He didn't care about the picture. He cared about what *you* thought of it, so he went away disappointed, all because you were too fixated on your operation. That's not like you, Laurie. Not being able to walk doesn't deny you the opportunity to appreciate your sons, but being focused on your disability does." I gulped as reality started to permeate my hardened shell. Ben sensitively waited a moment. "Don't let one dodgy leg rob you of the pleasure of life, Laurie. Don't let an operation (that may or may not work) rob you of five months enjoyment. There is so much more to you than one leg."

He stood up and put his hands in his pockets. I sat

contemplating his words. He shuffled nervously, awaiting my reaction. Slowly, I regained strength and uncurled my foetal disposition.

"Thank you!" I said softly. "I needed to hear that." He smiled and nodded gently and then ran his hand nervously through his hair.

"Right. I'll go then."

"Go? Why? I thought you were having dinner with us tonight?" I asked perplexed.

"You asked me to go. Remember?" he replied sheepishly. I snorted as I remembered my tempestuous outburst.

"That wasn't me! That was someone else!" I laughed. "But she's gone, now."

The departure of tension that evening left a void, which was filled to brimming with laughter and joy. For the first time in weeks, dinner was a relaxed, fun affair. Davina regaled us with some of her more elaborate, animated stories and Freddie laughed so much that he fell off his stool. Henry and Alfie clapped with delight at the Mexican banquet that was set before them and squealed as they wrestled to keep the filling in their fajitas. I relaxed back into myself, occasionally hopping mischievously from chair to chair to steal titbits from unsuspecting diners and to tickle the twins. A Mexican wave of conversation rippled around the table, closely followed by a game of Chinese whispers.

"The bell rang out too late?" offered Freddie. Henry guffawed victoriously.

"No! No! I said *The bull ran out the gate!*"

"Oh! That makes much more sense. Right, your turn Alfie." Alfie shot us all a toothy grin and whispered into Ben's ear. Ben raised his eyebrows.

Hope

"I'm not saying that!" he protested, causing Alfie to descend into peals of laughter.

"Go on Dad! Pleeeeeease!"

"Oh alright." Ben turned and whispered in my ear, causing me to squirm.

"That tickles!"

"Sorry," he said apologetically and then winked.

"Anyway, what did you say? I didn't hear you because it tickled so much."

"Well I can't repeat it."

"Why not?"

"Because those are the rules."

"Oh go on! Just this once. Pleeeeease!" I begged with a huge smile.

"Okay. I'll repeat myself, just this once, but make sure you listen this time because it's important." I leant over eagerly to hear him regurgitate Alfie's gem. Ben grinned and cupped his hand over my ear. The hotness of his breath set my ear alight and carried the words to deep within.

"I love you!" he whispered breathily. Instantly my pilot light ignited causing me to blush. I flicked around quickly and looked into his face. Did he mean those words or was it simply a mischievous quote from Alfie? He smiled and raised an eyebrow.

"Go on then! Pass it on." He gestured to me to continue the game, but I found myself at a loss for words. I couldn't bring myself to replicate the phrase, to leave myself so exposed, so I uttered the first similar thing that came into my head.

"Elephant poo." I whispered into Davina's ear.

"Alfie!" she exclaimed with mock disapproval and passed it on. I waited with baited breath as the sentence completed its circuit.

"Elephant poo!" declared Henry with a giggle.

"No!" squealed Alfie delightedly, clearly loving the

corruption of his sentence.
"What did you say then, Alfie?" I asked with trepidation.
"I love you! That's what I said. Not elephant poo!" The table descended into streams of laughter at the distortion. All except me. I was biting my lip hard, fighting back tears of disappointment. In that moment my innermost hopes and desires lay exposed, dashed on the rocks of misunderstanding. I realised now how much I had wanted those three words to have come from Ben, not Alfie.

"Coffee anyone?" I offered, pouring myself into my wheelchair. I left the dining room and wheeled myself sorrowfully along the corridor.
You had your chance! came the thoughts of condemnation – those destructive thoughts that so often try to steal our hopes and dreams by belittling our souls. *He wanted you back, but you turned him down! You blew it! Your future's gone!* I embraced the thoughts for a moment but was quickly repulsed by the negative sensations they evoked. I felt heaviness and hopelessness starting to crawl all over me, a complete contrast to the lightness and joy that I had felt only moments earlier. Immediately I rejected the thoughts and focused on the truth, swiping those repulsive feelings onto the floor.
"No!" I shouted inside. "I am blessed with an amazing family and an amazing future ahead of me. Maybe I have blown it with Ben and maybe I haven't, but either way, I will be fine." I gazed out through the back door and into the garden. There, painted across the sky in colours of promise, was a rainbow. Boldly it stood, confirming the hope and future of all mankind. I smiled inside as I embraced that promise.

Deep in thought, I never heard Ben enter the room.
"What are you looking at?" came Ben's gentle voice from

behind. He walked over and, placing a hand on my shoulder, looked out too. "Oh! A rainbow! It's beautiful!" he declared.
"Uh huh!" I agreed.

Silently we remained, dumbstruck by its radiance and colour, basking in its warmth and glory. Ben cracked the silence first by kneeling beside me and coughing nervously.
"Laurie?"
"Yes?"
"The game of Chinese whispers…"
"What about it?" I asked uncomfortably.
"I just want you to know…" He paused and so did my heart; I felt it skip a beat as time stood still. "That… that I meant what I said?" I closed my eyes and inhaled, allowing the warmth of hope to envelop me.
"What exactly did you say?" I asked, turning to face him. I was not being cruel, I just did not want another misunderstanding.
"I said that I love you… Although what I should have said is… that I love you more than ever." The last drip of ice melted from my heart as his blowtorch confession rekindled my love for him - a fiery love that I had kept caged for fear of the damage that it might allow into my life. Reassuringly, I smiled and took his hand in mine.
"I love you too Ben. I love you too."

Slowly our foreheads tipped forward until they rested together, our noses touching lovingly. There we rested peacefully with eyes closed, inhaling the presence of each other. This was no heady, lust-driven passion, but a deep love forged in the mines of old. A love created before the world began. We let it wash over us, allowing it to cover our failures and fill us with strength. We rested silent and still until the joining of hearts and entwining of souls was complete, sealed by the promise of the rainbow.

"Laurie?" Ben whispered. "Will you marry me?"

Chapter 39

Pin Cushion

Mr. Turner peered over his glasses and smiled. "Welcome back young lady!" Wearily, I roused myself and attempted a smile, but my muscles were slow to react, still half-paralysed by the anaesthetic. "Everything went well at our end, so it's over to you now, Laura. Your body needs to do its stuff!" He turned to Davina and Ben. "She needs to rest now. I'll pop in and see her tomorrow."
"When will we know?" asked Davina eagerly.
"Know?"
"If the operation's worked!" The keenness in her eyes warmed his heart and he placed a hand on her shoulder and let her down kindly.
"Let's not get ahead of ourselves just yet. This is going to be a long haul." The tension of the last 24 hours started to show as my mum broke down in tears. Ben stepped in and hugged her tight.
"She's going to be okay, Davina. Whatever happens, she's going to be okay," Ben reassured her. He nodded to Mr. Turner over Davina's shoulder; the consultant took his cue and left. Aware of my mum's heartache but unable to regain control of my senses, I drifted back to sleep leaving her in Ben's capable arms.

"Are you ready?" asked Mr. Turner optimistically the next afternoon. Let's see if you can feel anything yet." I glanced over at Davina and Ben and braced myself, smiling. The consultant leant over my foot. "Tell me when you feel something." I waited patiently... but there was nothing. No sensation. No pain. Nothing. Eventually he sat up. "Not to worry!" he encouraged. "These things take time. I'll pop in tomorrow and we'll try again. Your foot's been through a lot and it's still very swollen so there's still hope." I smiled weakly at him, trying to hang on to my courage, but disappointment was etched on my face. The deflation in the room was tangible.

"I'm going to get a coffee. Can I get you anything?" Davina asked, leaving the room hastily. The glisten of her tear caught the light as she left. Ben sat up straight; smiling, he squeezed my hand. I felt his strength rub off on me, leaving me with a small smear of courage.
"I'm scared, Ben," I admitted for the first time.
"What of?" he asked.
"I'm scared that I'll be stuck like this forever. Scared that you'll come to your senses and leave if this doesn't come good." I saw the shock hit him as I revealed that final fear. He was quick to interrupt.
"Don't you dare be scared of that, Laurie! I came to my senses a long time ago, when I realised what I had lost when I left you. I shall *never* make that mistake again! Whether you can walk or not is not important to me and never will be because all I care about is you and what's inside you." He rubbed my hand reassuringly and smiled gently.
"I guess, I just wanted to walk down the aisle to meet you this time. Unassisted – no Zimmer frame; no wheelchair! I want you to marry all of me and for nothing to be broken this time."

"So long as your heart is whole when I marry you, that's all I want. As for how you get there... You can ride down the aisle on a white quad bike for all I care!"
"I'm sure Freddie would love that!" I chortled.

Tomorrow came and went along with Mr. Turner. There was still no sensation in my foot.
"We're only on day two, Laura!" he reassured. "Let's see what happens tomorrow. Miraculous things can happen on the third day!" His optimism was contagious and I found myself smiling and nodding in agreement. However, his optimism was short-lived because he was called back early the next day by one of the registrars, who was concerned about the burning feeling that was developing in my leg. The pain was searing and restrictive, like burning wax.

"Right! Let's have a look," he said, unravelling my bandages. His facial expression slipped momentarily to reveal horror as he set eyes on my leg, but he was professional enough to recover a smiling façade again within seconds. However, that momentary slip was enough for me to engage with fear.
"Is everything okay?" I asked tentatively. He paused before answering.
"It will be!" he assured firmly. I stared at him, waiting for an explanation. He formed his words carefully. "You appear to have picked up an infection in the wound. I'm going to prescribe you a course of intravenous antibiotics. Hopefully that should do the trick. I'll also get one of the doctors to drain the site and clean it up. I'll be back later to see how you're doing." As he reached the door, he noticed the pained look on my face and returned to my bedside. "Don't worry about it! It's a setback we could've done without, but it's a hurdle that we'll overcome. We've not come this far to be beaten by some little bug now have

we?"
"No!" I agreed.

Painful draining and cleaning followed. Day after day. Bag after bag of antibiotics, copious notes and whispered conversations left me bereft of facts and at the mercy of my imagination. I felt feverish and faint and was glad for the daily reassurance of Ben's touch, but I no longer felt included in the truth of my situation. Ben knew more than he let on but remained steadfast in his outward support and optimism. My awareness decreased as the fever took hold. Finally, succumbing to the burning within, I drifted in and out of consciousness leaving Ben to hold onto reality for me.

"This is our last resort!" Mr. Turner confided to Davina, Freddie and Ben. "We've tried all the other antibiotics, but it's been resistant to them all. At best we've slowed its progress, but I'm afraid that if this one fails, then we shall have to consider some other options."
"Other options?" Davina enquired. Mr Turner fiddled with his glasses, the only external sign of his inner turmoil.
"Amputation," he replied, sombrely. This unexpected turn made my mum reel in horror. Mr. Turner took charge of her emotions. "I'm afraid that may be necessary to stop the infection from spreading to the rest of her body." He turned to Freddie and pointed at his dog-collar. "We could do with all the help we can get right now," he said.

Thankfully, I was not privy to that conversation, for if I had been, I think it would have sucked all my remaining energy from me. As it was, I was aware of very little. From time to time the excruciating pain would return and I would

Pin Cushion

writhe but that was always closely followed by a dose of super-strength painkillers and a comatose sleep.

The nurse approached my bedside with the new IV bag. It was crazy to think that so much hope rested on the contents of one flimsy, plastic bag. Carefully, she attached it to the hook and opened the valve so that the drips began to flow. Davina, Ben and Freddie watched solemnly as drip by drip hope was released into my toxic system. They closed their eyes and began to pray - the prayer of desperate people.

Minute by minute, hour by hour the battle raged within. Inch by inch the chemical army of hope pressed forward overcoming and arresting the toxic rebels that had so violently invaded my system. After 24 hours of hidden warfare my fever started to subside and the blotchy, purple hue of my skin disappeared leaving a reassuringly healthy flesh colour. I may have been mostly absent from the battle, but I was there to hear the victory cry.
"At last!" Mr. Turner cried out jubilantly a few days later. "We've beaten the damn thing! Young lady, you had me worried there for a while, but I'm pleased to say that this wound is looking as good as I ever intended. Finally, it's a suitable accolade to my handiwork!" he chuckled, looking around the room in a self-congratulatory way. "I reckon it's about time we tried that pin test again, don't you?" I nodded cautiously.
"Yeah! I've always fancied being a human pin cushion!" I quipped sarcastically. He guffawed his approval.
"If my theory is right, Laura, then the infection was pressing on the nerve before, preventing you from feeling anything. So, now that it's been cleared up I am once again optimi…"

"Ouch!" I yelled. "That hurt!"

Mr. Turner beamed at me and then prodded another area. Time and again I felt it and time and again he beamed. Joy flooded the room and Davina danced with excitement.
"Now wiggle your toes for me," he commanded. I concentrated hard and engaged with my internal GPS system. Everyone watched my toes with baited breath. Very slowly, a small but detectable Mexican wave of movement rippled across them. Mr. Turner sat back on the bed triumphant and adjusted his bow tie.
"I always knew I was good!" he declared playfully.

Jubilation was quickly followed by months and months of painful physiotherapy, which seemed to yield little fruit. The sensation in my foot was present but weak and my leg muscles had atrophied and needed rebuilding. After months of work I could now place my foot on the ground and shuffle it forward but only with the help of a Zimmer frame. My determination and stubbornness kicked in as I focused on the rapid approach of my wedding day.

"One month!" I kept repeating to Lindsay, my tiny physiotherapist, as I attempted to walk forward. "One month! I've only got one month." My leg buckled underneath me and she caught me as I fell. She saw the frustration on my face and sought to relieve me from my burden.
"No! Not a month. You've got a lifetime! You will get there, just maybe go a bit easier on yourself in the meantime. Ben doesn't mind whether you walk down the aisle or not. You've said so yourself."
"But I mind!" I complained tearfully.

"I understand that, but you still need to be realistic. One month is a very short time. I'll help you to be as mobile as I can for your wedding day, but just rest on the fact that you will be able to walk again one day, of that I have no doubt. Just look at the progress you've made already!"

"Hmmmm," was my impatient reply. My elusive final victory was just around the corner, so close that I could smell its sweetness, but so far away that I could not yet grasp it

Chapter 40
The Final Shuffle

Exactly three months later, I stood tearfully at the door of St Mungo's church. Uncle George, with his kind eyes and warm smile, stood protectively by my side, his arm around my waist.

"I'm feeling a bit of déjà vu here!" he quipped, pointing to my florally bedecked Zimmer frame and the church. I chuckled!

"Yep! Same wedding dress. Same Zimmer frame!"

"Just a different ending this time, eh?"

"Definitely a different ending!" I agreed.

With a racing heart and legs like jelly, I turned to the twins behind me.

"Are you ready?" I asked.

"Yes!" they chorused, grinning from ear to ear. This was the day they had dreamed of in their hearts - the day that their family was to be reunited. So enthralled were they that they had not even complained when I insisted that they wore matching three-piece suits (although maybe they were just relieved that my choice of page boy outfits was less embarrassing than my mum's).

Freddie nodded towards me.
"Shall we?"
"Yes!" I said firmly. With that, he opened the great oak doors and I started to inch my way down the aisle. No-one saw the pain or effort that it took to move my left leg forward, but I felt it with every step and leant heavily on the metal frame to relieve the pressure. Of course, there weren't many there to see it anyway because we had only invited a handful of close friends and family to this wedding - those who had accompanied us on our roller coaster journey and supported us through thick and thin. This was not about glamour and show but about the reforming of a three-chord-tie.

Davina was on stand-by with the wheelchair at the front of the church, eagerly watching my progress, which was slow but solid. I fixed my eyes on Ben ahead and kept shuffling, trying to maintain a semblance of rhythm. When I finally reached Marcie, in the third row, I stopped and she handed me my bouquet. She smiled proudly and winked supportively. Henry stepped forward and gently removed my Zimmer frame. I stood shaking in the aisle supported only by Uncle George's arm.
"You can do this kiddo!" he whispered.

Step by step and inch by inch, I walked the final few feet of the aisle. Ben, who had been patiently waiting for me at the front, turned as he heard the gasp from the congregation. Everyone waited with baited breath, each willing my every step. Uncle George's arm gave me the confidence I needed to overcome the wobbles and to remain upright and progress forward. Ben's beautiful smile and tears of pride gave me the courage to overcome the pain and step my way forward to the front. I had almost reached him when I teetered as my strength failed me and my leg buckled underneath.

"Go on, Mum!" I heard Alfie whisper to me encouragingly. "You can do it, Mum!" declared Henry. Uncle George gripped my waist tighter and smiled.

"Just two more steps," he encouraged. Ben offered his hand towards me, a bridge to lessen the gap. Uncle George released his grip on me and I stepped forward again unassisted. Reaching out, Ben grasped my hand and tearfully brought me into the safety of his loving arms.

My dress was not important on this day, nor my leg. Even the achievement of walking down the aisle unassisted paled into insignificance when I measured it against the weightiness of the vows that we undertook; vows that we had previously broken and cast aside. So much forgiveness had been ministered between us, so much painful learning and undeserved grace to bring us to this point of restoration. Our marriage and love was precious to us both now. This time it felt like it had weight and substance. Something to be cherished. Something to be nurtured. This time I knew that we would both fight to keep our vows with every breath in our bodies.

A Rampage Of Chocolate

"There are not many books that have made me laugh out loud. This is one of them! ..."
Margaret Cornell, Author

"... The book is light-hearted and fun, but at the same time profound... A great, laugh-out-loud read."
Joy Maddison, Editor

Laura is a smart, but clumsy, chocoholic with an ability to turn any situation into a disaster. Her chocolate-filled journey from childhood to womanhood is both hilarious and heart-warming, as the great learning curves of life are served up through her experiences of friendship, love, betrayal and loss. In order to survive, she has just one destination in sight, a place which every woman longs to find – that place where the events of our lives do not dictate the way we feel about ourselves.

Whether you laugh or cry on Laura's disaster-filled, emotional roller coaster, I hope that her rampage through life will bring peace to your storm, put a smile on your face and remind you that you are valuable!

If you have enjoyed this novel,

then why not visit

www.ARAMPAGEOF.com

or catch up with Anne-Marie Alexander on social media.

There will be another "A Rampage Of" novel coming soon!